WE WERE
SISTERS

BOOKS BY WENDY CLARKE

What She Saw

WE WERE SISTERS

WENDY CLARKE

bookouture

Published by Bookouture in 2019

An imprint of StoryFire Ltd.

Carmelite House
50 Victoria Embankment
London EC4Y 0DZ

www.bookouture.com

ISBN: 978-1-78681-943-7
eBook ISBN: 978-1-78681-942-0

This book is a work of fiction. Names, characters, businesses,
organizations, places and events other than those clearly in the
public domain, are either the product of the author's imagination
or are used fictitiously. Any resemblance to actual persons, living or
dead, events or locales is entirely coincidental.

For my mum

CHAPTER ONE

Kelly Now

I know something you don't know.

That's what I think as I wheel Noah's pram past the elderly woman who's sitting on the bench overlooking the sea, her little dog by her side.

Not that she's paid me any attention. If she had a mind to study me at all, she'd just see a young woman with mousy-brown shoulder-length hair and dark shadows under her eyes. She might notice the baby weight I'm still carrying around my middle and my anxious expression as my daughter, Isabella, breaks away to chase a seagull.

What she wouldn't see is the thing that sets me apart from the other people on Brighton seafront. Nor would she understand the relief I'm feeling at what I've just discovered. The release of tension. The easing of the intrusive thoughts that come into my head when I least expect it.

There are twenty steps between the lamp post we've just passed and the one before it. It's a fact I know because I've counted the gaps between every lamp post since we left home. And now I *am* sure, I can relax.

Stopping the pram, I pull at the fine gold chain around my neck and lift out the heart-shaped locket. With my thumbnails, I undo the clasp. Inside, are two photos – one of Sophie and Isabella. The other Noah. Closing it again, I press the metal case to my lips.

'I don't want to go, Mummy.' Sophie looks up at me and I see how pale her face is. How she's bitten her bottom lip so badly it's almost bled. Sophie is worried sick about starting school, and even though we've made a special trip to M&S to buy her brand-new uniform and the pencil case with Elsa from *Frozen* on the front, it has done nothing to help. If she had her way, she'd stay at home with me for the rest of her life.

I want to comfort her, to tell her that her first day at school will be fine, but a niggling doubt has wormed its way into my head. What if I've counted incorrectly? If I've made a mistake, will it mean something bad will happen? Before the feeling of dread can take hold, I force it away. We're safe. Nothing is going to happen.

'You'll have a lovely time,' I say brightly. 'You've met Mrs Allen and you said you liked her. There will be lots of children to play with and, besides, you'll have Izzy with you.'

Isabella is ahead of us, turning circles on the esplanade, her arms spread wide like a helicopter. Her dark hair is escaping its band and I wince as she nearly collides with a dog walker.

'Look what you're doing, Izzy.'

As we catch up with her, Sophie's knuckles whiten on the pram's handle and she seems paler than ever. 'Are you all right, poppet?'

If she says no, I can take her home with me again. Postpone this horrible day. But she nods miserably and carries on walking.

Telling Isabella to hold onto the other side of the pram, we leave the seafront and head for the main road. When we reach the pelican crossing, I jab at the button with my finger. It's early morning rush hour and a steady stream of cars pass by. A grey Fiesta, a white van, a motorbike, its rider anonymous under his leathers and helmet. Four… five… six… Another four cars drive past us. If the red man changes to green before ten more cars go by, it will mean bad luck for the rest of the day. Eleven… twelve… thirteen…

Don't change. Don't change.

Fourteen… fifteen… sixteen. With sinking heart, I see the green man light up, but I don't move. I'm wondering if I should wait and try again. There's a persistent beep and the green man flashes – warning that the lights will soon change. People are crossing. Some are looking at us strangely. Wondering why we're not going.

'For fuck's sake.' A teenager with a pink puffer jacket pushes past me, trying to get across before the lights change again.

'Come on, Mummy. We're going to be late.' Isabella's shaking the pram and it brings me out of my trance. She's excited – was out of bed this morning before my alarm had even gone off. She'd pulled at my duvet and thrust her school pinafore in my face. 'I can't get it on!'

'We've plenty of time,' I say, glad we left the house a good fifteen minutes earlier than we had to, allowing us time to go the longer seafront route. Knowing that the prospect of being separated from the twins for the first time in my life could spiral my anxiety out of control and hoping the sea air might help.

'Dad says that at the big school there's a massive climbing frame in the playground and the boys will let me play football if I show them I'm not a sissy.' She looks at me slyly. 'He said I can kick anyone who bullies Sophie.'

'I'm sure he said nothing of the sort.'

He probably did, though. Mitch can speak without thinking at times and Isabella's gung-ho enough without his encouragement. I feel a twinge of guilt. He'd offered to come with us for the girls' first day, but I'd put him off. I'm their mum; it's something I need to do on my own. I think of my own first day at school. How my mother had asked Mrs Ringrose from next door to take me in as it was on her way to the newsagent's. I was the only one not to have a parent kiss me goodbye. I feel my eyes fill with tears, but Isabella is tugging at my sleeve.

'We're here, Mum.' Isabella is pulling at the pram handle again, trying to make us go faster. 'It's the big school.'

We're approaching the school gates and I feel Sophie's body push hard against my side. She's crying openly now, clinging on to my hand as though to a life raft.

'There's nothing to be scared about, darling.' I drop a kiss onto the top of her fair head. Her hair smells of the detangling shampoo I used last night, in preparation for her big day. The action gives me time to close my eyes and count to twenty. When I reach my goal, I start counting back down again.

'Mummy, come *on*.'

People are filing in through the gates and gathering around the classroom doors. Isabella has left us and is already halfway across the playground. We follow, but as we get closer to the building, Sophie's feet start to drag. Already, I'm dreading the moment I must leave her, but I can't put it off. The best thing, I know, would be to slip away as soon as possible so as not to prolong the separation, but it's going to be hard.

The girls' classroom is in a new extension that's attached to the original Victorian building. Mrs Allen stands at the door, welcoming each child as they arrive. She's young and pretty and looks barely old enough to be a teacher, let alone married. As I wheel Noah's pram up to the classroom and push the brake on with my foot, I can't help wondering if she'll still look that way after a day of Izzy.

Bending to the tray beneath the pram, I take out the girls' lunch boxes – Sophie's Elsa one and Isabella's, which has Bob the Builder on the front. I turn it so I don't have to see the picture – I used to have one just the same when I was a child. I'd tried to persuade her to choose something different, but she'd insisted I buy it as it reminds her of Mitch. I'm just straightening up when a leaflet is thrust at me. Turning to ask what it is, I find I'm too late; the woman has already moved on to the next group of parents, and all I can see is the back of her black coat and a peacock blue scarf. On the front of the leaflet, in big letters, are the words South

Downs Tree Survey. Below it is a picture of a large beech tree, with a dense green canopy and smooth grey bark. A small box to the side shows a magnified leaf and a beechnut for identification.

My breathing becomes shorter. Hating the sight of it, I ball the leaflet in my hand and toss it into the nearest bin.

Isabella glares at me. 'What are you doing? I wanted to look at it.'

I don't answer as Mrs Allen is approaching, a big smile on her face. 'Ah, my twins are here. Welcome! At least I'm not going to get the two of you muddled up.' Crouching down, she helps Isabella with her coat.

Isabella brushes her hand away. 'I can do it. I don't need help.'

I'm mortified. 'Isabella! Don't be so rude. Say sorry to Mrs Allen.'

She folds her arms. 'I don't want to.'

'It's all right. It's all new and exciting,' Mrs Allen says, and I'm relieved that she seems unconcerned. 'I'm sure Isabella can be a very polite girl when she wants to be.'

Sophie is hanging back. She's yet to cross the threshold. Children push past her, and she flattens herself against the wall as though hoping they won't notice her. She's as white as a sheet. I hold out my hand to her, but she ignores it, her eyes fixed on the ground. Outside the classroom, Noah begins to cry, and a wave of exhaustion engulfs me. I know how I must appear to their teacher. A mother who has no control over her children.

'Please, Sophie. Don't be difficult.'

Not sure what to do for the best, I do nothing and am thankful when Mrs Allen comes to my rescue. 'Do you like Lego?'

Sophie nods. 'Well, that's very lucky because we just happen to have a huge box of it waiting to be played with before I take the register. Our classroom assistant, Miss King, is trying to make a fairy castle, but she's not very good at it. Would you like to help her?'

She holds out her hand like I did, and, to my surprise, Sophie takes it.

'You go,' Mrs Allen says, with a smile. 'They'll both be fine.'

I want to hug Sophie to me, but scared of spoiling things, I blow her a kiss instead. Isabella has already disappeared, clearly no longer needing me.

'I'll see you later, Sophie, and you can tell me all about your day.' Without waiting for her to answer, and fighting back tears, I quickly walk out of the door and into the playground, relieved that Noah has stopped crying.

I turn to where I left the pram and pull up short. It's not there. With racing heart, I look around wildly, fear gripping my stomach. I parked it here. I know I did. As though it will miraculously appear, I look back to where I think the pram should be, but there's nothing there but a dropped book bag. I'm properly scared now – all sorts of things going around in my head. None of them good.

'Is anything the matter, Mrs Thirsk?' Mrs Allen is holding open the door, looking at me questioningly.

'My baby. The pram.' I'm trying to calm my rising panic. 'It's gone.'

Mrs Allen turns back and calls across the classroom. 'Miss King. Could you hold the fort for one minute?' She comes outside and stands next to me. 'Where did you park it?'

'Just here.' I point to the wall. My voice rising. 'Someone has taken him. I don't know what to do.' People are looking at me. I'm crying now and don't care who sees. 'Where is he?'

The playground is still full of parents, standing in groups chatting or looking in the classroom windows, waving to their children. I stare at those who have prams and buggies. Is one of them Noah's? Could someone have taken his pram by mistake? I know it's a ridiculous thought, but I'm not thinking straight.

'Mrs Thirsk. You need to calm down.'

I barely hear her. The wall where Noah's pram should have been is constructed of red bricks. I start to count them under my breath. If there are twenty bricks along the top of the window frame, my baby will be safe.

'Mrs Thirsk.' Mrs Allen has her hand on my arm. 'There must be a simple explanation. Are you sure you parked him here?'

I'm about to shout at her. Tell her that of course I'm sure and that we need to call the police, when I hear a cry. It's coming from the covered porchway of the next classroom, just out of sight. I run in the direction of the sound, a cry of relief breaking from me when I see Noah's pram parked against the wall.

Picking him out of his covers, I clasp him to me. 'Oh my God. Thank heavens.'

I look around me, trying to comprehend. Did I park Noah here? I didn't think I did, but now I'm not sure. I was so worried about Sophie. Concentrating so hard on how I was going to be able to leave her, that maybe I did.

Mrs Allen comes up to me. 'It's an easy mistake to make,' she says sympathetically. 'These classrooms all look the same when you're not used to them. I'm just glad everything's all right.'

I feel ridiculous now. 'I'm sure I didn't park him here.'

'Tiredness can make your mind play tricks. He's safe and that's all that matters.'

I nod. Knowing that my sleepless nights are written in the dark circles under my eyes. She must be right. My mind's playing tricks on me.

'Would you like me to take you to reception? Lorraine can make you some tea.'

'No. I'm fine now. Really.'

'Well, if you're sure. Go home and get some rest. You look exhausted.' With a parting smile, she walks back into the girls' classroom.

Noah is getting restless, squirming in my arms. Quickly, I place him back in the pram, but as I tuck the blanket around him, my hand touches something cold. Picking it out from the covers, I see it's a locket.

My first instinct is that it's mine. That the clasp must have come undone and the necklace fallen into the pram as I picked Noah up. My hand rises to my chest, but immediately my fingers make contact with the telltale heart shape of the locket beneath my jumper.

I stare at the one in my hand, not understanding. It looks just like mine.

Easing my thumbnails into the crack, I prise the two sides apart. Even though I know it's not possible, I half expect it to contain photographs of my children, but of course it doesn't. Both sides are empty.

I turn the locket over, a feeling of unease creeping up my spine. On its smooth surface, someone has scratched a word.

Sister.

The necklace slips through my fingers onto the tarmac. I know this locket. I haven't seen it in fifteen years. It's the one Freya was wearing the day she died.

CHAPTER TWO
Kelly Now

Noah has cried all the way home and my nerves are jangling. Who could have put the locket there? When I reach the house, I'm weak with relief. More so when I see Mitch's white van still parked outside. Ours is an ordinary house, one of several in a small Victorian terrace, the number twenty-seven almost obscured by the pyracantha we never seem to get around to pruning. Ignoring Noah's screams, I search in my bag for the key and let myself in, pulling the pram behind me into the hall.

'Mitch,' I call.

As I try to take off my boots, Charlie, our Border Terrier, jumps up at my legs and I push him away, not wanting any more demands on me.

'I'm in the kitchen.'

Lifting Noah from his covers, I go to find him, the dog at my heels.

Mitch is at the table, finishing his breakfast. Reaching for the bottle of ketchup, he upends it and bangs on the bottom to release a dollop of red sauce onto his plate. I watch as he wipes a slice of white bread through it and then through the congealing yolk of his fried egg.

He looks up at me. 'You're back late. Isabella didn't play up, did she?'

'No. Nothing like that.'

I want to tell him about the pram. About finding the locket… but I can't. What could I say? He doesn't know anything about Freya or even that I once had a sister. He'd say I was imagining things – that the locket could have belonged to anyone. He'd tell me I was exhausted. Hormonal. That I'd simply forgotten where I'd put the pram.

Noah's cries are getting louder. Mitch puts down his fork and holds out his arms for the baby, but I ignore him. Pulling out a chair, I sit and undo my blouse so Noah can feed. As he latches on, I close my eyes and try to enjoy the sensation of giving sustenance to my child. It's hard to believe that my mother would have done this once, held me in her arms and whispered special things only a mother would say to her child.

'You look done in.'

I open my eyes again. 'You would too if you were up all night.'

Mitch pulls another slice of bread from the packet in front of him, there's a smear of ketchup on the bristles of his chin. 'If you gave him a bottle, I'd be able to do some of the night shift.'

I look away. 'I told you. I don't want that. The midwife said—'

'I know what the bloody midwife said, but I'm worried about you, Kel. Surely your health is as important as the baby's. If you'd just let me do my bit, it would make life easier for you.'

I feel the pull of Noah's little mouth on my breast and tell myself that this is what being a mother is all about. Nurturing. Being there whenever your child needs you. Keeping them safe. Without realising it, my fingers have strayed to my locket. 'There's nothing wrong with me.'

He doesn't reply but gives a look that tells me exactly what he's thinking. Popping the last piece of egg-soaked bread into his mouth, he looks at his watch.

'I have to be on-site today, but I can leave early. At least let me collect the kids from school.'

It's as though he hasn't been listening to a word I've just said.

'I told you I don't need you to help.'

It's said too quickly, and his eyes register his hurt.

'For just once in your life, Kelly, can't you think about what *I* might need?'

Mitch looks so dejected that I feel my guilt rise. It's easy to forget he's a parent too. I force myself to say the words.

'I'm sorry. Of course, you can collect the girls if you want to.'

Taking his hand with my free one, I link my fingers with his. It's a practical hand, the pads of his fingers roughened and the nails short. At the moment, they're crusted white with whatever he's been working with these last few days and he hasn't done a very good job of cleaning them.

I don't mind really. It's proof of how hard he works. Five days a week plus Saturday morning and it's all for us. For his family. One day, he likes to say, we'll have a big house with a garden with enough space for the children to play on the trampoline they so desperately want – not a scrap of grass with a high brick wall and a tiny shed like we have now. He doesn't realise that I'm not bothered. That it's my family's love I care about. Nothing else.

As I stroke his hand with my thumb, I wonder what I would have done if Mitch hadn't found me that night in the bar. Hadn't fallen in love with me. This house was Mitch's before I married him and there's no way I would have afforded a house of my own. I could barely afford the rent on my grotty bedsit by the station. We've done little to the house since then. The white patch on the back of the door, where a dartboard used to hang, has never been painted over and the oversized plasma TV is the same one that was there the first night I stayed. It's never bothered me.

He beams. 'That's great. I'll take the baby too. That way, you can go for a run. You haven't been since you found out you were expecting. It will do you the world of good.'

I know he doesn't mean to sound patronising and force a smile. He's right. I used to run every evening and I miss it.

'All right, but make sure you don't leave him. Take him with you if you go into the classroom.'

Mitch frowns. 'What do you think I am? An idiot? He's only three months old, of course I wouldn't leave him.'

But *I* did. Just for those few minutes. I left my baby and someone moved him. Holding Noah closer to me, I feel the weight of my guilt. It was my job to keep him safe and I didn't.

Mitch gets up and takes his plate to the sink and Charlie follows him, hoping to get a treat. Leaving the plate on the draining board, he goes over to the calendar on the wall and looks at it.

'I've been thinking,' he says casually, rubbing his hand over the top of his stubbled head. 'Next weekend, we should do something different for a change. Invite some people over for the afternoon.'

I stare at him as though he's mad, but he carries on.

'I could fire up the barbeque, buy a cake – we never have cake. Maybe we could invite your family.'

The last words are said breezily. He has no idea of the effect they'll have on me. My throat tightens and, as if sensing a shift in atmosphere, Noah bats at my breast with his outstretched hand and begins to squirm. There's so much I want to say, but I can't.

Instead, I burst into tears.

CHAPTER THREE

Kelly Before

Kelly sits at the polished table at the far end of the living room and waits. In front of her is her birthday cake with its eight mismatched candles, and three small plates – one for her mum, one for herself and one for her dad when he comes home. There are no holders on the candles. They've been pressed haphazardly into the cake and the wax has dripped down, leaving pools of colour on the fudge icing that she'd watched her mum spoon from a plastic tub.

She hates the cake. She hates chocolate. What she'd wanted was one from the supermarket like the one her friend Carly Freeman had, with smooth pink icing and a unicorn on the top. She'd also wanted a party in the village hall with a Disney princess to do the party games, but she hadn't been allowed to have that either. Parties were for spoilt girls her mum had said.

'Mummy?' When she doesn't answer, she climbs down from the chair and goes to get her comfort blanket, which she's stuffed down the side of the settee. She knows it's babyish, but she can't sleep at night without it.

Kelly stands in the doorway and listens. The house feels different – as if it's waiting for something. Even Ben, their dog, is lying with his eyes glued to the door that leads into the hall, as though expecting something exciting to happen. Kelly calls to him and clicks her fingers like her dad does if he wants Ben's attention, but he ignores her, rubbing his nose with one of his paws and letting out a little whimper. It's past his supper time. She hasn't seen her mum since the phone call that sent her running from the room. Where is she?

'Mum?' she calls again.

The big hand of the clock on the mantelpiece has crept to the top and the little hand is on the eight. Eight o'clock. It will soon be time for bed, but her mum has said that as it's her birthday, she can play one of the games from the high shelf in the cupboard in the playroom. It's what she's been waiting for all day. She could get a game out ready, but that would mean standing on a chair, which will get her into trouble. Anyway, she isn't allowed to touch these games without asking first and she doesn't want to make her mum cross. Not after she took the time to ice the cake.

On the table is a box of matches, a used one mixing with the crumbs on her mum's plate. She'd left the room so quickly, Kelly hadn't had the chance to tell her what she'd wished for. But she's heard that telling someone your wish will stop it from coming true, so it's probably a good thing. This wish is one she wants to come true more than anything.

Thinking she should do something, Kelly goes into the hall, dragging her blanket behind her, and stands at the bottom of the stairs. After a few minutes, she climbs halfway up and sits on the threadbare carpet worrying at her wobbly front tooth. She can hear her mum now through her closed bedroom door. She must still be on the phone.

Should she go and knock?

From their cheap brass frames on the wall of the staircase, the faces of her brothers and sisters look down at her. Her mum doesn't like her calling them that, telling her that foster children are not the same as real brothers and sisters, but she does it anyway.

Some of the faces Kelly doesn't know, because they lived in her house when she was too young to remember, but even these children feel like they belong to her. She'd asked her mum once why she never talked about them once their stay had ended, but all she'd said was it wasn't good to get too attached. Then she'd pressed her lips together and that had been an end to it. Kelly had known better than to ask again.

Despite her mum's words, Kelly likes to imagine that she's linked with invisible threads to these children who have taken it in turns to occupy the bedroom at the back of the house. The shortest and tightest thread being reserved for Mason. He'd stayed from Christmas until March and, after he'd gone, she'd cried herself to sleep, her sobs muffled by her pillow so that they wouldn't be heard. She'd never asked why he'd left and they'd never told her.

There's the sound of a key in the lock and Kelly glues her eyes to the front door, her heart thumping. Her dad's home! As he pushes the door open and steps through it, turning to shake out his umbrella, Kelly thinks, as she always does, how handsome he is, with his blond hair combed back from his face and his smart grey suit. She wants to rush to him, have him bend down to kiss her or spin her around like she's seen on the telly, but she doesn't. It's not what they do in this house.

'I'm going to have a shower,' is all he says to her.

Edging past her on the stairs, he goes into the bathroom and shuts the door. Soon Kelly hears the shower running. He hasn't even said happy birthday to her.

'Andrew?' Her mum is at the top of the stairs and, although it's her father's name she's said, it's Kelly she's frowning at as if she's somehow made him disappear.

Kelly sees the phone in her mum's hand. 'I wasn't listening,' she says quickly, in case that's why she's cross.

Twisting her blanket around her finger, she searches her mum's face for a clue to her mood and is surprised when, instead of shouting at her, she joins her on the step. Reaching an arm around her, she pulls her close and Kelly can smell the sickly fragrance of her perfume. This unexpected attention should feel good, but all it does is make her rigid with anticipation.

'I have some good news, Kelly. Great news, in fact.' Her eyes flicker to the faces of the children in their brass frames. Her cheeks are unnaturally flushed. Her eyes shining.

'What is it, Mummy?' Kelly holds her breath.

The bathroom door unlocks and Kelly's dad stands there, a towel around his middle. Her mum turns to him, her smile too bright.

'Great news,' she repeats, but her dad just shakes his head.

'Jesus. Not again, Karen.'

Kelly looks from one to the other, wondering how he knows what her mum's about to say.

'Why don't *you* tell her, Andrew?'

Ignoring her, Kelly's father strides into the bedroom, slamming the door behind him, and when her mum looks back at her, her smile isn't as bright as it had been.

'Well, we won't let him spoil things.'

'What is it, Mummy? Tell me, please.'

Kelly's mum takes her hand and places it on her chest. 'Feel how my heart's racing.' It's true. Her mum's heart is fluttering in her chest like a trapped bird and Kelly feels as if she too might burst with excitement.

'Is it true?' she asks, as she's guessed what it might be.

Her mum nods. 'Tomorrow,' she says, 'another girl is coming. Her name is Freya and she's ten years old.'

Kelly puts her fingers in her mouth to stop from shouting out; the tips are sweet with the chocolate icing she hates so much. She doesn't care, though, as she's just had the best news in the world. The candle fairy had been listening after all. Her wish has come true.

Tomorrow she will have another sister.

And maybe, this time, she'll stay forever.

CHAPTER FOUR

Kelly Now

As I run, trainers slapping on the wet concrete, I fall into a natural rhythm and start to relax. I've missed this. The sound of the waves breaking on the stones and the cry of the seagulls.

I carry on until my sleep-deprived body tells me it's had enough, then slow to a walk and steer a path to the seafront railings. They've been newly painted, their geometric patterns gleaming with raindrops. I watch one, as it trickles down the painted surface, and wonder how many breaths it will take before it drops onto the ground. Five? Six? If it does it in less, my family will be safe. If more…

I can't bear to think of this possibility and start to count. *One… two…*

Come on, Kelly. Get a grip. Balling my hand into a fist, I rub the drips away, weariness enveloping me. The girls will be home from school now. Safe at home with Mitch. What's wrong with me?

I lean my arms on the rail and look down. Today the sea looks mean, the broiling waves rolling one after the other onto the shore. The tide is on its way in and the beach is empty except for a woman with an Alsatian that's digging at the glistening shingle with its paws. When I look more closely, I see the woman isn't on her own. There's a child with her. I hadn't noticed him as he was crouched in the shelter of one of the wooden groynes, studying the pebbles. He runs towards the sea in his blue wellingtons, a stone clutched in his fist then, drawing back his arm, he throws the stone as hard as he can. When it doesn't make the foaming water, he stamps his foot and I can't help smiling.

A wave washes over the child's feet, threatening to send a spray of foam over the top of his boots, but the woman has got there just in time, sweeping him up and carrying him back up the beach, his little arms wrapped tightly around her neck. I'd thought she was his mother, but now she's turned, I see that she's too old. Possibly, it's his grandmother. The child's face is buried in her neck and I turn away, not wanting to see. Knowing that my own children will never know this special type of love. Noah will never run from the waves and into the safety of his grandmother's arms and the girls will never get to show her their special things.

I remember my meltdown when Mitch suggested inviting my family at the weekend. How he'd apologised and said he realised it was thoughtless of him. He knows I won't talk about them – have never talked about them. My mother doesn't deserve to feel the weight of my baby in her arms.

At the thought of the children, I feel a sudden tingling in my breasts and a telltale warmth spreads through my running shirt. Unzipping my sweatshirt, I shove my hand inside and feel the warm, wet dampness where my milk has leaked. Damn. I shouldn't have stayed out for so long. Pushing myself off from the railings, I start to jog again. If I run all the way, I'll be home in fifteen minutes.

Heading back along the esplanade, the rain, that had stopped earlier, starts to fall again. Cursing myself for not having brought a waterproof, I pull up the hood of my sweatshirt and run faster. At least the rain that's soaking my top will hide the embarrassing damp circles I can feel spreading.

I stop at the crossing as I did this morning, jogging on the spot and waiting for the lights to change. I've counted twenty before the ~n man appears to tell me I can cross, and I should feel relieved, but I don't. I'm looking at the Mini that's first in the queue and however much I want to tear my eyes away from the driver, I can't. There's something about her white hair and narrow face. The pale eyes raised to the red light in front of her, waiting for it to change. As I stand mesmerised by the windscreen wipers that sweep arcs across the glass, a sense of inevitability floods through me.

It's Freya. I know it.

CHAPTER FIVE
Kelly Before

When Kelly wakes the next morning, she doesn't jump out of bed as she normally does but keeps her head still on the pillow, her comfort blanket draped over her face and her eyes squeezed tightly shut.

Please don't let it have all been a dream.

She turns the events of the previous evening over in her mind: the vile chocolate cake with its dripping candles, the game from the forbidden shelf that had never been played and the conversation she'd had with her mum on the stairs.

It must be true. It must.

And even as she pushes herself up onto her elbow, letting the blanket slide down her face onto the covers, she can tell that the house has already changed. There's the whine of a hoover in the bedroom across the landing and the rasp of furniture being moved across the polished wooden floor.

Sunlight's creeping through the blinds, slanting tiger-stripes across her duvet. She hates these blinds and wishes she had proper curtains like Carly Freeman's, pink ones with stars.

Slipping out of bed, she goes to the window and parts the blind with her finger and thumb. She'd tried to open them once, using the white cord that hung down at the side, but instead of the gaps between the slats widening, the whole blind had moved,

‌ng up at one side. She hadn't been able to get it down again and knowing no one would be bothered to fix it, had got used to sleeping in pools of light from the street lamp.

Outside, there's nothing to be seen except the lane full of potholes, the hedgerow and some telegraph wires, but at least from here she'll be able to see when her new sister arrives. Kelly's tummy fizzes with anticipation. Sometime today, a car will pull up outside their house and a woman, or maybe a man, will get out. With them, will be Freya.

That's what happens every time a new foster child arrives and this time, as with every other, her heart will race with anticipation. She'll study their faces for clues. Will this child be the one who'll stay?

Already she has a picture in her mind of what the girl will look like – a head taller than her with glossy black hair and laughing brown eyes. When they see each other, it will be like they've known each other all their lives. Freya will curl her pinky finger around her own. *Best friends forever*, she'll say. But the bond will be greater than that – the invisible threads tighter. For Freya will be her sister. Her best one yet.

There's the sound of a car door, but it's only her dad. He'll be driving to the station in Shoreham where he'll leave his car in the car park with lots of others and catch the train to London. Her mum took Charlene and Jasmine to London last summer to see the queen's palace, leaving her with Mrs Ringrose from next door. She's old and smells of rose petals and something else she doesn't like to think about. Maybe this year it will be *her* turn to go.

As her dad reverses out of the drive, her mum, still in her dressing gown, bangs on the car window. He winds the window down and, from the look on her mum's face, she knows they're having a row. It's been a warm and muggy night and her mum's words float in through Kelly's open window.

'Why can't you just be pleased?'

Kelly steps back, not wanting them to know she's seen. The front door slams and there are footsteps on the stairs. Jumping quickly back into bed, she pretends to be asleep when the door to her bedroom opens.

Her mum stands there, her wiry, brown hair wet and straggly from her shower. Bags under her eyes. 'Time to get up, Kelly. It's a big day today.'

Kelly stretches and fakes a yawn. 'When will she be here?'

'Soon,' her mum says distractedly. 'Very soon.'

Despite Kelly's excitement, she knows what this will mean. Her mum will fuss around Freya, asking her questions about what she likes to eat and what time she goes to bed, as if the answers haven't already been given to her. Then she'll show her around the house like she's the queen, leaving the bedroom, with its view across the wild meadow, until last.

'This will be your room,' she'll say, as she's said so many times before.

She's seen it with Charlene and Jasmine. Even Jade had been made to follow her upstairs, her face sulky and her hands curled into fists. Kelly had looked on in awe as the teenager's heavy black boots had scuffed the skirting whenever she thought her mum wasn't looking. It was only Mason who'd missed out. He'd had to sleep in the spare room downstairs as he had legs that didn't work properly.

Don't forget me, she wants to say. *I'm here too.*

Instead she says, 'I'll get dressed, shall I?'

'Yes, do that. I need to get myself ready.' Her mum points to the pile of new clothes she's left on the chair by her chest of drawers. New brothers and sisters always mean new clothes, even if they're ones she'd never choose herself.

As her mum's bedroom door closes and she hears the hum of the hairdryer, Kelly pulls on her pants and vest, then picks up the tartan skirt from the chair. It looks very small and, when she pulls the label out, she sees that it says Age 6-7 years. Nearly two

~~ small. Not knowing what else to do, she steps into it and pulls it up. The elastic waistband is tight, cutting into the flesh of her stomach and she knows it will leave a red mark. Trying to ignore the discomfort, she slots her arms into the puffed sleeves of the white blouse and does up the buttons, relieved when it fits.

The doorbell rings. In a fever of excitement, she goes back onto the landing. Her mum is already there, looking in the landing mirror. Checking her make-up.

'How do I look?'

She looks as she always does. Overweight, with skin prone to eczema. She's put on a summer dress that is straining over her bosom. Usually, her dark, wiry hair is scragged back into a band, but today she's taken more care over it. It's newly washed and bounces off her shoulders, the side sections drawn away from her face and fastened with diamanté clips. When she turns and flashes Kelly a red-lipped smile, a sickly floral fragrance fills the hall.

'You look nice, Mummy.'

Her brows pull together. 'Only nice?'

Kelly swallows. 'Pretty… and clever… and…'

She's relieved when her mum helps her out. 'The perfect mother?'

Her head nods urgently, like a chicken pecking grain. 'Yes.'

'Then everything is all right with the world.' The flushed cheeks from the evening before have returned. She looks feverish, as though she's starting with a cold.

'Come on then,' she says, taking Kelly's hand.

Then, together, they go down to meet Kelly's brand-new sister.

CHAPTER SIX

Kelly Now

A sharp blare of a car horn brings me roughly from my trance. The woman is looking at me now, gesticulating for me to cross the road, and I see I'm mistaken. It isn't Freya. How could it be? Just like the other times, it's simply someone who looks like her, someone who just happens to share her blonde hair and pale eyes. Seeing the woman on the beach reminded me of my mother and, in turn, has brought back memories from the past.

For several years after it happened, I'd seen her everywhere, but once I'd moved away, the incidents had become fewer until I'd managed to tell myself that I was over it. Over *her*. After Noah was born, though, I'd started seeing her again. Started remembering what happened. And now I have her locket. Since it appeared in Noah's pram, I haven't been able to put it out of my mind. How did it get there? I search my memory for clues… Did Freya give it to me all those years ago? Did I steal it? Even if it had been in my possession, it doesn't explain how it came to be nestled inside my baby's covers. But even as I'm wondering, an image is in my head of Freya the last time I saw her – the gold of the locket caught in a flash of lightning.

Another car sounds its horn. Feeling foolish, I cross the road, then continue my jog home. It's miserable now and I'm soaked, running around the puddles that spring from nowhere. When I eventually reach my house, I slow, telling myself it's because I want my heart rate to return to normal but knowing, in truth, it's because I'm dreading I'll find Noah red-faced and screaming, the twins fractious for their tea and the house a tip.

As I search in the pocket of my sodden tracksuit bottoms for my key, I notice the newspaper that's sticking out of the letter box. It's soggy with rain and I pull it out before letting myself in.

As predicted, the place looks like a bomb's hit it. One of Mitch's work boots is by the door, covered in mud. The other is further down the hallway. Two black patent shoes, also caked in mud, have been discarded at the bottom of the stairs along with a fleece and Noah's car seat. Picking up the shoes, I place them with the others that are neatly lined up against the wall, smiling as I remember how Isabella had insisted I buy them even though it was plainly not what the uniform guidelines had meant by sensible school shoes. She'd argued and argued in that crowded shop, knowing, even at the tender age of five, that she'd wear me down, and when she had, Sophie, of course, had wanted the same.

There is only one pair of patent shoes here, though, and the house is suspiciously quiet. Something that a house with Isabella in never is. Unfolding the newspaper, I look at it. It's a copy of *The Argus*. What's it doing in my door?

From the living room, I can hear the unmistakeable commentary of a football match. For Mitch, watching the game is the next best thing to playing with the lads on a Sunday morning, something he had to give up after he'd damaged the tendon in his knee.

Putting the newspaper on the hall table, I hang my sweatshirt over the banister. There's a jumble of other jumpers and jackets slung across it, and I resist the urge to sort them out. Instead, I go into the living room, nearly tripping over the change bag that's spilled its contents onto the floor.

The first person I see is Sophie. She's sitting on the floor, her fair head bent to the Disney princess dolls she's playing with. She looks miserable and when she sees me, she lifts up her arms, but Mitch shakes his head.

'You're a big girl, Soph. You don't need picking up.'

He's sprawled across the settee next to her, his feet resting on the worn arm – the cigarette burn they cover, testimony to his previous thirty a day habit. Noah, in his white blanket, lies along his legs. He's fast asleep and my instinct is to ask Mitch why he didn't put him in his crib. I say nothing, though. Noah is quiet for a change and, for that, I can forgive my husband anything.

I crouch beside Sophie and stroke her hair back from her face. 'Not had a good day then?'

'Don't put words into her mouth, Kelly.' Mitch tears his eyes away from the television. 'Christ. You're soaking.'

'Did anything happen, sweetie?' I say, pulling Sophie to me.

'Don't fuss her, Kel. Everyone has a first day at school. Everyone survives. All they do on day one is play and listen to stories.' He chuckles to himself. 'That and working out who's the class bully.'

I throw him a look. 'Don't say things like that, Mitch. You're supposed to be making things better not worse.' Releasing Sophie, I kiss her cheek. 'Take no notice of silly Daddy. I'll make some tea and you can tell me all about it after.'

A copy of the *Daily Mirror* lies on the floor next to a half-eaten packet of crisps. Picking it up, I put it into the magazine rack. As I straighten up again, I see Mitch is still wearing his work jeans from this morning – they're covered in dried plaster and splashes of paint.

'Oh, Mitch. You could have changed.'

He grins and wiggles his toes. 'I took my shoes off. That must be worth half a brownie point at least.'

I've never been able to stay cross with him for long. Being careful not to wake the baby, even though the ache in my breasts tells me I should, I lean over and kiss my husband, thinking that I should change my damp top before getting Sophie's tea. Mitch's stubble is sandpaper-rough against my cheek, but I don't care. It's what I love about my husband, the unapologetic maleness of him. Straightening up again, I pick up the can of lager that's on the table beside him and the one he's crushed and dropped onto the floor, wondering as I do if I should be worried.

As I come back from the kitchen, having put the cans in the recycling, I remember the newspaper.

'Someone put a copy of *The Argus* through the door.' I glance back into the hall. 'Is it something to do with you?'

'What? No. Get in there!' Mitch cranes his neck to see around me as the crowd roars, but his excitement turns to a groan as he realises it's the other team who have scored.

'Fuck!'

'Mitch!'

He widens his eyes. 'What?'

'Not in front of Sophie.'

He has the decency to look sheepish, nodding towards the TV where a player in a green shirt has just skidded under the legs of another. 'Sorry, I got sidetracked.'

'So I see.'

The crowd groans as a ball skims the goalpost. Mitch looks at the screen, then back at me. 'How was your run?'

'It was okay. Thank you for collecting the kids.' I try to keep my voice neutral, not wanting to give away how stressed I've felt at not being the one to collect them. 'Where's Izzy? She's very quiet. Is she up in her room?'

His eyes don't leave the television. 'She's round at Maddie's.'

'At Maddie's? Why?'

'We'd just got back, and she was passing – on her way back from a holistic fair, whatever the hell that is.' I hear the defensiveness in his tone. 'Izzy was playing up and I was struggling to undo the clasp on Noah's buggy. She asked if the twins wanted to go over and see her new kitten. She could see that I had my hands full.'

'If you couldn't cope, then you should have let me—'

'I didn't say I couldn't cope.' He sounds offended.

Not wanting to make things worse, I turn to Sophie. 'And you didn't want to see the kitten, sweetie?'

My daughter looks up and shakes her head.

'She wanted to wait for you,' Mitch says.

Of course she did. Ever since she was born, Sophie has never liked to be too far away from me – unlike Izzy who's happy wherever she is as long as there's something to entertain her. Bending down, I kiss the top of her soft fair head, and feel her small hand reach up to touch my cheek.

Mitch looks at the clock. 'Where were you anyway? You were gone ages.'

'I just lost track of the time.' He doesn't know about the counting. I haven't wanted to tell him, sensing he won't understand. Worried in case he thinks I'm losing it. 'I'm going to go upstairs and change.'

Just as I get to the stairs, the doorbell rings and Charlie rushes to it, barking madly. It's a welcome distraction and I go and answer it. As soon as I do, the whirlwind that is Izzy rushes past me. When she reaches the end of the hall, she gives a twirl, then waves her arms in the air.

'I've seen a kitten. I've seen a kitten,' she chants to anyone who might be listening.

'Lucky you,' I say, catching her and giving her a squeeze. Pressing my cold cheek against her warm one. 'Thank you for having her, Maddie. It was kind of you, but there was no need. I'm sure Mitch could have managed.'

Maddie smiles, a dimple showing in her cheek. 'It was no problem at all. If you want to bring Sophie round to see the little furry monster sometime, you're very welcome. I don't want her to miss out.'

'Thank you,' I say again, taking in her long, indigo wrap-around skirt, the white T-shirt that clings to her slim body and the orange espadrilles that are completely inappropriate for a rainy day such as this. Her look is bohemian. Not a look I could ever carry off – not until I shift the baby weight anyway. I fold my arms across my chest, aware of how I must look. 'Maybe I could bring her over at the end of next week… when she's settled in at school a bit more.'

'Isn't she keen? Izzy couldn't talk about anything else.'

'No,' I say, glancing into the living room. 'Not really.'

Maddie pats me on the arm and I try my hardest not to find it patronising. 'I'm sure she'll be fine in a week or so,' she says. 'I remember being petrified on my first day. Anyway, she has Isabella.'

'I know. I just hope you're right.'

Maddie turns to go, but when she reaches the gate, she turns back. 'I've been thinking about Noah. Have you thought of trying baby massage?'

I'm surprised by her question. 'No, why would I?'

'It's just that it can do wonders for soothing a colicky baby. It's hard when you're up all night, not knowing what to do.' She pauses and a flush of pink climbs up her neck as she reads in my face my unspoken question. 'Mitch told me. He says Noah wakes a lot at night and that you're finding it hard. I thought I'd just mention it.'

My fingers grip the door frame. How could Mitch be so disloyal? Making it sound as if I'm not coping… even if it's true. And what right does she have to tell me how to look after my baby? It's not even as if she's a mother herself. Only someone who's carried a baby could understand.

'Thank you,' I say stiffly. 'I'll bear that in mind.'

I close the door and rest my back against it, my nails digging into the soft skin of my palms. The newspaper is still on the table where I left it and I pick it up, hoping to find something in it to calm me down before I go back to the others. As I flick through it, I notice that the corner of one of the pages has been folded down. It's the page with the horoscope on and immediately I see that the symbol for Leo has been circled in red pen. I start to read.

This is a time to re-evaluate your life. Looking to the past will help you put things in perspective. This is not the time to be divulging secrets.

There's a prickling at the back of my neck. My zodiac sign is Leo. Who put this through the letter box? Unable to stop myself, I search for something to count, my eyes alighting on the wooden floorboards that run along the hall. I close my eyes, not allowing myself to cheat. If there are more than twenty, I can relax and forget the stupid newspaper.

I'm just counting them when Mitch calls out to me from the living room.

'Kel. What are you doing?'

The interruption has made me lose my place and I stop, frustration washing over me. Now I'll have to start again. 'Nothing.'

'Can you come in then? Noah's woken up.'

I count faster, but Noah's cries are sudden and impossible to ignore. With a huge effort, I force myself to leave the hall and go into the living room. Noah's little head, with its soft fuzz of light brown hair, is bumping at Mitch's broad chest, looking for milk.

'You're not going to find anything there, buddy,' he says, lifting the baby up and settling him on his shoulder. He looks up at me. 'Are you all right?'

'Of course I am.'

Taking a deep breath, I hold out my arms so he can pass Noah to me. Mitch looks so comfortable with him, so confident, that I feel a twinge of envy – knowing that as soon as I take him, Noah's little mouth will pucker, his face will turn red and the crying will start again. A noise that will only stop when I settle him to feed.

'Good,' he says, 'because I've been thinking some more about the weekend and I've come up with a better idea. One that I know you're going to love. But I'm not going to tell you what it is; I'm going to surprise you. Surprises are the best thing, don't you think?'

I look at him, then away again, unsure how to answer. In my experience, surprises are a herald of worse things to come.

CHAPTER SEVEN
Kelly Before

The girl who stands behind the young woman with the briefcase looks nothing like the picture Kelly has been holding in her head for the last few hours. Despite being two years older, she's not much taller than Kelly and in place of the dark brown curls is a halo of pale hair so fine she can see the sun shining through it.

The woman steps forward and holds out her hand to her mum. Her smile's apologetic. 'I'm sorry it's such short notice. Sometimes these things are tricky under a Section Twenty.'

'There's no need to apologise.' Her mum takes her extended hand between her own plump ones. 'I understand. Really, it's no problem.'

The woman looks down at the girl. 'Freya, this is Karen. And you must be Kelly.'

Kelly says nothing. She doesn't like the woman in her trouser suit and shiny black shoes. Has never liked any of them. They smile and ask her questions they already know the answers to, but even as they write the things she's said in their notebooks, she knows it's not really her they're interested in. But that's not the worst of it. What she hates most, now this woman is here, is that everyone will start acting differently. Even her.

The girl doesn't move. Just stares at Kelly with an ice-cool gaze before covering her eyes with her arms. Kelly can't drag her own eyes away from the blue veins beneath the skin of her forearms.

Pale skin. Pale eyes. Pale hair. She's never seen anyone so colourless. Even her T-shirt is pale pink.

'Don't stare, Kelly. Say hello.' Her mum's fingers are digging into her shoulder.

'Hello.'

The girl doesn't answer, just stands where she is beside the lady, her jeans hanging from her thin frame. Her white arms raised like a shield.

'It will take time.' The woman turns away from Freya and lowers her voice. 'It's been a difficult time, but I'm sure it won't take long for her to settle in. And with your experience…'

'Of course.'

Kelly stands in her white blouse and too-tight tartan skirt watching her mum's face soften in a way it never does when she looks at her. A deep well of despair opens up as her mother kneels in front of the girl and places tender hands on either side of her arms.

'Take your time, Freya. There's no hurry. One day at a time, eh?'

Still the girl says nothing.

Kelly is wracked with disappointment. This is not how it was meant to be. She wants to take Freya by the hand and show her Ben… the games cupboard… the garden. Most of all, she wants to show her the photographs of all the children who've come before her and tell her that she knows she will be different. But she doesn't. Instead, she waits for a signal from the girl. A smile. Anything.

When none comes, she ignores her mum's scornful look and leaves them to it, going into the living room where Ben is waiting. Lying next to him, she drapes an arm across his warm body and pushes her face into his fur, not caring that her mum will think it's disgusting. As she flips his ear around her finger, she feels his heart beating against her chest. Soon they will all come inside and Mummy will offer the lady tea in a delicate cup decorated with pink roses, its rim and handle edged in gold. She learnt a long time ago that a new sibling and their social worker deserve nothing less than the best china. They'll sit at the polished table and, instead of the chocolate birthday cake, there will be forms passed between them.

'I suppose you've told her.' They are in the hall now and Kelly can hear their voices clearly.

'Of course.'

It can't be Kelly they're talking about. They never tell her anything.

'Because it's always best to familiarise.' It's the lady's voice again.

'Please don't worry,' her mum says. 'We have it all in hand.'

They don't come into the living room as she'd thought they would but stay in the hallway. She hates how Freya didn't even look at her, even though she's going to be her sister. It's Kelly who'll be looking out for Freya in the school playground, the one who'll be sharing the books from the shelf above her bed and showing her the secret hiding places she has in the garden. Doesn't she know that?

When the door opens, Kelly thinks it will be her mum and the lady with the briefcase, but it isn't. It's Freya. Dropping Ben's ear, she sits up and folds her arms around her knees. She expects the girl to say something, but she doesn't, just stands inside the room, her arms wrapped around her body, her pale blue gaze fixed on her.

Kelly stands up, unsure of whether to go to her or not. There's something about the girl's paleness that both attracts and repels her. She wants to ask so many things. Why are you here? Where are your mum and dad? What have you done? Are you scared? But she doesn't ask any of these things as her mum has made it clear that if she asks too many questions when a new child arrives, she'll scare them off. Instead, she takes in the twig-like fingers that clutch the sides of her pale pink T-shirt and the jeans that are too big for her and way too hot for the time of year. She's never known anything about the children who have joined their family.

The voices in the hall murmur on. Mostly, she can't hear what they're saying, as they've deliberately lowered their voices, but occasionally some of the conversation drifts through.

'You have the number,' she hears the woman say. 'Ring any time if there's a problem. Though I'm sure there won't be. Despite the obvious, Freya appears to have adjusted well.'

Although Freya's eyes don't leave Kelly's, her head turns fractionally towards the door and the grip on her T-shirt whitens her knuckles. What's she thinking?

'Considering…' From the way her mum says it, it's like she and the lady are sharing a secret.

'Yes, of course. Considering.'

The voices dip again and Freya's fingers release their hold on the T-shirt. Her eyes are shining and Kelly wonders if she's going to cry. She hopes not. Feeling sorry for her, she takes a step towards her and then another, fearful of what this strange, pale girl will do when she reaches her. Ben is behind her and she's thankful, the thought of his soft brown eyes and the warm bulk of his golden-furred body giving her courage. Kelly covers the rest of the distance quickly and then they are face-to-face.

Close up, the girl's eyes are even more unusual, watery-pale like the eyes of a ghost. Kelly blinks and swallows. Now she's in front of the girl, her courage has run out and she doesn't know what to do. But while she stands in a fug of indecision, something happens. Something that shifts the balance. For she feels Freya's hand creep into hers, her thin fingers curling around her own.

Kelly looks down at their linked hands. 'Do you want to play?' she asks uncertainly.

When she sees Freya nod, the movement so tiny she nearly misses it, she thinks her heart will burst.

CHAPTER EIGHT

June 7th

You don't know me and I know I probably shouldn't be doing this, but I want you to know that I understand how you must be feeling. The pain of losing a child must be the same pain a child feels when they lose their mother. I want to tell you about the girls. In some strange way, I'm hoping that by getting in contact, it might make the loss more bearable – that it might make up for everything. I've included photos of them when they were much younger so you can see how beautiful they were. I think you'll agree, they're very different.

All the best

CHAPTER NINE

Kelly Now

Freya is taking me by the hand, leading me through the woods. It's cold and dark and she's wearing just a thin nightdress while I am dressed in my navy anorak with the fur trim around the hood. Aren't you cold? I ask, but she just laughs. How can I be cold when I'm dead? I ask where we're going but she doesn't answer and I realise she doesn't need to, as I know already. I don't want to go there, but she's pulling harder, tugging at my hand to make me go faster. I see my father through the trees. He's wearing his work suit. Please don't make me go! I scream, but he just shakes his head sadly.

I think I'm still screaming as I wake, but as I force my eyes to open, I realise I'm not. Mitch is there beside me in the bed, snoring gently. Other than that, the room is quiet. I lie on my back, sweat cooling on my face and chest, trying to calm my racing heart. It was only a dream, I tell myself. Dreams can't hurt you.

On the other side of the room is Noah's cot. Mitch had wanted to move him into his own room, but I'd put my foot down. The health visitor has said we should keep him with us for at least the first six months and, as far as I'm concerned, her word is law. We did the same thing with the girls. Even though it was hard.

As I lie awake, I can hear his little sighs and mewls. Sounds I've come to recognise as the prelude to him waking. Closing my eyes tightly, I breathe from my diaphragm, counting back from a hundred. If I manage to get to twenty before he cries, he'll go back to sleep straight after his feed. Tonight, though, it's not working. Instead of feeling calmer, by the time I've reached my goal, my anxiety has escalated as thoughts crowd into my head: What if he won't feed properly like last night? What if he won't stop crying? What if, God forbid, I drop him? Thoughts I'd never had with the twins even though they were my first. Maybe it was because, with two, I never had time to think, let alone worry.

As the mewls become cries, I feel the tears gather. Looking at the clock, I see it's only three fifteen. Just two hours since Noah's last feed. The cries are getting louder, more insistent, and I put my hands over my ears, wishing for one treacherous moment that everything could go back to how it was before I had him. A time when it was just me, Mitch and the girls and I still thought I was a good mother.

Mitch turns to me sleepily. He pushes himself up onto one elbow and looks over at the cot.

'Kelly, are you awake? He'll disturb the twins.'

I want to pretend that I'm not, bury my head in the pillow and go back to sleep, but it will only be putting off the inevitable.

'Just give me a minute.'

I continue my count then, when I've reached twenty, I push the duvet back and slide out of bed, my lack of sleep making me stumble like a drunk across the carpet. Between the wooden bars of the cot, I can see Noah's little fists waving in the air. I know that when I bend to pick him up, his face will be red and scrunched. Reaching down, I pick him out of his cover, feeling his tiny body stiffen as I lift him onto my shoulder.

'Hush,' I say, as I place my hand against the back of his head, holding him close and rocking him from side to side. 'You can't still be hungry.'

But already, he's searching for my breast through the nightdress, soaking the jersey material with his tears. Taking him back to the bed, I prop up the pillow and pray that he'll feed properly and not fight me. I'm lucky this time. As I feel the pull of his lips, it's a struggle to stay awake. I'm scared I might fall asleep and roll on him, but that's not the only reason I force my eyes to stay open.

I'm afraid of what else I might find in my dreams.

CHAPTER TEN
Kelly Before

The lady is leaving. From their hiding place, in the cool darkness of the laurel hedge in the back garden, Kelly hears the slam of the door and the sound of a car's engine.

Parting the leaves, Kelly peers out, wondering why the woman didn't come out to say goodbye. It seems strange. She looks behind her at Freya. She's sitting cross-legged in the leafy shadows, her head bowed. Her lap is covered with the detritus you find in such a shadowed spot: leaf mulch, twigs and dry earth.

'Mummy won't like it if you get dirty,' Kelly says.

The girl only stares back, her arms slack at her sides. Beside her, Ben dozes, letting out little whimpers every now and again as he chases rabbits in his dream.

Kelly sits down again. 'I've got some of my birthday cake. Do you want a piece?' Reaching behind her, she feels beneath the shrubbery for the Tupperware and pulls off the plastic lid. She holds it out to Freya. Freya takes a piece and Ben, a sixth sense telling him food is near, opens his eyes.

When Freya offers it to him, Kelly bats it out of her hand, horrified. 'Are you stupid? Dogs aren't allowed to eat chocolate. They could die!' She scrabbles to pick up the pieces from the ground before Ben can reach it.

The girl flinches and Kelly's immediately sorry she shouted. She's probably never had a dog. Putting the lid on the box, she tries to make her voice friendly. 'Now you know, you won't do it again.'

It's nice out here, just the two of them, but Kelly knows that soon her mum will come out and ruin it as she always does. She'll call to them and she and Freya will have to crawl out of their hiding place. The smile her mum will put on won't quite reach her eyes and she'll take Freya's hand and pull her away from her, fussing over her and asking annoying questions.

But for the moment, Kelly has Freya to herself. She still hasn't said anything but has followed her meekly around as she's shown her things. Squatting next to her to look at the millipedes in the woodpile, eating the early blackberry Kelly handed her from the bramble that's made its way over the top of their fence and turning Kelly's shell collection over in her hand. Showing Freya her special things makes her feel warm inside.

'I'm happy you came,' she says, watching the pattern of leaves flicker across Freya's face. 'I really, truly am.'

'Kelly? Freya? Where are you?' Her mum's at the French windows and the mood is shattered. 'Come inside. I want to show Freya her room.'

Kelly turns to Freya. 'Do you want to go?'

Freya is holding a snail in the palm of her hand, tracing the spirals with her finger. She looks up at Kelly, her eyes squinting as the leaves move in the breeze and a camera-flash of sunlight breaks through the gloom. Slowly, she shakes her white head.

Gratified, Kelly turns and peers through the leaves once more, seeing her mum step back into the house. But it isn't long before her fear of displeasing her mum overrides her desire to keep Freya to herself a little longer.

She backs out of her hiding place into the sunlight. 'Come on.'

At first, Kelly's scared Freya won't come out, but then there's a rustle of leaves and she appears, the snail still cupped in her hand.

She drops it onto one of the squares of crazy paving that winds its way down to the end of the garden, then hovers her trainer over it.

Kelly stares, appalled and fascinated in equal measures. Surely, she's not going to step on it? With her eyes fixed on Kelly's, Freya lowers her foot a centimetre until it makes contact with the delicate shell. It's as if she's waiting for her to give her permission.

Kelly's stomach does a flip. Miss Dunlop has taught them to respect all living things and the snail is as much a living thing as Ben. As if reading her thoughts, Ben pushes his nose into her hand. It's cold and wet. She worries at the edge of her white blouse with her free hand, rolling it between her fingers, exposing a narrow strip of squashed flesh above the too-tight skirt. Freya is still looking at her, the eyes, with their pale, unblinking lashes, watching her with interest. Before she can stop herself, Kelly nods and Freya's foot comes down with a nauseating crunch.

Kelly steps back, her hand across her mouth, her eyes wide with horror. She doesn't look when Freya lifts her foot, but the image is in her head, nonetheless. The soft, viscous body of the creature smeared on the paving, mixed with fragments of its broken shell. Water rushes into her mouth and she thinks she might be sick, but Freya has stepped off the path and is standing next to her on the grass. For the second time since she arrived, Kelly feels Freya's hand creep into hers. It's as if the untimely death of the snail has been an offering, a present to cement their friendship.

Hand in hand, they walk towards the open French windows, their arms swinging. When finally, Kelly looks behind at the shining jelly-like mass on the concrete, she feels like she's passed a test.

CHAPTER ELEVEN

Kelly Now

'Where are we going?'

Lifting Noah from his car seat, I hold him under the arms and dangle his legs over the holes in the baby sling that Mitch is holding out.

'Want me to have him?' he asks.

'No. I'll have to get used to it sometime.' Holding Noah firmly to my chest, I slip one arm and then the other through the straps and then wait while Mitch snaps the clasp closed round the back. I close my eyes and sway a little, drunk with tiredness after my sleepless night.

The additional weight at my front reminds me of my pregnancy. One that was full of problems: morning sickness that lasted into the fifth month, a couple of scares with my blood pressure and sacroiliac pain that sent shooting pains down my hip.

'Okay?'

I nod, taking some of Noah's weight with my hand under his striped canvas bottom.

Mitch releases the girls from their seats, and they climb out, Sophie immediately comes to my side and tucks her hand inside my free one. The thumb of her other slips into her mouth. Since starting school, she's been quieter than ever. I make a mental note to go and see Mrs Allen on Monday.

'Take it out, Soph. You're a big girl now. You don't need to suck your thumb.' Even as I say it, I realise the hypocrisy of my words. Remembering when the warmth and softness of my old blanket was the only comfort I had in that house devoid of love.

During the drive here, I hadn't taken much notice of where we were going, too busy checking off the things we may have left behind: the baby wipes, nappy sacks, extra drinks for the children. So many things to remember. So much responsibility. At least we haven't brought Charlie with us – it's enough having the children to worry about. I'll make sure Mitch gives him an extra walk later.

'I've got the picnic bag,' Mitch says. 'I had a look online and up there is the perfect spot for a picnic. There's plenty of shade and a view to die for. There's even a pub in the village if we fancy it later. What more could you ask for on a day out?'

I give a half-hearted smile. It's certainly better than his first barbeque idea, but what I'd have really liked was a day in bed. A day without worries. A picture of my bed drifts into my mind and I imagine the deep softness of the pillow. The bliss of floating into a dreamless sleep in the cocoon of my duvet, knowing that I wouldn't be dragged awake a few hours later by Noah's cries.

We've parked in a rough lay-by at the side of the road and, through a kissing gate, a hill rises ahead of us. The thought of climbing it makes me wearier still, but Mitch is smiling expectantly – waiting for me to give him a verbal pat on the back for his idea. However much I want to, I haven't the heart to deflate him.

'It was a great idea,' I say instead. 'Well done *you*.'

He grins and rubs the top of his stubbly head with his hand. 'Anything for my gorgeous wife. Come on, tribe. Let's go.'

He picks up the green-striped cool bag and leads the way with Izzy. I follow, letting Sophie go through the gate first before pushing through myself, taking care not to catch Noah's legs as it swings opens.

The track is not particularly steep. It's long, though, winding through stubbled cornfields dotted with hay bales, the margins edged with pale violet chicory flowers and the tall, spiky heads of teasels. In the field to our right, a skylark rises skywards with rapid wingbeats, its trills filling the air as it stops and hovers, poised between heaven and earth. Sophie and I stop and watch it for a moment, her head leaning against my leg. It's a beautiful day and the sun is warm on our backs. For the first time in ages, I feel relaxed. Not feeling the need to guess the number of steps to the nearest waymark or the number of fence posts before we reach the first hawthorn hedge pregnant with red berries.

Up ahead, I can see Isabella. She's running in front of Mitch, her strong little legs taking her away from him with every step. Every now and again, I see her jump over the tufted line of grass that runs down the middle of the chalky track, as deft as a gazelle. She's quick on her feet – just like I was at her age.

Sophie squeezes my hand. 'Are we nearly there?'

She's always the first to tire, but we haven't gone far. 'Are you all right, sweetheart?'

She doesn't answer, just holds out her arms.

'I can't carry you, Sophie. You can see I've got Noah. It's not much further.' I cross my fingers as I say it, having no idea where we're going. 'Let's play a game.'

Without thinking, I break a stalk of purple Yorkshire fog from the side of the path. Lowering it, so Sophie can see, I run my finger down its soft seed head. 'Here's a tree in summer.' I tickle her under the chin with it, then, placing the grass between my first finger and thumb, I run my thumbnail up the stem until the seeds are bunched between them. 'Here's a tree in winter...'

I stare at the seeds, trying to remember where I've heard the rhyme before and then it comes to me. It was Freya who taught it to me.

Sick to my stomach, I drop the seeds onto the ground and stare at them, my eyes filming with tears.

'Mummy?'

Sophie wraps her little arms around my legs, sensing something's not right and I pull myself together. It's just a rhyme.

'Come on. Let's go and see Daddy.' Taking her hand, I pull her gently away from the scattered seeds and catch up with Mitch who's waiting for us by a stile.

'You okay?' He looks at me curiously. 'You look as if you've seen a ghost.'

'I'm fine. Just tired. Are we nearly there?'

He laughs. 'You sound just like the kids. See that copse of trees at the top of the hill? I thought we could have our picnic near there. Tired legs, Soph?'

Sophie nods and Mitch bends down and taps his back. 'Hop on.'

She climbs onto his back and he carries her, and the cool bag, up the hill to where Isabella is already waiting, her little legs raised to the blue sky in a handstand. Sometimes I wonder how my twins can be so different. Even when they were babies, Isabella cried the loudest, woke more often and demanded my attention. Maybe Sophie learnt early that there would be no point in competing with her spirited sister.

I follow behind, smelling the sweet cakey aroma of Noah's head through his sun hat. He's moving his head from side to side against my chest and I know I'll have to feed him soon.

When we're all gathered at the top, Mitch spreads out a picnic rug beneath one of the trees and I reach behind and unclip the sling. Lifting Noah from it, I lay him on the rug and circle my shoulders.

'That's better.'

Mitch is standing with his hands on his hips, a twin on either side of him, looking out at the view. Turning to me, he grins. 'What do you think?'

I join him. Below us, a patchwork of fields in different shades of green and brown follows the dip and sway of the land and I can see a white farmhouse and two tiny tractors that look as though they've come from the twins' farm set. In the distance is the sea – the line where it meets the sky dotted with white wind turbines as straight as tiny soldiers. It's beautiful, but however much I want to enjoy the view, I can't. Always there, at the back of my mind, is the locket that's in my jewellery box. The one whose heart-shaped casing is empty of any faces. Whenever I think of it, a cold lick of fear curls around my heart. If I'm right that Freya was wearing the necklace the day she died, there's only one person who would have kept it. Would that same person have put it in Noah's pram? But, where there was once certainty, there is now doubt. However hard I try, when I attempt to fix the last image of Freya in my head, it breaks into pieces.

'I asked you what you think of this place, Kel.' Mitch is searching my face, worried that, once again, his idea isn't up to scratch. He's desperate for me to enjoy my surprise and I can't disappoint him.

'It's perfect.' I slip my arm around his waist and try to draw comfort from his warm body. 'Thank you.'

Mitch beams. 'Thanks for being my missus.'

Behind us, on the blanket, Noah is starting to fret. Reluctantly, I go back to him and settle myself down to feed him. As I do, I watch the girls who are trying to do cartwheels. As usual, Isabella is in charge. She's telling Sophie what to do and showing her where to put her hands. I wish that Sophie would stand up to her sister more – not always do as she says. But I know that, more than anything, Sophie wants to be liked by her sister. I chew my lip, knowing what that feels like.

'Come on, kids.' Mitch points to the food he's set out on the rug: sandwiches, mini sausages, packets of Wotsits and Swiss rolls in shiny purple wrappers. 'Your banquet awaits.' He turns to me and laughs. 'Nothing fancy, I'm afraid. I wanted to make sure I put together something the kids would eat. Sorry.'

'It's the thought that counts.'

Lifting a rather limp Marmite sandwich from the foil, I take a bite, a few crumbs landing on Noah's side. Brushing them off, I watch as my husband hands sandwiches to the children and tears open bags of Wotsits with his teeth. The girls are quiet, Sophie picking at her sandwich and Isabella tipping back her head and emptying the crumbs from her crisp packet into her mouth. Her teeth are stained orange.

It would be perfect, except that tomorrow is a school day and again I will have to relinquish control of my children to someone else. Ever since that first day, last week, Sophie has been tearful, and Isabella overexcited, when I've collected them from the classroom. Even though I know I have no choice, it's hard to trust that their teacher can look after them as well as I can.

I watch my husband throw Hula Hoops into the air, tipping his head back to try to catch them in his mouth. How can he be that carefree when there is so much danger in the world? I could tell him my fears, but I know he'd just laugh them away. Turn them into a joke. If only he knew that the unimaginable can sometimes happen when you least expect it.

'I need to pee.' Isabella has got up and is jiggling on one foot, her hand between her legs. 'I need to pee now!'

I look around for inspiration, but the spot where we're sitting is pretty open. 'Just squat over there. No one will see.'

Isabella's face screws up. 'I don't want to. I want a toilet.'

'There isn't a toilet here, Izzy. We're in the middle of nowhere. Look, if you're that bothered, we'll go over to those trees.' I point to where the trees are closer together. 'Can you hold on until we get there?'

'Yup.'

She runs ahead, like a puppy, and, when she gets there, begins the search for the perfect tree before pulling down her shorts and shouting at me not to look. Wondering when my children became so prudish, I face the other way and look out at the valley below.

The view is different here. Below us is a village, its squat church tower rising from the rooftops. It's very pretty. Moving a little closer to the edge, I see how the downs have drawn back, revealing and protecting a field of waving meadow grass.

I grow cold. Recognising it.

Memories come flooding back. Freya and I are lying on our backs. She giggles and holds out fingers bulging with grass seeds. *Here's a bunch of flowers,* she says, scattering them into my lap. *Here's an April shower.*

Her face is everywhere I look.

Squatting down, I press the heels of my hands into my eyes, my breathing ragged. Blood pulses in my ears and I start to count. I've reached twenty-five before Mitch finds me, Noah in his arms. Behind him, Isabella and Sophie are looking at me curiously.

He crouches beside me. 'Someone cried out. Was that you?'

I lower my hands and look at them. They're shaking. 'I don't know.'

'What happened, Kelly?'

I look around me, my senses extra heightened – the sun that shines through the trees behind me too bright, the rhythmic metronome of a chiffchaff calling from high up in the canopy, too loud. 'I thought I saw... thought I heard...'

Mitch looks around him. 'What, Kelly? What did you hear? Look, you're worrying the children.'

Isabella is sitting cross-legged, her back to me and Sophie has crept behind Mitch's legs.

'I'm sorry. I was fine and then...' I point to the combe below. 'It's this place. I don't want to be here.'

Mitch rubs a hand across his stubbled head. Once. Twice. 'I don't get you, Kel. We've only just got here.'

There's a hint of impatience in his voice and I long to tell him the truth. Tell him what happened to Freya and that it was all my fault. But that would mean telling him her secret and that's something I swore I would never do.

I try to laugh it off, telling him that the sleepless nights have got to me, but I can tell he's not convinced. As we finish our picnic, I feel his eyes slide over to me. Wondering what it is I'm holding back.

I owe it to him to give him something.

'That village below us. It's where I used to live.'

CHAPTER TWELVE
Kelly Before

It's been two weeks since Freya arrived at their house. Two weeks since Kelly's mum helped her empty her little rucksack into the drawers of the bedroom which looks out onto the meadows. In all that time, she's said nothing. Not a word.

At first, Kelly didn't mind, but now she's upset. Why won't she speak? She knows she has a tongue and teeth and a throat. She's even heard her humming to herself when she thinks no one is listening and, sometimes, after they've gone to bed, she's heard her crying. Once, when she couldn't stand it any more, she got out of her own bed and tiptoed to Freya's room, pressing her hand to the door as if that might somehow comfort her. She'd been too scared to go in, as her mum had told her she wasn't allowed, but she hoped that in some strange way, Freya might feel her presence outside her door. That she'd know Kelly realised how lonely she was. That she understood.

Although it's the summer holidays, and Kelly usually looks forward to them, she's quickly discovered that it's no fun talking to yourself. Asking questions and getting no answers. She wants them to be like Tabby and Ava at school, whispering behind cupped hands, laughing at silly jokes, having a made-up language only they can understand. What she has instead, is a girl who follows her around, her arms always wrapped across her body as though she's cold. Her candyfloss hair covering half her face.

Having a sister is not turning out how she imagined it to be. On the shelf above Kelly's bed is a book of fairy tales. Her favourite is *Snow White and Rose Red*. Sometimes Jade would read it to her and she knows some of it off by heart. *'We will not leave each other,' Rose Red answered. 'Never so long as we live.' And her mother would answer, 'What one has she must share with the other.'* Kelly wishes her mum would say the same to Freya; her sister never shares anything with her – not even her voice.

Her parents don't seem to think it strange that she doesn't speak. They act as if it's normal. Answering questions for her or giving her multiple-choice options to which she can nod or shake her head.

Today, Kelly's come down early for breakfast. As she nears the kitchen door, she hears voices. Her mum and dad are together for a change. Instead of going in, she waits. The only information she ever gets is the information she overhears when they think she's not there.

'Look, Andrew. I've bought her this locket. If you open it, you'll see I've put in our photographs – one on each side. What do you think?'

There's a silence and I picture my dad taking it from her hand.

'I think you're bloody obsessed. She's not our child, you know.'

'No, but she's a blessing.'

'If you say so. You don't think she's a bit…' There's the rush of water into a kettle and Kelly misses what her dad has said.

'How, could you say that, Andrew? She's so much easier than the rest. You'll grow to love her, I know you will.'

There's the clatter of a plate in the sink. 'It's just that it's not something we've had to deal with before.'

'Deal with? What do you know about dealing with things? You're out before she gets up and even when you *are* here, it's me who does everything. You're in your office listening to your bloody music.'

'And why do you think that is, Karen? You tell me?'

There's a rasp of chair legs being scraped across the tiled floor and footsteps coming nearer. Kelly melts back against the wall, her blanket bunched in her fist. If she's caught snooping, there will be trouble. But the footsteps stop and she hears the clunk of the dishwasher being opened. The metallic clink of cutlery being dropped into the basket.

Kelly holds her breath. She hates it when they argue. Tabby's mum and dad got divorced last year and now she hardly sees her dad. She closes her eyes, imagining a life with only her mum. She doesn't like the thought of it one bit.

When her mum speaks again, her voice is softer. It's the one she uses when she wants to get around her dad. 'I know it hasn't been easy and that you didn't want to do it again, but it's not the same this time. The poor kid has been through such a lot.'

Kelly leans her back against the wall and looks up at the stairs. She thinks of Freya asleep in the best bedroom in the house. Imagines the white hair spread across the pillow, her closed eyelids patterned with a spiderweb of tiny blue veins.

What has she been through? Why will no one tell her?

Freya isn't asleep, though. As if conjured up by Kelly's thoughts, she appears at the top of the stairs, wearing a nightie that once belonged to Charlene that comes down to her ankles. Slowly, she descends and, when she reaches the bottom step, sits down and puts a finger to her lips. It seems Kelly isn't the only one who wants to know what her parents are talking about.

'And the publicity. Christ, that must have been hard.'

'She won't remember that. She was too young.'

As they talk, Kelly is aware of Freya's ghostly presence. What is she thinking?

'It's not like with Kelly,' her mum says. 'You said that…'

The voice becomes muffled and Kelly steps closer in frustration.

'What time will you be home?' She says it as though she doesn't care, but Kelly knows she does. If her dad is late home, she'll pace in front of the kitchen window like one of the tigers in the zoo her class went to. Her eyes growing cold when he walks through the door.

'Can't say.'

Kelly imagines her mum gripping the edge of the worktop, her eyes wild. She's scared that her bad mood will drift like a storm cloud out into the room and hover above their heads. Kelly's eyes had been fixed on the door, but now she glances back at Freya. The girl is no longer sitting on the stairs but has got to her feet. She walks the few steps to the kitchen door and Kelly thinks she's going to go in, but she doesn't. Instead, she stands silently in her white nightdress and waits, her arms crossed. Her hands rubbing at her upper arms.

Moving out of the shadows, Kelly goes over to her and, this time, it's she who takes Freya's hand.

CHAPTER THIRTEEN

Kelly Now

'Want to talk about it?'

Mitch stands in the doorway of their living room. The children have gone to bed and it's just us downstairs. As he'd driven us home from the failure of a picnic, he'd flicked me uncertain glances and I knew he was wondering what to say. How to approach it.

The television is on and I'm staring at the screen, although it's a programme about gardening and I hate gardening. I don't want this conversation. I want to forget the rooftops and the church tower. The restless grass in the meadow. But above all, I want to forget the path that leads through it, rising up the hill to a place I never want to see again.

'Kel? Did you hear what I said?'

I look away from the television, not bothering to try and hide the fact I've been crying. I know my eyes are red-rimmed. My face blotchy.

Mitch frowns slightly. Hating to see me like this. Coming over to my chair, he kneels beside it, in a cameo of when he asked me to marry him and takes my hands in his.

'If you don't tell me, how am I supposed to fix it?'

I give a half-smile. 'You don't have to fix everything, Mitch.'

'I know that, but I like to try. Please, Kel. Tell me what's going on in that head of yours?'

I consider telling him, then shake my head. 'Did you know, Mitch? Did you know all along where you were taking me?'

He looks away. 'Of course not. I just thought it would be somewhere different to go. A change of scene. Since you've been on maternity leave, apart from the odd run at the weekend, you've been stuck in the house. You don't go to a baby group. In fact, you never see anyone.'

I turn on him. 'I don't need anyone and I don't want to go to a baby group. It's enough effort just to get dressed in the mornings, let alone drag myself to a sodding group full of perfect mums and perfect babies who never cry.'

Mitch stands and walks over to the window, his hands shoved deep into the pockets of his jeans. There's nothing much to see outside, except his white van and the houses in the terrace opposite. I see his broad shoulders rise as he takes an intake of breath.

'Okay, so you don't want to go to a baby group. I was just using it as an example.'

The room is silent except for the sound of Charlie sniffing at something that's under the settee, out of his reach. Usually, I'd be grateful for the peace, but now it feels awkward – pregnant with the words we've left unsaid.

Mitch turns and looks at me, helplessness written across his face. At times like this, he doesn't know how to play it. Whether what he says will make things worse.

'What happened today, Kel? That's all I'm asking. So the village you saw was the place where you used to live. What's the big deal?'

To Mitch, things are either black or white. He can't understand that there might be a multitude of answers to his question. Each one dredging up emotions so intense I can almost taste them: love, hate, envy... guilt.

I don't want to answer, but I need to tell him something. I owe him that much. 'It wasn't a happy place. Bad things happened there.'

Mitch nods, grateful that I've shared this small morsel. 'You've never told me that. I'm sorry.'

All he's ever known about me is that I left home as soon as I was old enough. Moved to Brighton and worked in the bars and clubs. When he met me, I was living in a rundown bedsit having spent the previous months dossing on people's sofas.

'There are some things it's better for people not to know.'

'What? Even your husband?'

I look at him sadly. 'Especially my husband.'

The change in his expression is slight. A thinning of his lips and a tightness around his eyes. Mitch looks at his watch.

'I said I'd meet the guys at The Crown tonight for a quick pint. There's a new project I want to discuss.'

'Don't go!' I hadn't expected the rise of panic at his words. The dread at being left alone in the house with the children. Not after today.

He stiffens. 'I won't be long. It's important.'

I can see Mitch wants to be out of this room. Away from the emotion he can't understand. He needs to be somewhere else, with people who speak the same language. Not a neurotic wife who talks in riddles.

'Do you have to?'

Suddenly, the baby monitor springs into life. Noah's awake again. Mitch glances at it, unsure of the right thing to do. 'I'll see to him.'

'No, I'll go. He'll need feeding. You go to the pub, I'm just being stupid.'

Mitch hesitates, torn between staying and going. As another cry comes through the monitor, he rubs the back of his neck, crippled by indecision.

'You weren't like this with the other two, Kelly. You sailed through it like a pro. But having another baby seems to have knocked you for six. Like I said before, if you got out more, made some friends, you might not be so…'

'So what, Mitch?'

He looks at me lamely. 'So weird. Sometimes I see you standing in the hallway just staring at the floor or the wall. You don't move even if the baby cries. It's not normal. The midwife mentioned the baby blues. It could be something like that. Maybe if you saw Dr—'

'I don't need to see a doctor,' I snap. 'There's nothing wrong with me. I just wish people would stop asking me questions.'

For a second, I'm back in the thatched house of my childhood. Someone is leaning over me. *What really happened, Kelly? Tell me the truth.*

A tear runs down my cheek and I know Mitch has seen.

'I'll stay if you want,' he says half-heartedly.

I wipe my face with my sleeve. 'No. You go. I'll be better on my own. I'll feed Noah, then get an early night.' I force a smile. 'Maybe this will be the night he sleeps through.'

'Well, if you're sure.' Mitch squeezes my shoulder, looking relieved. 'I'll be back before you know it.'

I place my hand on top of his. 'I know and I'm sorry. One day, when I'm ready, I'll tell you everything, I promise. And Mitch.'

'Yeh?'

'Go easy tonight. You know how persuasive the lads can be.'

'Just a couple of pints. I promise.'

He walks to the door and opens it, his shoulders relaxing. He's keen to leave and, for the first time in our marriage, I wonder whether my husband might have secrets of his own.

CHAPTER FOURTEEN
Kelly Before

Kelly's fast asleep when her mum wakes her the next morning. She feels groggy as though she hasn't slept properly. It was too hot last night, the air thick and still.

'Get up, Kelly. We've a busy day.'

Sitting up, Kelly rubs the side of her face, feeling the imprint of her cellular blanket on her cheek. 'Where are we going?'

Her mum smiles brightly. 'To the sports centre. Freya changed her mind.' She holds out a lined page that looks like it's been torn out of a notebook. On it, in felt pen, her sister has written *I will go to holiday club.*

Could this be a mistake? Only yesterday, Kelly had thought she wouldn't be going. Had sat, heartbroken, as Freya had shaken her head and covered her hands with her eyes when her mum had suggested it. Kelly had always wanted to go to holiday club, and now she's old enough, her dream had been snatched away from her.

For the rest of the day, she had refused to play with Freya. Had sat in the shadows of her hiding place in the laurel bush and wished that the girl had never come to them. Had hated her for spoiling everything.

As she'd peeped through the leaves, she'd seen Freya standing alone by the flower bed, reaching out a hand to the late-summer blooms and breaking their stems with her thin fingers. Finding one she couldn't break, she'd let the flower head loll heavy and broken against the bruised stem. When her mother had walked across the grass and seen the wilting posy in Freya's fist, Kelly had put her hands over her ears, waiting for the raised voice… but it had never come. Instead, her mum's face had softened into a smile as Freya held the flowers out to her.

If Kelly had done the same, she'd have been rewarded with a slap.

Now, Freya's standing behind her mum, her fair hair freshly washed. She's wearing a pair of denim shorts that emphasises the thinness of her legs, the white skin mottled as if its winter. Beneath her T-shirt, Kelly can see the shape of the locket her mum gave her.

She's never had a locket.

The room lightens as her mum twists the blind to open it, and Kelly sees what's in Freya's hand. It's Amber, her favourite doll, her white, nylon hair gleaming in the morning sunlight. She holds it out to Kelly.

Last night, still angry with her, Kelly had stopped by Freya's open bedroom door on her way to the bathroom. On the floor, beside Freya's bed, she'd seen a row of dolls, their plastic faces turned to the wall, as though they'd done something wrong.

Freya was lying on the pale pink duvet, Amber clasped to her body.

In seconds Kelly had been on the bed, prising Freya's fingers to make her let go, but she'd only clutched Amber more closely to her body. Grabbing one of the doll's arms, Kelly had pulled harder until she'd fallen back on the bed, Amber's plastic arm in her hand.

Kelly can still hear the terrible sound that had come from between Freya's pale, thin lips as she rocked the armless Amber in her arms. A low keening that had frightened her. Wanting her to stop, she'd thrown the plastic arm at the girl and Freya had taken a juddering breath. With the doll tucked under her chin, she'd closed her eyes and within seconds was asleep.

Kelly stares at the doll in Freya's outstretched hand and sees that the arm is back in place. Is she trying to say sorry for taking what wasn't hers? For breaking Amber's arm? Is she feeling guilty for not being a good sister?

She turns away. 'I don't want her now.'

Kelly's mother grabs the doll out of the Freya's hand and thrusts it at her. 'You should be ashamed of your behaviour. Why can't you be more like Freya, Kelly, instead of always thinking of yourself?'

Kneeling next to Freya, she cups her hands around her face. 'She doesn't mean it, sweetheart. It was a lovely thing to do and she's just ungrateful.'

Kelly's eyes ache with the tears she's holding back. She wants to tell her mum that it was Freya who took her doll, but she doesn't. She knows it will only make things worse. Instead, she climbs out of bed and puts on her slippers. 'I'm sorry.'

'I expect you are.' She takes Freya's hand. 'Come on, Freya, it's time for breakfast.'

It's only when they've left the room that Kelly realises she hasn't seen or heard her father this morning.

'Where's Daddy?' she calls after them.

Through the half-open door, she sees her mum stop, her free hand on the banister. 'He had to go to work early.'

As always, Kelly considers the way she's said it. Cross-referencing it against other conversations for signs of crossness or disappointment. She thinks she hears both.

'Okay.'

Her clothes have been laid out for her and, as she puts them on, she wonders what Carly will be wearing and what she'll say when she shows off her new big sister. She can't wait to see her face when she tells her that this one will be staying forever. But then doubt creeps in. What will Carly make of this strange girl with her baby-fine hair, the blue veins visible beneath the translucent skin? What if she doesn't like her?

When she gets downstairs, her mum has made them both packed lunches. They are in plastic lunch boxes on the kitchen worktop. One box is shiny pink and has Beauty and the Beast on it. On the lid of the other, Bob the Builder smiles out from the scuffed blue plastic, his yellow helmet almost rubbed away. She hates it.

Her mum points to the blue one. 'You don't mind taking that one, do you, Kelly? It seemed silly to buy two new ones.'

Kelly thinks of the Disney princess at Carly's party and the unfairness wraps itself around her, making it hard to breathe. Her mum knows how much she loves Beauty. How, even though no one has taken her to see the film, she's read the book from cover to cover. Sliding it out of the box set of Disney stories that sits on the shelf in the large bedroom that's now Freya's.

The girl is sitting at the table, an empty breakfast bowl in front of her. Kelly knows she's waiting for her to make her choice so she can have the same. Can't she make up her own mind? But then she remembers Freya's change of heart, how she's tried to make amends, and the irritation slips away. How horrible it must be to sit in someone else's kitchen with different cupboards and different food and a new sister who you've only known a few weeks. She looks at the Bob the Builder lunch box. It was once Mason's. She liked Mason.

'I don't mind having that one,' she says, even though it's a lie.

Her mum is stacking the dishwasher. 'On the holiday club timetable, it says it's swimming today. Your costumes and towels are in your rucksacks by the door and I've rung Anne Johnson to let her know you're coming.' She looks at Freya meaningfully. 'I've explained everything and she's going to keep a good eye on you, but I expect you to look after her too, Kelly.'

'Of course, I will. She's my sister.'

'No, Kelly, she's… Oh, for goodness' sake, I haven't got time for this.'

The dishwasher door slams closed and Kelly flinches. Not wanting to make her crosser, she says nothing more but takes the box of Honey Nut Loops and tips them into her bowl before pushing the box to Freya.

As the girls eat, Kelly's mum comes round behind Freya, a hairbrush in her hand and a stretchy black band around her wrist. Gently, she pulls the brush through the girl's wispy hair, then, putting the brush down, uses both hands to smooth the hair away from her face before securing it with the band. It's so fine she has to twist it four times around to stop it from slipping off. With her hair tied back, Freya's face looks odd, the pale eyes too large in her head, the neck too long, the chin too pointed.

'There.' Her mum nods at her work, satisfied. 'That will make it easier to put on the swimming cap.'

She doesn't offer to do Kelly's hair and she's glad. Sometimes, when she does it for school, she brushes too hard, the bristles raking across her scalp. At other times, the band is twisted so tightly that the skin around her hairline aches.

They have the radio on all the way to the sports centre and her mum doesn't mind when she sings along with her. She looks across at Freya who has her forehead pressed against the glass.

'We're going to have a great time. There will be bouncy, inflatable things in the water and later we might have races.' A thought occurs to her. 'You can swim, can't you?'

They've pulled into the sports centre car park. Her mum reverses into a space, then puts on the handbrake. She turns round in her seat. 'Anne says it's fine to join in with the others as long as you wear your armbands, Freya. Just make sure they're blown up properly.'

Freya gives no indication that she's heard. She's watching the girls who are climbing out of the people carrier that's parked next to them. It's Carly. Tabby and Ava are with her.

'Wait for me, Carly!' Leaning out of the window, Kelly waves her arms, but it's too late. The girls are already running towards the double doors of the sports centre. She wants to run after them, but she knows she'll have to wait for Freya.

Carly's mum walks over to the car. She smiles apologetically at her mum through the open window.

'They're just excited. I'll take the girls in if you like.'

Kelly's pleased. If her mum went in, she'd only make a fuss about Freya and everyone would stare.

They follow Carly's mum into the sports centre and she has to listen to her twittering on about how lovely it is to meet Freya at last. The shy smile Freya gives in return makes her feel grumpy. When they get inside, a young woman, dressed in navy shorts and a yellow T-shirt with ClubActive embroidered on it, is waiting for them.

'Hi, girls. I'm Anne. You can change in here.' She points to a door with Changing Room written on it. 'I'll show you.'

She pushes the door open and leans against it to let them through. Immediately, Kelly is hit by the smell of chlorine and the echoing voices of the girls who are changing there. Spotting a bench with enough space for both their bags, Kelly leads Freya over to it. The floor is wet in places, strands of hair collecting in the joins between the tiles. She tries not to look at it, or at the used plaster she can see through the slats in the wooden bench.

'When you've put on your costumes,' Anne says, 'put your clothes in your bags and hang them on the hooks above the bench. I'll come back to take you to the pool area in ten minutes.' Turning to Freya, she lowers her voice and points to the row of blue metal doors that line the wall. 'If you want, you can change in one of the cubicles, Freya.'

Kelly had been looking at a lone sock that someone's left on the windowsill above her, but now she drags her eyes away to stare at

Anne. Like the other girls, who have stopped what they're doing to listen, she's wondering why Freya's getting special treatment.

Beside her, Freya stands with her head bent, her hands bunched into fists. Slowly, she shakes her head, then takes her rucksack off her back. Unzipping it, she takes out her towel.

Anne looks doubtful. 'Well, if you're sure.'

The door swings shut as she goes back out and Kelly waits to see what Freya will do. The other girls have lost interest; they're stuffing clothes into bags and stretching swimming hats over their hair. The talk is of the races they'll have and how warm the water's going to be.

At the other end of the changing room, Carly, Tabby and Ava have finished changing and are looking at them with interest. She'd wanted so much for them to meet her new sister, but now they're here, she's not so sure. What if they think she's weird?

Unrolling her towel, Kelly takes out her costume and lays it in front of her. She'd have liked to have worn the red one with frills around the legs, but that's the one her mum's given to Freya. Instead, she's got the polka dot costume that she's had for ages. The material has gone thin and see through in places where it's stretched, and she suspects the elastic around the legs will cut into her.

Using the wall for balance, Kelly stands on one leg and takes off one trainer, then swaps legs and takes off the other. She places them both under the bench, then sits and pulls off her socks, trying to find a dry piece of floor for her feet as she bends to push them into her shoes. Her T-shirt is next and then her shorts.

Standing in just her pants, she looks across at Freya and sees that she hasn't moved. She's standing with her arms by her sides, the red swimsuit in front of her, her face a picture of misery.

'Come on, Freya. Anne said we only have ten minutes.'

Freya looks at her, her eyes barely blinking, then picks up her towel and wraps it around her body. It's a long towel and the end trails on the wet floor. Holding it closed with her right hand, she tries, with difficulty, to wrestle her arm out of the sleeve of her T-shirt. Kelly watches, fascinated. At school, nobody changes under a towel. When one arm is free, Freya bunches the top of the towel in her fist and tries to free the other arm. The other girls are mostly changed, standing by the benches waiting to be told they can enter the pool area. Soon, their attention will be taken by the strange girl who is changing inside her towel.

Kelly can't bear it. 'I'll help you.'

She pulls at Freya's sleeve, trying to free her small pointed elbow from the stretched material, but as she tugs, the towel loosens from Freya's fingers and slips down. Her face white, Freya grabs at it and drags it back, clutching it to her but not before Kelly has seen. From her chest to where her shorts start, the skin is pale pink, puckered and ridged as though someone has ironed it on a too-high setting. Kelly stands mesmerised. Fascinated and revolted in equal measures.

Forcing down her T-shirt, Freya backs away. Her pale eyes fixed on Kelly. 'I hate you.'

When she turns and runs, her feet sliding on the slippery tiles, Kelly realises these are the first words she's heard Freya utter.

CHAPTER FIFTEEN

July 28th

I know it's been a while, but I was sorting through some things and came across this picture. It's a copy of one we took on her birthday and I think you'll agree she looks very happy. I just wanted you to know that. It made me wonder whether the two of you look alike. Anyway, I just thought you might like to have it.

All the best

CHAPTER SIXTEEN

Kelly Now

Maddie opens the door at the first ring. 'Kelly, what a nice surprise.'

I force a smile, knowing it's not true. Whenever I see Maddie without Mitch, it feels awkward. We try to pretend this isn't the case, but it's hard to ignore the uncomfortable silences when he's not with us. It was Isabella who had insisted we come. She'd said it wasn't fair that she'd seen the kitten and Sophie hadn't, and even though I'd known it was just a ruse for her to hold the kitten again, I'd agreed. After the afternoon I'd just had – Noah's constant crying, the girls arguing – I'd have agreed to anything that got me out of the house. Now I'm wondering if it was such a good idea.

'Can we see the kitten? Can we see the kitten?' Isabella does a little jig on the doorstep, craning her neck to see inside. 'I want to hold him again.'

I pull her back by the sleeve of her coat. 'Izzy, mind your manners. I'm sorry, Maddie. We were just passing, but if you're busy...'

Maddie shakes her head. 'Don't be silly. You're here now. I was just getting things ready for my next client, but she's not due for another hour and a half. Mitch not with you then?'

It's said lightly, but I can tell she's disappointed.

'He went to the site.' Even as I'm saying it, it sounds unlikely. Why would he go on a Sunday? He didn't stay long at the pub last night but, even so, after the conversation we had, we've both been walking on eggshells and, to be honest, I'm glad he's not come with me.

'Are you feeling all right, Kelly? You look very pale.'

What can I tell her? That I'm kept awake at night, not only by my baby, but by the thought of the locket in my jewellery box. Or maybe I could say that since I saw the village where I used to live, memories have been crowding in – threatening to tear me apart and leave me in pieces.

'I'm fine,' I say.

I'm feeling more uncomfortable by the minute; I know my company isn't enough. 'We won't stay long. Noah will be wanting his next feed soon and then all hell will let loose.'

Maddie looks down at Noah, who's kicking at his blanket, then back up again. 'Honestly, it's not a problem. Come inside and I'll make us all a drink.'

The girls run in and Maddie helps lift Noah's pram into her bright hallway. Although her house is almost identical to ours in layout, it looks very different. It's warm and inviting, the saffron-yellow walls adorned with colourful prints advertising local art exhibitions. A rag rug, in geometric patterns, runs down the centre of the floor and twisted around the banisters are fairy lights in the shape of dragonflies. I look at all these things and wonder why I've never felt comfortable here.

'He's in here.' Isabella runs ahead into the living room and by the time we've joined her, she's laying on her stomach, peering under the settee. 'He's hiding. Come out kitty cat.'

Sophie crouches down next to her and Maddie and I watch them in an awkward silence. I'm grateful when the kitten at last emerges from its hiding place.

Isabella scoops it up and holds it to her chest before Sophie gets the chance to touch it. 'If you're good, you can hold it too,' she says to her sister, and I smile because Sophie is always good.

'Come on, Izzy. Let Sophie have a turn.' Lifting the kitten from Isabella's lap, I hand it to Sophie, who buries her face in its fur. Isabella scowls, but I ignore her.

'Can I get you anything? Tea? Coffee?' Maddie asks.

What I want to do is to say no and go back home as soon as Sophie has had enough of the soft ball of fluff she's holding on her lap, but I don't. It would be rude and that's something my mother would have hated. I bite my cheek – annoyed that she's wormed her way into my thoughts. Why should I care what she would have thought? It's not as if I've seen her in years.

Crouching next to the twins, I stroke the kitten's head, trying to relax. 'A coffee would be nice, thank you.'

As I turn my head to smile at Maddie, Isabella uses it as an opportunity to take the kitten out of Sophie's hands. I stop her and tell her off, but it worries me. How on earth can I expect Sophie to manage at school if, at other times, I'm constantly there to help her? No wonder she's unhappy. I picture her in the playground waiting patiently for a turn on the slide while others push in front or, worse still, standing on her own with no one to play with. Mitch is right. I need to start letting her fight her own battles.

Leaving the children to it, I go into the kitchen to see if there's anything I can do to help, but Maddie waves away my offer. Pulling out a wooden stool from the breakfast bar, she gestures for me to sit, then hands me a mug with *You are what you want to be* written on it.

There's an earthenware vase filled with fat spikes of lilac on the breakfast bar and Maddie picks it up. 'Sorry, they're a bit overpowering, aren't they?' She takes them over to the Welsh dresser on the other side of the room where they join an assortment of paperwork and a wooden bowl filled with gourds of all shapes and sizes. Next to me, her mug of tea steams, its fragrance astringent.

'Ginseng and thyme,' Maddie says, even though I haven't asked. 'It's good for you. Supposed to keep you calm yet focussed.'

Pulling out the stool next to me, she perches on the edge of it, one long leg reaching to the floor. Her other foot rests on the wooden bar. Whatever she drinks, it must be doing her good as she looks a picture of health. Needing the caffeine, I take a sip of my coffee, trying hard not to compare Maddie's clear skin with my own, which is in dire need of sleep and attention.

'How's Mitch?' she asks brightly. 'Work going well?'

I wonder if she's just making conversation. Does she really want to know or has Mitch already told her and she's just being polite? That's the problem with Mitch having known Maddie for so much longer than he's known me. He tells her things about our life. Some of which should stay private.

'He's good,' I say, deciding to give her the benefit of the doubt. 'In fact, he's just started a new project in Hove that he's excited about. It's bigger than his usual contracts so will mean he'll have to take on more labourers. Should be pretty lucrative, though.'

Maddie runs a finger around the top of her mug. 'That's good,' she says. 'And what about you, Kelly?'

'Well, you know. Mitch told you about Noah. How difficult he is at the moment.'

'What you need is a change of scene. If you and Mitch want to go out, I could look after the kids.'

From the living room, I can hear Isabella telling Sophie how to hold the kitten. How to stroke it properly. I think about intervening, but I'm just too tired. 'I couldn't ask you to do that. It's not just the girls, it's Noah. Besides, I'm still breastfeeding him.'

'You must come here then.' Maddie spreads her fingers on the table. Her nails are painted a dark blackberry. 'The girls can sleep in the spare room and you can bring a travel cot for Noah. I'll invite some others too. It will be fun. Tell Mitch it's about time we had a proper catch-up.'

I want to say no. Tell her that all I want to do, when the long day turns to evening, is sleep, but I'm not sure what Mitch's reaction would be if I did that. After all, Maddie was his best friend before I took over that role.

'What about next Saturday?' Maddie is looking expectantly at me and I know I'll have to answer.

'I'll check with Mitch when he gets home.' If we go this once, then, hopefully, we won't have to do it again for another year.

'Great.' Maddie lifts the calendar from the nail on the wall, finds the correct date and writes *Mitch* in big letters in the empty box. 'I'll start thinking about what to cook.'

Trying not to let it bother me, I drink my coffee and look around the kitchen. On the worktop, under a large, modern print of a fig cut in half, which looks strangely pornographic, is a row of brown bottles with black lids. Each one has a different coloured label and I can just make out the names on the nearest two: *patchouli* and *sandalwood*.

'How's the aromatherapy going?' I say, in a bid to be pleasant.

'Not bad.' Maddie pushes up the sleeves of her top to reveal slim, freckled arms. 'Since I finished the course, I've had several bookings.'

'You must be pleased. It looks like you'll make a success of your business.'

'Hopefully. Although it'll take a while for me to pay back the bank loan for the equipment. The massage table alone cost an arm and a leg.'

I roll my shoulders, imagining firm fingers releasing the tension in them. My whole back aches from the endless nights pacing with Noah. As if on cue, I hear him cry. I know I should go to him, but instead, rest my elbows on the table and press the heels of my hands into my eyes. Counting how many ticks of the clock it will be until one or other of the girls calls out to me from the living room to complain about the noise. If it's more than twenty, he'll settle after his feed. If it's less, he won't.

Maddie's voice cuts through my counting. 'Kelly? Are you okay?'

Quickly, I lift my head from my hands, letting the stars at the back of my eyes disperse. 'Sorry, yes, I'm fine. It's just that I wish he'd settle for more than an hour at a time, that's all.'

'I'll check him if you like.' Lowering herself from the stool, Maddie goes into the hall. She's back almost immediately. 'It looks like he's gone off again.'

I breathe a sigh of relief. 'Thank God.'

Maddie picks up one of the bottles of oils. 'The children are happy playing with the kitten. How about I give you a quick shoulder massage? I can pretty much guarantee it will make you feel better and I could do with the practice.'

I'm surprised by this offer. 'I don't know. I really should be getting home. The children will be wanting their tea and then there's the supper—'

'Get Mitch to make it. You know he's a pretty good cook when he wants to be.'

'Of course, I know. I live with him, don't I? I just meant he'll still be on-site.'

The words have come out sharper than I meant them to. Looking uncomfortable, Maddie puts the bottle of oil down on the table. 'I'm sorry. I didn't mean…'

Heat rises to my face. My mother's voice is in my head again, telling me I should be ashamed of my behaviour. *Why can't you be more like Freya, Kelly, instead of always thinking of yourself?*

'No, it's me who should be sorry. I'm tired and it's been a long day. A massage is probably exactly what I need.'

'You don't need to apologise.' Opening a drawer, Maddie rummages inside, then brings out a tortoiseshell clasp. 'Why don't you clip your hair up with this?'

I twist my hair behind my head and secure it with the clasp. 'Five minutes then.'

Maddie's hands rest lightly on my shoulders. 'Take a few deep breaths for me. It'll help you relax.'

Doing as I'm told, I take a deep breath in, letting it out slowly through my mouth. Maddie moves closer. Resting her forearms on my shoulders, either side of my neck, she rolls her arms outwards and immediately my shoulders relax. She knows what she's doing. Her hands slide either side of my backbone. With gentle pressure, she moves her thumbs in small circles up my neck towards the hairline. Her touch is light and, as her thumbs work their magic, her fingers curl round the sides of my neck.

I'm no longer in my body but out of it looking down. Where her fingers touch, I picture a ring of dark bruises. Imagine how easily the fragile bones could crush.

'Stop it!'

Maddie drops her hands and steps back, startled.

'What is it?'

I don't answer. Screwing up my eyes, I start to count my breaths. In for five. Out for five. I've got to push away the hideous images. Put them back in the box marked *never open*.

'Kelly?'

The warm kitchen with its colour and clutter and the cloying smell of lilac is too much. I want to be back in my own home with Mitch – the curtains closed against the world.

I've reached twenty. Is that enough? I drag the clip from my hair. 'I'm sorry. I've got to go.' Unwilling to explain further, I hurry to the living room and tell the children we're leaving. Isabella isn't happy, but I don't care. I just want to be home.

Maddie frowns as she opens the front door. 'Are you feeling unwell? I know there's a bug doing the rounds.'

'Yes, that's probably it.'

We're in the hall now and Isabella's complaining loudly, telling me I'm mean. Pushing her in front of me, I release the brake on Noah's pram and wheel it into the street. We leave Maddie standing at the door and take the shortcut home through the park. As we walk, I try to empty my mind, but it's impossible. I've allowed Freya to slip in and now she's with me, all I can think of is my guilt.

CHAPTER SEVENTEEN
Kelly Before

'Are you going to tell me what happened, Kelly? Anne Johnson says Freya wasn't feeling well.'

Her mum is cross, sweat making her forehead shiny, her puffy hands bunched on her hips. Kelly can tell by the creases on her cheeks that she's been napping while they've been at the sports centre and she's made no attempt to hide how unhappy she is to have been called back to pick them up so soon. Kelly looks across at Freya. She's standing by the French windows, her forehead pressed to the glass. Why doesn't she answer? She knows she can.

Her mum taps her on the shoulder. 'Kelly, I'm talking to *you*. You didn't do anything to upset her, did you?'

Kelly's not sure what to say. What to tell her. She pictures again the shiny pink skin, imagining what it would feel like under her fingers, and shudders. Should she tell her mum or is it a secret?

'She had a tummy ache.' It's the best she can do.

'Is that all?'

'Yes. That's all.'

Freya's no longer looking out of the window but is staring at Kelly and she doesn't like it. She doesn't know if she's done right or wrong. Whether she's said the right thing or whether it will make her even more upset with her.

Kelly's mum goes over to Freya and runs a hand down her hair. 'How are you feeling now, love? Any better?'

Freya nods and her mum looks relieved. 'That's good.' She pinches her lower lip between her thumb and forefinger and looks at the phone on the sideboard. 'Maybe I should call the surgery, just in case. We shouldn't take chances.'

Freya steps back and shakes her head so hard, hair escapes from the black band. Kelly doesn't blame her – she doesn't like going to the doctor's either. If Freya goes to the surgery, they might ask her to lift her T-shirt and then they'll see what *she's* seen. She likes the idea that if no one else knows, it can be their secret.

A thrilling gruesome secret.

'Look,' she says, taking Freya's hand and raising it like a boxer who's just won a match. 'She's better, now.'

Her mum frowns. 'Please don't interfere, Kelly.' She studies Freya's face. 'Are you sure you're okay?'

Freya nods.

'Well, if you're certain.' Lifting her arm, she wipes the sweat from her brow. 'I'm going upstairs for a lie-down. It was so hot last night I could barely breathe, let alone sleep. You can call me if you need me.'

'We'll be fine, Mummy. Won't we, Freya?'

The girl nods again.

Kelly waits for her mum to leave the room, then turns to Freya. 'I know you can talk.'

From the kitchen, Ben gives a bark. His signal to be let out. When nothing happens, he pads into the living room and slumps down, his big head resting on his paws.

'I'm going to take him outside.'

Kelly goes into the kitchen and Ben follows. She twists the key in the door, then pushes down on the handle and lets him out. Tail wagging madly, he runs down the side passage to the back garden. Kelly follows him. When she gets to the garden, she looks back and is surprised to see Freya. She's standing at the side gate, her fingers on the metal bolt.

'What are you doing?'

Freya doesn't look up but draws the bolt across and back again. Across and back. Across and back.

'Don't do that. Mum will be cross.'

'She's not my mum.' Freya's staring at the ground.

'I knew you could speak.'

Kelly can't take her eyes off the thin fingers that are now twisting the metal handle. The gate opens an inch or so and Ben comes up to sniff at the gap. Kelly makes a grab for his collar, then pushes the gate shut with her bottom.

'Stop it!'

'He wants to go out.'

'No, he doesn't. He's not allowed out and neither are you.'

Ben paws at the gap under the gate and whimpers.

'See,' Freya says. 'He does want to.' Her face breaks into a smile. 'Let's explore the meadow… the woods.'

Glancing nervously at the house, Kelly lowers her voice. 'We can't.'

'Please. Please, Kelly. You're the best sister ever.' Freya's voice is rising.

'Be quiet. She'll hear you.' Her mum's bedroom window is right above them. The pane is blank, the clouds reflected in the glass. 'Anyway, I'm not allowed there.'

Freya looks at Ben. 'We'll say he escaped and had to go after him. Then we won't get into trouble.'

Kelly twists her hands until her fingers hurt. She's never been out of the garden on her own. If she's found out, she'll be in the biggest trouble ever.

Freya's looking at her curiously. 'Are you scared?'

'No.' She is, though. She's scared of the unknown, scared they might get lost, scared that they'll get caught.

'I'm ten,' Freya says. 'I'll look after you.'

Everything's changed. It's no longer Kelly who's the protector; it's Freya who's in charge now. It's like someone has taken the girl who arrived only a few weeks ago and put a new one in her place. Kelly stares at her.

'You're different.'

Freya shrugs. 'Being quiet and good makes people want me more. With my sister I don't need to pretend.'

'But you said you hated me.'

'Sisters always fight. Don't you know that? If you don't want to come with me, I'll go on my own.'

Kelly looks at the house. Maybe her mum will stay asleep and never know. Sometimes she takes tablets to help her and, when she does, it takes an earthquake to wake her.

'I'll come.'

With a smile, Freya holds out her hand to her and this time Kelly doesn't hesitate. Instead, she steps forward and takes it, then shuts the gate behind her as quietly as she can.

They run down the track beside the house and climb the stile into the meadow. From the upstairs window, it's always looked far away, but here it is already, stretching away from them towards the rolling hills.

Freya is ahead of her. 'Come on then.'

But something is stopping Kelly. Far away at the very end of the meadow, just a strip of red against the green, she can see the disused rifle range that Jade told her about. She's imagining the graffiti-strewn wall that hides the machinery. She knows all about it as a man came in to talk to them in school assembly. He showed them photographs of the place as it used to look and told them how cadets used to fire rifles at the targets that were pulled up on big metal frames. After the boys had finished firing, the targets would be wound down again and a new target fixed on. No one uses it now and all that's left are the rusting metal frames behind the long-roofed markers' gallery.

As she thinks of the targets covered with bullet holes, Kelly puts her hand to her heart and shivers.

'What are you looking at?' Freya stands, hands on hips, squinting at her through the sunlight.

'Nothing.'

Kelly follows Freya through the field of grass, the soft heads brushing against her arms. It's hotter here, the air filled with the buzz of insects. Half of her wants to go back, but the other half is exhilarated by the enormity of what she's doing. The daring.

They're climbing towards a belt of trees. It's steep and Kelly's legs are getting tired, the merciless sun making every step an effort. She slumps down onto the scrubby grass. Pushing her fringe away from her forehead, she looks down to where they've just come from. Beyond the restless grass of the meadow is their house, its blank windows pointing towards the rolling downs, and just visible above the rooftops, she can see the square tower of the village church. Has her mum noticed they've gone yet? Will she call her dad? Call the police?

'I don't want to go any further.'

Freya comes back to her. Crouching beside her, she flings an arm around her neck and holds her close. 'Please, I want to see the wood. Sisters must stick together.'

Kelly slips her arm around her waist, feeling the sharp ridges of her ribs. 'I suppose so.'

She lets Freya pull her to her feet and lead her on, their bodies pressed together as if in some sort of three-legged race. A barbed wire fence is in front of them, broken by a kissing gate, and beyond it is the wood. As they step through the gate, the air becomes mercifully cooler and Kelly tips her head to look at the dense green canopy. It's silent here, the only sound the clang of the gate as Freya closes it. Her mum's never taken her here and she wonders why. Maybe it's because Hansel and Gretel got lost in a wood such as this one and she knows Mummy doesn't like losing her children. She's heard her crying after they've left.

Kelly rubs at the goosebumps on her arms. 'I don't like it here.'

Freya links her arm through Kelly's. 'Don't be silly. Let's explore.'

A narrow path, knotted with roots, disappears into the wood and they take it, threading their way between the trees that stretch upwards to the sky either side of them. To begin with, their interlocking branches afford glimpses of the parched, sunlit slopes of the downs they've just left, but all too soon, the path veers away and it becomes darker.

Suddenly, Ben breaks away, heading towards a gap in the trees.

'Ben. Come back!' Kelly pulls at Freya's arm in panic. 'We can't lose him.'

Leaving the path, they go after him, stumbling over tree roots and rotting logs, pushing through the brambles and undergrowth. As they run, they call Ben's name and when Kelly hears his answering bark, she's giddy with relief.

They've broken out of the trees and are standing in a clearing lit with sunlight. It isn't empty, though. At its centre is a huge spreading beech tree, with two massive trunks pushing away from each other, the ground beneath littered with the previous year's leaves. It's a tree from a fairy tale or a picture book.

Freya claps her hands. 'Let's climb.'

Kelly's not sure. She's never climbed a tree as big as this one and there's something else she's seen. Something she hadn't noticed earlier.

'Look.' Her voice is a whisper.

Branches fan out from the joined trunks and from one of the lower ones, someone has fixed a rope. It hangs straight and unmoving, its end tied into a perfect hangman's noose – just like the one Miss Dunlop showed the class in her book about highwaymen.

She doesn't want to touch it, go near it, but Freya is running her hand down one of the trunks, her fingers exploring the secret creases of its bark. Her eyes are closed, her lips moving soundlessly.

Ben, who had earlier been running around the tree, jumping at the trunk and barking, now lies flat on the ground, his ears down.

'Freya?'

Freya doesn't answer. She's acting weirdly again and Kelly doesn't like it. She wants to be back home – not here in this horrible wood. But just as she's reaching out a hand to shake her shoulder, Freya pushes herself away from the tree. She looks up at the rope and pulls a face. 'I can't reach it. It's too high.' She turns to Kelly. 'What star sign are you?'

The change of subject is abrupt. Unsettling. She scuffs at the dead leaves beneath the tree. 'I don't know what a star sign is.'

'It's when you were born.' Lifting her thin leg, Freya places her foot in the cleavage of the two trunks. 'When is your birthday?'

'August twenty-second. You came here the day after my birthday. Remember?'

Freya had been her birthday present.

'You're a Leo then.' Pushing her hands against the inside of the two trunks, Freya pulls herself up and finds a purchase for her other foot. She looks down at Kelly, a pattern of leaves on her face.

Kelly shrugs. 'Am I?' Leos are lions and she doesn't feel much like a lion. Lions are brave and she's definitely not that.

'I'm a Gemini,' Freya continues. Steadying herself with her arms, she cups her hands under her chin and moves her head from left to right. 'Two-faced. But don't worry, Geminis and Leos are like best friends.'

The branch with the rope is stretching away from Freya, and Kelly knows there's no way she can reach it. Feeling bored, she walks away, calling Ben to follow. She only turns back when she hears Freya calling her name.

How she's managed it, she's not sure, but Freya is clinging to the rope, her legs clamped around the twisted cords like a fireman, searching with her foot to find the noose.

Kelly runs back, her arms outstretched. 'Don't fall.'

'Don't be an idiot. Why would I fall?'

Freya's face is pressed against the rough strands of the rope, her arms straining as she tries to keep herself stable. She manages to fit the other foot next to the first, then looks down at Kelly, her eyes shining. 'Now swing me.'

Kelly reaches up her arms, but she can't reach. 'You're too high.'

'I'll do it myself then.'

Leaning back, she pushes her feet forward, but instead of swinging, the rope starts to twist. Tipping back her head, Freya laughs wildly, bucking her body to make the rope move faster. It twists and tightens and, when it won't tighten any more, it stops and the branch creaks. Slowly, the rope starts to twist the other way. As it spins faster, Freya squeals in delight.

Ben is jumping at her, his barks ringing through the trees, but Kelly stays where she is, petrified she'll fall.

Finally, the rope stops spinning. Taking her foot out of the loop, Freya drops to the ground. Her face is pink. Her breath coming in gasps.

'Now you have a go.'

'I don't want to.'

She doesn't like the tree with its two thick trunks. Neither does she like the rope that hangs from it. Taking Ben by the collar, she leads him to the edge of the trees. 'I'm going home.'

Freya's face falls. She runs over to Kelly, her shorts covered in dead leaves. 'Don't leave me.'

She looks so distraught that, immediately, Kelly feels guilty. She drops Ben's collar and straightens up, chewing the inside of her mouth. 'I wasn't going to. I was only joking.'

Tears glitter on Freya's pale lashes. 'I know you were. You wouldn't leave me like everyone else.' She leans her head against Kelly's. 'If you like, I'll tell you a secret. The reason I don't live with my mum any more.'

Kelly stares. No one has ever told her a secret before. 'Would you?'

Freya looks back at the rope. It's still now. Her voice is grave. 'Yes, but if you tell anyone. Anyone at all. Ever. I will hang myself by that rope and my soul will haunt you forever.'

Kelly moves away from her, horrified. 'I wouldn't tell. I promise.'

'I mean nobody ever. Not your mum, not your dad, not anybody. If you do…' Circling her neck with her hands, Freya drops her head to her shoulder. Her tongue lolls from her mouth grotesquely.

Kelly pulls at Freya's hands, appalled. 'Stop it! I said I wouldn't tell, didn't I?'

The wood is quiet, just the odd rustle of leaves and the shrill cry of a bird in the canopy. Freya stands defiant, her eyes fixed on Kelly's.

'I killed my sister,' she says.

CHAPTER EIGHTEEN

Kelly Now

I'm getting the children's breakfast, bouncing Noah in his bouncy chair with my right foot while trying to persuade Sophie to finish her toast. She's pushed away her plate and her head is resting on her folded arms, her blue eyes looking up at me. They're filled with tears. I hate to see her like this and am worried about how she's coping. Twice she woke in the night and eventually, exhausted from getting up for Noah too and craving sleep, I'd allowed her to come into our bed.

Feeling my throat tighten, I hold up a piece of toast. 'Just one more bite, Sophie, please. It's a long time until lunchtime.'

On the other side of the table, Isabella is still sulking. 'It's not fair. Why aren't *I* allowed in your bed?'

I look at Izzy and can't help smiling at the crescent of milk that follows the contours of her little mouth like a clown's. 'It *is* fair when Sophie's had a bad dream. If *you* had one, I'd let you too.'

If that happened, I know just how it would be. Instead of curling herself into my body and going back to sleep as Sophie had, Izzy would take advantage of the situation, spreading her limbs into a starfish and pushing us to the edge of the bed. She'd regale us with stories of zombies and ghosts until Noah's next feed or until Mitch conceded defeat and left us to it, sleeping in Isabella's bed instead. Sometimes it's hard to cope with Izzy's overactive imagination.

Sophie looks up at me, her fine fair hair falling into her eyes. I make a note to tie it back before we leave. 'I don't want to go back, Mummy.'

I hear the thrum of panic in her voice and wish there was something I could do to make it better. I brush her hair back from her face. 'You'll have fun when you get there. I know you will. Your topic is fairy tales and I know you love them.'

It's said without conviction. I can't imagine my quiet, sensitive daughter in a noisy classroom, knowing that if anyone tries to speak to her, she'll clam up and withdraw into herself. My heart breaks at the thought of it.

'Cheer up you lot. It might never happen.' Mitch turns round and looks at the three of us. He's filling thick doorstep sandwiches with corned beef, flattening them with his large hand before cutting them in half. He'll eat them in the site office or outside with the other guys. I nod in Sophie's direction, not wanting to speak my fears aloud.

'She'll be fine,' he says, wiping his hands on his jeans. 'She'll get used to it.'

Noah has started to cry and I grit my teeth, weary of his continual demands for feeds. Feeling my body react to the sound, I pick him out of his chair.

Mitch looks at us both. 'You could always leave him for a while longer. It wouldn't hurt him to wait.'

It's just the thing my mother would have said and I shut out his words, unclipping my nursing bra and latching Noah on. If we're quick, I can get him fed before we leave and still have time to spare once we get to school. I need to speak to the girls' teacher. Make sure she understands how different the two of them are. That while one needs a firm hand, the other needs understanding and a gentle touch.

Isabella has finished her breakfast and is sitting on the floor, trying to put on her patent shoes. I'm impressed with her perseverance, her tongue sticking out of the corner of her mouth as she tries to buckle them, despite the fact she's got them on the wrong feet.

'Can you help her, Mitch? You can see I've got my hands full.'

My husband crouches down beside her and slips the shoes onto the right feet, buckling them carefully with his practical fingers. 'There you are, beautiful,' he says, kissing her on the top of her dark shiny head. He looks up as the letter box clatters. 'There's the post. Fetch it for me would you, love.'

Izzy leaps up and runs out of the room. When she returns, she's holding a clutch of letters to her chest, trying not to drop them. Mitch takes them from her.

'Bill... bill... bank statement... Cotton Traders catalogue.' As he speaks, he flicks them onto the kitchen table until there's just one left in his hand. He studies it, bringing it closer so he can see the postmark. 'Now this looks more interesting.'

I look up. 'What is it?'

'I'm not sure, but it's addressed to you. Can't remember the last time anyone sent an actual *letter*.' He says the word as if he's talking about something from the dark ages.

'Give it here.' I reach out my free hand and Mitch passes it to me. The envelope is thick vellum, not something cheap you'd pick up at the supermarket in a multi-pack. My name and address have been written on the front in small neat writing.

I stare at it and my heart goes cold.

'Aren't you going to open it?'

'No.' Placing it on the kitchen table, I push it away from me, as far as I can without disturbing Noah. I feel sick at the thought of the hand that's written whatever is inside.

Seeing my face, Mitch frowns. He slings his donkey jacket onto the back of the chair and picks up the envelope.

'Kelly, tell me what's going on? If you've an admirer and that's their love letter, you'd better tell me now.'

His attempt at a joke falls flat. I'm in no mood to laugh and Sophie, knowing something's the matter, slips off her chair and presses herself against my body. I look at her, her little face pinched with concern, and feel guilty. I'm doing nothing to make it better. Unlatching Noah from my breast, I take a fresh pad from the box beside me and position it inside my nursing bra before clipping it back up. My head is aching with the weight of all that is unread in the letter, but I can't let it affect me.

'It's nothing,' I say, taking Noah out into the hall and putting him in his pram. 'I'll read it later.'

Mitch starts to say something, but I throw him a look that says, *just leave it*.

Kissing each of his daughters in turn, he pulls on his jacket and picks up his sandwiches. 'I'll see you later then. Have a good day, tribe. Oh, and I'll let Maddie know it's fine for Saturday.'

He hesitates, then comes over to me. 'You know who it's from, don't you?'

I say nothing, not trusting myself to speak. Of course I know who it's from. It's from my mother.

CHAPTER NINETEEN
Kelly Before

Kelly runs, desperate to get away from the terrible thing she's been told. She hates this place. Hates the sunlight that flickers through the branches. Hates the tree. Hates the rope. But most of all, she hates the terrible thing that Freya has just told her.

Being so far from her house is no longer exciting. No longer an adventure. Why did she ever let her sister persuade her to leave the garden? *Her sister.* The very words bring goosebumps to her skin. Is Freya following her? She doesn't want to stop to find out. The kissing gate's in front of her. Not far now.

Bursting from the trees into the open and hearing the gate clang shut behind her, she stops to catch her breath. The grassy slope that leads down to the meadow is in front of her, her house just visible. After the coolness of the trees, the heat is shocking, the sun blinding.

'Wait!'

Freya's call is faint. She's not close. If her mum knew she'd left her behind, she'd be angry. Kelly runs faster, Ben jumping at her legs, thinking it's a game. Her feet pound the ground. One two. One two. She's glad she's the best runner in her year. Not once does she look behind to the belt of trees they've just left or to the far end of the meadow where the rifle range is. Instead, she looks straight ahead, being careful not to slip on the loose chalk. Then she's back in the meadow, the grasses whipping at her legs as she runs through them.

It's only when she reaches the stile and is about to climb over that she dares to look over her shoulder. Freya is no longer running but is walking through the grass, her head bowed. Biting back the guilt, Kelly climbs over and runs down the track beside the house, Ben at her heels. Her mum's not in the garden and when she lets herself in through the kitchen door, there's no sound from inside either. Not sure what to do, she shuts Ben in the kitchen and tiptoes up the stairs.

'Mummy?'

When there's no answer, she creeps to her mum's bedroom door and pushes it open. The room is in darkness, the curtains drawn to shut out the sunlight. Her mum's fast asleep on top of the covers – her wiry hair spread out on the pillow, a packet of white pills peeping from an open packet on her bedside table. Hardly able to believe her luck, Kelly tiptoes out again and into her own room to wait.

She hears Freya come in. Hears the back door closing. Then silence. When she can wait no longer, Kelly creeps back downstairs and looks around the living room door. Freya is lying on the settee, but she hears her before she sees her – the dreadful sound her lungs are making as she tries to drag air into them. If it's possible, her face is even paler than before.

'Don't tell,' Freya whispers.

Kelly can't meet her eye. 'Your secret's stupid. Who cares if anyone knows? Maybe I'll tell Mummy.'

It makes her feel strong standing up to Freya. Important. For once, it's she who's in control. But even as she's thinking this, guilt is creeping up on her. She left Freya alone in the wood. Despite the awful thing she told her, that makes her a terrible sister.

Freya turns onto her side. Beside her, on the settee, is Kelly's doll, Amber, wrapped in her cellular blanket. It's where she left her that morning. Slowly and deliberately, her breath coming in gasps, Freya unwraps the doll from Kelly's blanket and starts to twist the soft material. When it's in a tight rope, she holds the ends to make a loop and slips it over Amber's head. Kelly watches in horror as she holds the twisted blanket high so the plastic body swings by its neck.

Running to the settee, Kelly grabs the doll from Freya's hands.

'I hate you,' she says, the words mirroring Freya's in the changing room. 'I wish you'd never come.'

CHAPTER TWENTY

Kelly Now

I've been looking at the letter for a good half hour, trying to pluck up the courage to open it. There's nothing my mother can say that I'd want to hear. All the way to the school, I'd thought of nothing else, knowing that when I got home with Noah, the letter would still be there waiting for me.

As we'd reached the classroom door, Sophie's hand had tightened in mine, but she hadn't cried and, somehow, this had been worse. If it hadn't been for Mrs Allen, coming out to meet us, taking Sophie by the hand and telling her all the lovely things they were going to do that morning, I don't know if I would ever have managed to leave her.

I've left Noah in the hall in his pram, knowing that if I take him out, he'll wake and scream. It's bad enough when I haven't anything else to worry about, but I can't cope with a crying baby as well as Sophie and my mother's letter.

Picking the envelope up, I take it into the living room. Without realising what I'm doing, I begin to pace the room, counting the number of steps between the door and the fireplace. Steeling myself to slide a finger under the flap.

When I've counted twenty paces, I stop and take a deep breath, a sudden realisation dawning on me – I don't have to open it at all. I can throw it in the recycling bin and never know what it is she wants to tell me. Whatever it is, it will be poisoned.

But what if the letter is about Freya? What if she knows something about the locket?

Before I can change my mind, I rip the envelope open and slip out the page. The letter is short, barely one side, and it doesn't take me long to read it.

My hand drops to my side and numbness spreads through me. It's not about Freya. It's about my father. He's dead.

I sit heavily on the settee, trying to process my thoughts. Once I idolised this man, would do anything for his love, but that's all changed. I'm older now and know that you can't make someone love you if they don't want to. If only that little girl had known, maybe she wouldn't have tried so hard.

Lifting the letter again, I re-read it. He died of a heart attack two days ago and the funeral is next week. My mother wants me to go. I think of the village I looked down on from the hill on our day out, the way my blood had frozen at the sight of it. The funeral will be held in the church with the square tower, and if I go, it will be the first time in years that I've set foot in the place where I grew up.

In the hall, Noah has started crying and I feel like joining him. Mitch has his faults, but there's no denying he is a loving father and would do anything for all his children. My own father was dispassionate. A figure of no substance who came in and out of our home with barely a look my way.

I'll write and say I can't come. That I'm too tied up with the children. But how can I say that when she knows nothing about them? No. I'll say nothing. Pretend the letter never reached me.

I put the letter down on the coffee table, relieved I've made a decision and get up to see to Noah. As I do, I catch sight of the envelope with my address written in my mother's neat writing.

In the shock of receiving it, I hadn't given it a thought, but now there is something nagging at me.

I've kept where I live a secret for so long. How did she find me?

CHAPTER TWENTY-ONE

Kelly Before

Kelly takes Amber into the kitchen and sits at the table wondering what to do. Placing the doll in front of her, she moves her plastic head from side to side, imagining the feel of the blanket around its neck. It isn't long before she hears her mum's footsteps on the stairs and when she appears at the kitchen door, she looks dazed. Her skin blotchy.

She rubs at her eyes with the heel of her hand. 'Where's Freya?'

Kelly stares straight ahead. She smooths Amber's shiny blonde hair. 'I don't know.'

'What do you mean, you don't know?'

Kelly points behind her to the half-open door. 'She's in there.'

Her mum folds her arms and leans her back against the door frame. 'I hope you haven't had an argument. Freya is…' She stops as if searching for the right word. 'Freya is delicate.'

Delicate is for flower petals and snowflakes. It has nothing to do with the girl who swung from the rope, her hands gripping at the twisted strands, feet wedged in the noose.

She looks up. 'Why is she delicate? What's the matter with her?'

Walking over to the cupboard, her mum opens it and get out two plates. She puts them on the table. 'It's nothing for you to worry about. What have you two been doing with yourselves while I've been upstairs?'

Kelly wants to tell her about the meadow, the wood, the creepy tree. Most of all she wants to tell her about the hangman's noose that swings from it and Freya's secret, but she doesn't. She can't. Instead, she twists Amber's legs in their plastic sockets to make her do the splits.

'We were playing in the garden with Ben.' Reaching down to him, she picks off some of the dried brown leaf litter that has caught in his fur and pushes it into the pocket of her shorts. Ben's yellow tennis ball is over by the back door. 'We played fetch.'

'Freya,' her mum calls as she gets a sliced loaf out of the bread bin. 'Come here, love, and choose what you'd like in your sandwich.'

When Freya doesn't appear, she puts her head around the kitchen door and calls louder. 'Freya? Did you hear me?'

Kelly follows her into the living room, feeling uncertain. Freya is still there, lying on the settee where she left her, but her eyes are now closed, and her cheeks are flushed. Instantly, her mum's beside her, feeling her forehead with the back of her hand.

'She's very hot.'

Kelly knows Freya's pretending. Just the way she did when they thought she couldn't speak. When she's been too noisy or asked too many questions, her mum calls it attention-seeking. It's what Freya's doing now.

'Freya?' her mum says in a choked voice. 'Can you hear me?'

Freya's eyes open and she tries to smile. She pushes herself up onto her elbow, her white hair falling around her face. Her mum puts an arm around her, brushing the hair from her face and Freya leans into her.

Kelly wonders what that must feel like.

'Are you feeling unwell, Freya?' her mum asks. 'Is it your tummy?'

Freya says nothing but nods her head.

'Is it sore? Do you have any pain? Do you feel sick?' All the time she's speaking, her mum is rocking her to her plump bosom, smoothing her hair with gentle fingers. 'Kelly. Get the thermometer from the medicine box.'

Normally, Kelly isn't allowed to touch the medicine box, but today is no ordinary day. Running to the kitchen, she drags a chair to the worktop and climbs onto it. The box is where it always is and she lifts it carefully out, then jumps off the chair and hurries back to the living room.

Without thanking her, her mum opens the box and searches through the packets of paracetamol and boxes of plasters until she finds the thermometer. She slides it under Freya's T-shirt, pinning Freya's arm to her side to keep it in place. After a minute or so, she pulls the thermometer back out and looks at it.

'It's high. I'll give you some Calpol and then I think we should call the surgery, just in case.'

Freya pushes away from her, but she's firm. 'I'm sorry, Freya, but while you are living here with us, I am in loco parentis. I can't take any chances.'

She acts as if Freya understands what she's talking about, but Kelly doesn't know what she means. Loco parentis – it sounds foreign and exotic. She watches her mum take her phone out of her pocket and listens as she tells the receptionist what the problem is.

'Tell Dr Bradley it's Karen Harding. It's about Freya – he'll understand.' She waits for a few minutes, then Kelly sees her nod. 'Certainly. I'll bring her in straight away.'

That night, Kelly's sleep is restless. She dreams she's at the clearing in the wood, but the trees that surround it have knotted their branches together to keep her from entering. They can't stop her, though, and she pushes through them, knowing she has to see what they're hiding from her. The giant beech tree stands in the middle, but now it's grown to fill the space. Its roots, instead of being underground where they should be, are pushing up through the soft earth. As she watches, the great tree moves towards her, heaving its two trunks. Its branches creak. The rope swings.

She wakes and cries out, her heart beating so hard she thinks it will burst out of her chest. Pulling the covers over her head, she knows she won't sleep again until it gets light. She wants her mum to come and comfort her. She wants her to tell her it's all just a bad dream but knows she won't. All her mum's worrying is for Freya who is lying in her bed in the big bedroom overlooking the meadow. She's had too much sun, the doctor said, and not enough to drink. That's all.

When her dad got home from work, she'd heard her mum tell him what had happened. Kelly had seen her through the door, sitting at the kitchen table, her head in her hands and her fingers pushing through her hair. 'They'll say I'm not fit to look after her. I can't bear it. What will I do?'

She'd reached a hand out to her father, but he'd moved away. 'Don't be ridiculous, Karen. You're being hysterical.'

It's dark under the covers and there's no air, but Kelly's too scared to push them back. Instead, she tries to think of nice things: the tickle of the meadow grass against her legs and the tiny orange butterfly she'd seen on the blackthorn. It doesn't work. Pushing through these thoughts are darker ones. The tree's monstrous trunks. The swinging rope. When she hears her door opening, she thinks she might scream, but she bites it back and pushes down the cover. It's better to know what's out there.

Kelly stares into the darkness, terrified of what she'll find, but it's just Freya. She's standing in the doorway, her nightie hanging from her tiny frame, her face marble-white in the gloom of the room. At least she has legs and arms – not those terrifying white roots. At least she's real.

Coming into the room, Freya sits on the edge of the bed. In her hand is the nightlight from her bedroom. Bending down, she pushes it into the socket in the wall next to Kelly and a dim light shines out.

Kelly pulls back her covers and Freya climbs in. She feels her thin arms wrap around her, pulling her body close against hers. They lie like that, their hearts beating as one, until Kelly can stand it no longer.

'I'm sorry I was mean,' she whispers. 'I don't hate you really.'

'I know,' Freya whispers back.

The warmth of her sister's body is comforting and it isn't long before she drifts back to sleep.

The next morning, Kelly wakes up alone. Reaching out a hand, she smooths the sheet beside her to see if it's still warm, but it's not. She can hear voices downstairs and the slam of a car door outside. When she parts the blinds, a blue light flashes into her room, then slips away again. Over and over.

She runs onto the landing. Freya's door is open and her dad is in there pushing clothes into a bag.

'What's happening? Where's Freya?'

'Complications,' he mutters.

Her blanket is around her shoulders and she sucks the end of it. 'Where's she going?' It's easier to ask her dad these things, especially when he's distracted.

He's dressed in his work clothes, but he's yet to put his tie on and the top button of his shirt is undone. 'To hospital,' he says. 'In London. They've got specialists there. Your mum is going with her.'

'She's my sister. I want to come too.'

'She's not your sister,' he snaps. 'Not really.'

A sudden anger grips her. 'She *is*. She *is* my sister and you can't let them take her away. They all go and you promised it would be different.'

Her dad takes a breath in, his fingers whitening around the bag. 'We never promised you anything, Kelly.'

'But—'

'But nothing. It's all been in your head.'

He pushes Freya's sweatshirt into the bag. 'Christ Almighty. Why can't the woman see the damage she's doing?'

Kelly hates the way he's speaking. 'Who? Who are you talking about?'

'Nobody. It doesn't matter.' He zips up the bag. 'I'll give this to your mum, then I've got to go to work.'

'What about me? What will I do?' She pulls the sleeves of her pyjamas over her hands and stares at him.

'I suppose you'll have to stay with Mrs Ringrose until your mum gets back. Get yourself dressed.'

'Will Freya be coming back?'

He doesn't answer. Just picks up the bag and leaves the room.

CHAPTER TWENTY-TWO

August 16th

I took the girls to have their hair cut today. It's the first time they've been to a hairdresser. There was a bit of a to-do as Miss Fusspot didn't want to sit in the chair, but I managed to persuade her eventually. I had the chance to pick up a lock of hair and I've attached it with the photograph I took of them both. I've also kept a piece for myself too. Hoping this makes you happy rather than sad.

All the best

CHAPTER TWENTY-THREE

Kelly Now

The trolley outside the girls' classroom is piled high with lunch boxes waiting to be collected by the children when they come out. I can see Bob the Builder's hat peeking out from under a plastic box with a picture of a Minion on it. I can't see Sophie's and wonder if she ate any of the food I packed inside. I'd chosen things I know she loves. Cheese strings and cucumber and a little pot of grapes. I think of my own school sandwiches when I was a child. Sliced processed cheese in warm white bread. An out of date chocolate bar if I was lucky or an overripe banana thrown in as an afterthought. Unless a new child was with us, of course. Then my mother would send us off with food fit for a king.

As I remember, my fingertips close around the letter I pushed into my coat pocket before I came out. I've no idea why I've brought it with me as by receiving it, I feel like I've been cursed. Why couldn't she have let things be? Why did she have to come back into my life now and ruin everything?

Through the classroom window, I see Mrs Allen collecting books from the tables. There are no children to be seen; they must be lining up at the door out of sight. Looking at my phone, I see there's still another ten minutes to go.

Other people have joined me in the playground. Some, like me, have younger children, others are on their own. It's not just mothers but fathers and grandparents. There are childminders too with gaggles of smaller children running around them. They stand in groups, the voices of the nearest ones drifting over to me. There's mention of *The X Factor* and a police drama I've never heard of. I turn my back on them, not wanting to be drawn in. There was a time in my life I was desperate for friends, companions, a sister. But I don't need that any more. I don't trust my judgement.

At last the door opens. Mrs Allen latches it onto a hook on the wall, and as each child comes out, she makes them wait, her hand resting on their shoulder until the person who's collecting them has been identified. I'm on edge, craning my neck around the other parents to see the twins, but there's no sign of them. I hover anxiously by the door and when Mrs Allen sees me, she mouths *have you got a minute?* I'm not sure if I should be worried or not.

It seems to take forever for the children to leave, but finally, the last mother and child moves away from the door. Mrs Allen steps back to let me inside, but I hesitate, not happy to leave Noah.

'Would you like to bring him in?' she asks kindly.

Remembering the scene I'd caused in the playground the first morning, I shake my head, embarrassed. 'No, the walk here has got him off to sleep. I don't want to wake him again. Maybe, once we get home, I'll get a bit of quiet time.'

Sophie runs to me and presses her face against my legs. I look around for Izzy and see her in the play corner. A folding screen has been covered over with a brick-patterned paper to make it look like a castle and Isabella sits on a plastic chair beneath a sign saying *Fairy Tales*. She's brushing the white, nylon hair of a doll with fierce strokes and, when she sees me, she turns her chair so her back is to me.

'Go away.'

Ignoring her, I turn to Mrs Allen. 'Is it Isabella? Has she misbehaved?'

She shakes her head. 'No, it's not Isabella. It's Sophie I wanted to have a word with you about.'

My hand strays to my daughter's blonde hair. 'What about her?'

Mrs Allen smiles at Sophie. 'Would you do something for me, love? Could you make sure the cushions in the reading corner are nice and tidy?'

Sophie looks at me for reassurance and I nod. 'Go on, Soph. That would be really helpful.'

When she's out of earshot, her teacher continues. 'It's nothing to worry about, and obviously early days still, but I've noticed how hard Sophie finds it to engage with the other children. We're doing our best to make it easier for her, but the only person she'll speak to is our classroom assistant, Miss King. I read in the girls' notes that they didn't go to a nursery school? Is that right?'

I look down at the tiled floor of the classroom, noticing there are three light grey tiles followed by a dark. Is Mrs Allen judging me?

'No, the twins didn't go to nursery. They had each other to play with.' What I don't tell her is how I hadn't wanted to let them go. Scared that if I did, something might happen to them.

Mrs Allen smiles. 'Please don't think I'm in any way putting blame on you. It's just that sometimes, if a child hasn't had the opportunity to socialise, it can be a bit daunting for them. I'm sure that in a few days she'll be just fine.'

'I hope you're right. Come on, Izzy. Sophie. Time to go.'

Putting down her doll, Isabella runs over to us. I think she's going to hug me, but she doesn't. Instead, she's out the door and is peering into Noah's pram. 'Wakey, wakey, baby.'

She's answered by a cry and Mrs Allen smiles sympathetically. 'There goes your quiet afternoon.'

I peel Sophie's arms from my legs, and taking her hand, lead her out of the door. 'Come on, we'll stop at the newsagent's on the way home and we can get some sweets.'

Isabella waves to her teacher. 'Bye, Mrs Allen. See you tomorrow.'

Sophie already has a hold of the pram handle. She says nothing, but I can tell she wants to get away as quickly as she can. I let off the brake and we make our way across the playground. As we do, my thoughts turn back to the letter that's in my pocket and fresh uncertainty nudges in. How did my mother find me?

There are other parents and children in the newsagent's when we get there, and we stand in a queue to be served. Sophie has chosen a necklace of candy sweets and Izzy's ice lolly is already unwrapped and in her mouth. It's melting in the warm shop, and as I watch, she licks at the red dribble that's run down her arm. On a high shelf next to the counter, is a display of after dinner chocolate: tall blue tubs of Roses, gold foiled Ferrero Rocher and the distinctive purple design of Milk Tray. It reminds me that I ought to take something to Maddie's on Saturday. After some deliberation, I choose a large box of Belgian truffles and put them on the counter.

'Hello, girls.' June, the manager, leans her elbows on the counter and looks down at them in their uniforms. The blue sleeve of Isabella's sweatshirt is already covered in yellow paint. 'I haven't seen you for a while. Don't you look smart now. How's it going?'

Isabella is quick to answer. 'I love it, but Sophie hates it.'

'Well, I'm sorry to hear that.' Reaching over, she takes two small fudge bars from the display. 'I'm sure this will help make it better.'

Izzy snatches hers up, but Sophie just looks at the one left on the counter. With a sigh, I pick it up and put it in my handbag. 'Thank you, June. That's kind.'

'And how's the baby?' It's only a small shop with not enough space between the shelves to bring him in, but I've parked the pram outside the window where I can see it.

'Fine.' I say automatically.

June pats my hand. 'It will get better. I expect it was the same with the girls and, remember, there were two of them.'

'I know. I shouldn't complain.'

I hand over some change and am just turning to leave when I hear June's voice again.

'I nearly forgot. I have your magazine.'

I turn my head. 'My magazine?'

'Yes, the one you ordered. It came this morning.'

'But I haven't ordered anything.'

June frowns. 'It was my assistant, Tom, who took the telephone call.' Getting off her stool, she disappears behind the counter, reappearing again with a magazine in her hand. She holds it out to me.

'Here you are. *Spirit and Destiny.*'

Taking the magazine from her, I flick through the pages, something making me stop when I reach the one with the horoscopes. My eyes skim down, searching for Leo, half expecting it to be circled as it was in the newspaper. When it isn't, I tell myself off for being so foolish and put it back on the counter.

'I didn't order it. There must be someone with the same name.'

She looks doubtful. 'Anyway, it's been paid for. I found the money in an envelope on the counter. Someone must have come in and left it there while I was out the back. I thought it was you.'

My heart's beating heavily in my chest. 'It wasn't.'

'Well, you might as well take it as it's been paid for. You might like it.'

'Yes, I suppose so.'

We leave the shop and I shove the magazine in the tray of the pram, but as I do, the pram moves slightly. Straightening up, I take hold of the white plastic handle and push. The pram rolls forward.

The brake is off.

Fear grips me and I grab the girls' hands, drawing them to me.

'Stop it, Mum, you're hurting me.'

Ignoring Isabella, I scan the street. Everything seems normal. An elderly woman crosses the road, bumping her shopping trolley up the kerb when she reaches the other side; a couple of boys, in the same uniform as the twins, run ahead of their parents until they're called back; a white van with Adams Builders printed on the side drives past us.

Everything's as it should be, but the ordinariness is not enough to alleviate my unease. There's someone out there who put a locket, just like Freya's, in my baby's pram. Someone driven enough to go to the bother of ordering a magazine in my name. To move Noah's pram.

I look at my fingers clutching the pram's handle, and imagine another hand holding the plastic, a foot flicking off the brake. My stomach gives a fearful twist. I'm not imagining it. Someone wants to take my baby.

CHAPTER TWENTY-FOUR

Kelly Before

'Kelly Harding, I'm talking to you.'

Kelly looks up, aware of Mr Seymore's eyes on her. He's pointing his marker at a baffling set of numbers and letters on the whiteboard and, as he taps the shiny white surface, his fitted shirt strains across his back. The girls in Year 10 all think he's cute with his highlighted hair and trendy clothes, but she doesn't. She's heard the rumours about him and one of the girls in his A-level group. Even if it's not true, the idea that anyone under the age of thirty would be interested in him is gross. He's married with two young kids after all.

'Come up to the front and solve this equation. It shouldn't be difficult if you've been listening. Your father's an accountant. Let's see if he's passed on his genes.'

Not daring to look at anyone's face in case they're laughing at her, Kelly pushes back her chair. Slowly, she gets up and walks between the tables. Straightaway, she sees her homework; it's sitting on Mr Seymore's table, a red circle around her workings. She'd heard some of the others say they'd had help with their homework from their parents, but she'd had to do hers on her own. Mr Seymore thrusts the thick black marker at her, his hand pale and freckly. She hates it. Hates *him* for doing this to her when he obviously knows she has no clue what to do.

Kelly stares at the numbers on the board, but they start to swim. She can't cry. Not in front of the class. Trying to concentrate, she blinks and brings the numbers back into focus. She knows that what she does to one side, she must do to the other. Lifting her arm, she writes something on the board. Someone scrapes their chair and she loses concentration. *X divided by seven.* She needs to move the number to the other side but can't remember the rule. Panic rises.

'We're all waiting, Miss Harding.'

Hating him even more, Kelly writes her answer quickly, knowing that it's wrong. Knowing how stupid she looks. Her hand is slippery with sweat and the pen drops at Mr Seymore's feet. Face burning, she bends to pick it up and hands it back to him.

'I suggest,' he says smoothly, his thin freckled lips stretched into a smile that has no warmth, 'that you go back to your seat and pay attention in future. Oh, and you can take this and redo it for next lesson.'

He hands Kelly her homework and she takes it, knowing that her next attempt won't be any better.

Maths was the last lesson before lunch. Finding a space by herself on the field, Kelly sits and takes her sandwiches out of her bag. As she releases them from their cling film prison and takes a bite of the moist bread, she watches Carly, Ava and Tabby. She gave up being friends with them years ago. Gone are the days when she'd tried to impress them – following them around like Freya used to follow *her*.

The girls are sitting with their backs against the Portakabin that serves as an English room, watching a group of boys trying to do backflips and failing. She can hear their laughter and the odd word as they call out to them.

Trying not to care, she fishes in her bag for a breakfast bar she found in the cupboard. It's past its sell-by date, but she doesn't care – she's used to it.

There was a time when the kitchen cupboards had been full of delicious things: family-sized bags of crisps and packets of chocolate wafer biscuits. Maybe a cake tin containing a delicious home-made cake. She'd come downstairs in the morning to find her mum standing at the kitchen worktop, her flowered dressing gown wrapped around her large body. She'd be buttering bread for sandwiches, which she'd fill with egg mayonnaise or tuna, or whatever else they fancied, before neatly packing them into lunch boxes.

This was before Freya left and everything changed. And even though the few short weeks with her foster-sister were strange ones, as the years have passed, she's come to view these times with nostalgia.

A picture of Freya's white hair comes into her head, the pale eyes that were so unsettling. After she failed to return to their house from hospital, Kelly had felt more alone than she had before Freya had come to live with them. Maybe it was because, since that day, no one else had come to sleep in the bedroom overlooking the field of waving grass. Or maybe it was because she had simply grown used to having someone around who was as desperate for love as herself.

After Freya left, leaving a hole that couldn't be filled, it was as if her mum's heart had broken. Not wanting anyone to take her place, and no longer needing to keep up the pretence that theirs was a happy family in order to secure another child, she'd stopped bothering. It wasn't long before the house had become untidy, the weekly shopping trips replaced with a quick trip to their local Co-op when the milk ran out. And, rather than spending more time with Kelly, her mother withdrew from her, leaving her confused and abandoned. Feeling as though it wasn't only Freya who had left her.

As the months slipped by, she'd expected things to get better, but they hadn't, and six years on, nothing's changed. She suspects her dad doesn't care. More often than not, he takes clients out to dinner, or orders from the local Indian. Eating it in his office, while listening to his classical music. But *she* minds. She's sick of ready meals and takeaways. Also, she's noticed her mum is piling on the weight.

It's not this that saddens her, though. Worst of all is that she misses her mum. Not the woman herself but the *idea* of her. Ever since she can remember, she's spent each day, each month, each year, living in hope that her mother might grow to love her – but recently, hope has turned to resignation. She knows she's been grieving for a mother she's never really had.

It's almost the end of lunch break. There's a rubbish bin at the edge of the field and as Kelly goes over to it to throw her wrappers away, she's surprised to see one of the girls making her way across the field towards her. It's Ava. Dropping her wrapper into the bin Kelly waits, wondering what she wants.

When Ava reaches her, she gives an awkward smile. 'Hi.'

Kelly's heart twists as she remembers how the two of them once played together in primary. How much she'd liked her. 'Hi.'

'I just wanted to say…' Ava looks back at the other two girls who are packing their lunch boxes into their bags, '*we* wanted to say, that it was shit what Mr Seymore did to you in maths last lesson.'

Kelly feels herself colour at the memory. She doesn't want to talk about it. Doesn't want Ava's sympathy. She just wants to forget it.

She looks at the ground. 'Thanks.'

'We're going to Truffles after school and wondered if you wanted to come too.'

It feels as though the ground is shifting. She isn't used to people making overtures of friendship and she can't remember how to respond. It seems a long time ago that the girls would come to her house to play, making dens in the garden and eating the marvellous teas her mum would lay out for them in the dining room. But, gradually, they'd stopped coming. First Ava and Tabby, then later,

Carly. It didn't take a genius to guess they found her mother's constant fussing over them weird.

Ava shifts her feet, waiting for her reply.

'I can't,' Kelly mutters. 'Mum likes me to come straight home.'

As soon as she's said it, she feels her blush deepen. Why did she have to mention her mum?

'That's okay. Just thought I'd ask.' There's a definite note of relief in Ava's voice and Kelly feels even worse. They didn't really want her to go; they were just feeling sorry for her.

The bell's ringing for the end of lunch and Kelly's just wondering how to get away when Ava gives a groan. 'What does *he* want?'

Kelly turns to see Ava's brother, Ethan. He's two years older than them and she knows a lot of the girls in her year fancy him. In his hand is a cat-shaped key ring with a key attached. He jangles it in front of Ava's face.

'How did you think you were going to get in tonight? You know Mum's not back until six.'

'Shit.' Ava grabs the key from Ethan's hand. 'Thanks. Where did I leave it?'

'By the front door, numpty.'

Stuffing the key into her bag, Ava zips it up, then looks around to see where Carly and Tabby are. They're going in through the double doors of the school and she calls out to them to wait for her.

'Got to go,' she says. 'See you in English.'

Ava runs across the field, leaving Kelly with Ethan. When he doesn't walk off too, she's unsure what to do. Being alone with him is excruciating. She tries not to stare at him but doesn't know where else to look. He's a head taller than her, blond hair falling into his eyes. When she was in primary school, Kelly had sometimes managed to persuade her mum to let her go to Ava's house and it was there she'd learnt what it was like to be in a normal household. Ava's mum would leave them to play on their own or watch TV, calling them into the kitchen later for fish fingers and beans, followed by a scoop of vanilla ice cream. She didn't smother her or pull her into a hug when it was time to leave, making her promise she'd come again, making her squirm with embarrassment. No, she was what a mother should be.

Usually, when she was there, Ethan would be out playing with his friends, but once he'd been there too. She remembers how he'd let her have a go of his remote-control car and hadn't minded when she'd crashed it into the skirting board. She'd liked him but, now he's older, it's a struggle to see that little boy inside this tall, long-limbed youth.

He's looking at her. Scratching his jaw with his fingernail. 'I saw you in the paper last week. You won that cross-country thing, didn't you? Mum was showing it to Ava. Asking if you're still in the same form at school.'

Kelly dares to look at him properly now, noticing how his eyes are an unusual shade of green beneath sandy brows. Why is he even talking to her? Everyone knows she's the girl whose family once had all the different kids living with them.

Swallowing down her embarrassment, she makes herself answer. 'Yes. The race was last week. I'm in the athletics club.'

'Impressive.'

Kelly glances at him to see if he's being sarcastic, but he's grinning. 'I'm pretty quick myself.'

'Oh.' She doesn't know what else to say.

'Well, see you around.' Hefting his rucksack onto his shoulder, he walks away across the field, leaving Kelly red-faced and flustered.

It's only as she's walking back towards the school building that a realisation dawns on her. How she's feeling now is the way she feels on the rare occasion her dad bothers to talk to her.

When Kelly goes home later, the humiliation she'd felt in the classroom is eclipsed by a feeling of unbridled joy. Ethan is two years older. Boys never like her, but he must – or he wouldn't have stayed and talked to her after Ava had gone.

Hugging the feeling to her, she fits the key into the lock and pushes open the front door. Immediately, she's hit by the lemony smell of some sort of cleaning product. That's not the only strange thing, though, as all the bags and coats that used to junk up their small lobby have been removed. They've been hung on a new pine coat stand and a matching rack on the floor is filled with their shoes.

'Mum?'

There's no answer, but she can hear the whine of a hoover somewhere above her head.

Taking her bag off her shoulder, Kelly goes into the living room. The first thing that catches her eye is the dining table at the far end of the room. Over the last few years, she's got used to the magazines and papers that have been dumped on it. The piles of bills, random junk mail and menus from takeaways waiting to be filed. Now, though, the table has nothing on it except a cut-glass vase of pink carnations. That's not all. The tabletop that she hasn't seen for a long while, has been polished, giving off a rather unpleasant waxy smell. When she runs her hand over it, it's slightly tacky.

Leaning her back against the table, she takes in the rest of the room. Gone are the piles of *Radio Times* by the chair her mum likes to sit in when watching daytime TV. In their place is a copy of *Good Food* magazine, yellow Post-it notes peeping from between its pages. She picks it up and flips it open at one of the marked pages. *Butternut Squash with Lentils and Spinach*, she reads.

The hoovering has stopped. 'Mum?' she calls again, but either her mother doesn't hear her, or she doesn't want to answer.

Ben's bed has been moved too. It's now in the kitchen instead of its usual place in the living room. Bending down, Kelly strokes his big head and smiles as he rolls over onto his back in the hope she'll rub his tummy.

'What's going on, boy? Any idea?'

Ben wriggles on his back and Kelly leaves him to it. As she climbs the stairs, she notices that the carpet has been freshly hoovered and the frames of the photographs on the wall shine. She stops on the landing and listens. Strange clunks and scraping noises are coming from the large bedroom across the landing from hers – the one her brothers and sisters once slept in. The one that hasn't been used in the six years since Freya left. Even though the room is twice the size of her own, she's never been allowed to move into it. It's as though it's been kept as a shrine.

She sees her mum straightaway. She's reaching into the wardrobe and hooking coat hangers onto the rail. Sliding them along to make room for more. The drawers of the chest near the window have been taken out and are on the double bed, which has a new duvet on it. Each drawer has been lined with flowered paper that's been cut from the long roll that's on the bed next to them and she can smell a faint aroma of roses.

Her mum turns her head to look at her. 'What are you staring at, Kelly?'

She runs her fingers through her dark hair and as it parts, Kelly sees the strands of grey her mum no longer bothers to hide. She can't remember the last time her mum went to the hairdresser's.

Kelly folds her arms across her school sweatshirt. Even at fourteen, her mum has a way of making her feel like she's said the wrong thing… asked the wrong question. She searches desperately for something that will appease her. Make her smile. 'I just wondered what you were doing.'

There's a pink spot on each of her mum's cheeks. A strange, distracted look in her eyes. She stares at the newly lined drawers, the freshly hoovered floor, the panes of glass that gleam in the sunlight. 'What do you think I'm doing, Kelly? You have eyes.'

'You're cleaning. You never clean.' As soon as she says it, she wishes she hadn't. It will only anger her and sometimes her mum's moods can last for days. 'I mean, it's a Wednesday and it's a funny day to be doing the housework.'

Her mum puts the last of the hangers on the rail and closes the wardrobe door. She picks up one of the drawers and carries it to the chest and, with difficulty, fits it onto its runners and slides it into place before going back for the other two.

'You could help, you know. Rather than just standing there.'

Kelly looks around the room. Her mum's been busy – everything's clean and tidy and she hardly recognises the place. She doesn't know what to think. After she'd started to make new tentative friendships at secondary school, she'd been too embarrassed to invite anyone back to her dirty, cluttered house. If anyone had shown an interest, she'd tell them her mum worked from home and needed the quiet. Is it any wonder that, just like Carly, Ava and Tabby, they'd eventually drifted away?

But today, everything is different and it's unnerving.

'What shall I do?'

'Put these in the drawers.'

Beside the bed is a large plastic carrier bag that she hadn't noticed earlier. When she squats down and opens it, she sees that it's full of clothes. Taking out a T-shirt, she looks at the label inside. Topshop. The price tag is still on it and she's surprised to see it cost almost ten pounds. There are other tops – skirts and trousers too. Things that Carly and Ava might wear. Fashionable things, like the tracksuit bottoms she's holding with the Adidas logo on the front.

Her mum smiles. 'They're nice, aren't they?' She looks around her. 'The room's scrubbed up well too. You see, patience is always rewarded.'

Pressing the tracksuit bottoms she's holding to her chest, Kelly feels her heart leap. After waiting for years, after holding her tongue and not asking, she's finally going to be allowed this room. It's because of the cross-country. They never said anything, but it's their way of rewarding her. She'll leave her tiny bedroom with its blinds and functional cupboards and move to this room where she'll sleep in the double bed with its view over the meadow to the downs. She can almost feel the plumpness of the pillow and the cool, crispness of the new duvet cover.

'Shall I get my things?'

Her mum is opening the windows, letting the sweet summer air into the room that hasn't had anyone in it for years. She stops with her hand on the catch.

'What things?'

'*My* things… my clothes and stuff.'

Her mum looks puzzled. 'Why would you do that?'

Kelly falters. She was so certain and now she's unsure. 'Aren't I moving into this room? Aren't these things for me?'

Even before her mum replies, she realises her mistake.

'For you? Why would they be?'

Dropping the tracksuit bottoms onto the bed, Kelly turns and leaves the room, fighting back the tears until she can reach the safety of her own bedroom. Of course, she wasn't going to be allowed to sleep in the new room or wear the new clothes. Her mum's feverish excitement, the spotless house and the smell of lemon and furniture polish can only mean one thing.

By tomorrow, there will be a new brother or sister in the house.

CHAPTER TWENTY-FIVE

Kelly Now

'Anyone home?'

From my vantage point at the top of the stairs, I watch Mitch shoulder the front door closed. Taking off his donkey jacket, he's about to hang it up when he changes his mind and throws it over the others on the end of the banister instead. In the living room, Isabella's voice is loud above the television.

I walk a few steps down the stairs, the letter in my hand, wanting, yet not wanting, to show him.

Mitch opens the door wide and I see, on the wide plasma screen, that a red dinosaur is talking to a small blue one, but neither girl is watching it. Instead, they're rifling through a box of Lego that's upturned onto the carpet.

'Hi, girls. Where's your mum?' He bends and drops a kiss on both their heads.

'Up there with Noah.' Isabella points towards the ceiling, but Sophie says nothing. She looks pale and withdrawn.

'What's up, chick?' Kneeling beside his daughter, I watch him scoop her into his arms, noticing how thin her legs look under her stiff grey school skirt. 'Not had a good day?'

Sophie shakes her head and buries her face in his neck.

'Jack Long called her a baby.' Isabella's voice is unconcerned. Running her arm through the Lego, she drags the pieces towards her and starts to pick out all the yellow ones, looking pointedly at Sophie. 'You can't have any.'

I bite my lip, wondering where her cruel streak has come from. But it's obvious where. My hand tightens around the letter.

Thankfully, Mitch is quick to pick up on it. 'That's enough, Izzy. You should be extra nice to Sophie if she's unhappy. Sisters should support one another.'

'Why?'

'Because they're family and family is more important than anything.'

'That's stupid.'

'No, it's not.'

Picking up the remote, Mitch points it at the television. As the red dragon's voice fades to nothing, he looks towards the hall and I quickly step back up.

'Kel?' he calls. 'What are you doing up there?'

When I don't answer, I know he'll come and find me. I'm going to have to make a decision. Shall I tell him or not? There's silence and I imagine him rubbing his hand twice over the top of his bald head, unsure whether or not to come up.

There's a cry from Noah, and with a shock, I realise I've left him on our bed on the change mat. What was I thinking? Running back into the bedroom, I'm relieved to see that he's fine. He's lying on his back, his legs paddling the air.

I hear Mitch come up the stairs and soon he's at the door, his jeans covered in what looks like creosote.

'Everything all right?'

Getting up from the bed, I go to the window and part the net curtains. The letter is still in my hand and I know that, if I want to, I can make something up. There's a movement in the street, and for a second, I wonder if someone is watching me.

Mitch is beside me, taking the letter from my hand, and I'm grateful the decision has been made for me.

'Come on then. Who's it from?' he asks.

I don't look at him. 'It's from my mother.'

'Your mother?'

'Yes, she's written to tell me my dad is dead.'

I can tell by his silence that he's shocked at my bluntness. Is he wondering at my emotionless voice? Painting a picture in his head of a father I've never talked about?

Outside the window, the sky has turned to navy and the street lights are starting to come on. I want to pull the curtains and switch on a light, but I don't. I'd rather Mitch didn't see my face.

He goes to the bed and sits next to Noah, placing a gentle hand on his stomach. He'll be searching for words of comfort. He's not good at this sort of thing.

'Do you want to tell me about it?' he says gruffly.

Ignoring his question, I scan the street again. The window is wet with condensation – all the windows are like it, but despite being a builder, Mitch has never got around to doing anything about it. I run the tips of my fingers down the glass, leaving two perfect lines on the misted pane, even though I know that I'll have to clean the whole window later if I want to get rid of the marks. 'How did she know I was here?'

Mitch folds the letter carefully. 'It's not hard to track someone down if you've a mind to.'

Downstairs, we can hear Isabella doing dinosaur impressions in the living room. Letting the net curtain drop, I walk over to the bed and sit next to him.

'Tell me something about him. What was he like?' He settles down on the covers as though I'm about to tell him a story.

I look at the letter and then into the distance trying to conjure up an image. 'He was never there. I hardly knew him.'

'That's all?' He's disappointed, I can tell.

'What else is there? Like I say, he was never there.'

Mitch frowns. To him the bond between a child and their parents should be the strongest there is, but in my case it wasn't.

'The funeral's next week,' he says. 'I'll leave the site manager in charge and go with you. I can look after the kids at your mum's house and—'

'I'm not going.'

Mitch stares at me. 'You have to go. He's your father.'

'A father who couldn't care less if I was alive or dead. Who all through my childhood made me feel that I was unwanted even though I adored him.'

My husband clearly can't believe what he's hearing. 'But you haven't any brothers or sisters. Your mother's alone now. You're all she's got, Kelly. You and the children.'

The street light outside the window casts a faint light into the room. Mitch's face looks ghostly.

'Keep the children out of this? She knows nothing about them.'

Mitch rubs his thumb across the back of my hand. 'Don't you think she should? She *is* their grandmother.'

'No.'

'Oh, for Christ's sake!' It bursts out of him, echoing in the room.

'Why are you shouting?' The twins are standing in the doorway. Sophie's voice is muffled from the thumb that's in her mouth.

Mitch gets up wearily and places a hand on each of their shoulders. 'Mummy's upset. She's had a letter from your gran.'

Isabella's eyes widen. 'What gran?'

'Don't call her that!' Leaping up, I snatch the letter from his hands.

'But that's who she is, Kelly.'

'I don't want you talking to them about her.'

'Okay, okay.' He raises his hands in supplication. 'I just thought…'

'No, Mitch. You didn't think.' Tearing up the letter, I drop the pieces into the wastepaper bin beside the dressing table. 'Go back downstairs, girls. I'll be down in a minute. Why don't you choose a book for me to read?'

They look at each other, then run downstairs. Mitch waits until he hears their voices in the living room, then sits back on the bed, lifting Noah to his shoulder.

'I think you're being unfair, Kelly.'

My jaw tenses. 'You think it's unfair that our children don't know that somewhere out there is a twisted, bitter old woman intent on ruining everyone's lives.'

'But she gave birth to you. She's your own flesh and blood.'

'My past is nothing to do with you or anybody else.'

My words have cut him. Now it's his turn to be angry. 'I'm not anybody else. I'm your husband, Kelly. You can't fucking accuse me of not understanding something if you won't share it with me.'

I flinch and lower my head, the fight gone out of me. 'Don't swear at me, Mitch.'

Before Mitch met me, he'd been a bit of a lad, calling out to pretty girls from his vantage point on the scaffolding. At weekends he and his mates would practise their cheesy chat-up lines on the hen parties that frequented the Brighton pubs and often he'd wake up with the hangover from hell and a strange face in his bed to tell Maddie about later over a strong mug of black coffee. Meeting me, that night in the pub as I'd pulled his pint, had put an end to all that. He'd become a different man.

Reaching out, he takes my hand and pulls me on to the bed next to him, the old bed frame squeaking. He moves closer and kisses my hair. Noah stirs in his arms and we must look the perfect tableaux: father, mother and the baby we both adore.

'Look, Kelly. I'm sorry, but you've got to see how frustrating it is for me. It's like I'm living with someone with no past. I want to know all of you. Not just the part you want to show me. Please don't shut me out.'

Outside, a group of teenagers are laughing and kicking a can along the pavement, but for once I know Mitch isn't thinking about whether they might steal his car aerial or fall into his wing mirror.

'When you smiled at me that first time in the pub,' he continues, 'I felt as though someone had got hold of my gut and twisted it. Did I ever tell you that?'

I manage a smile. 'Yes, you did. Maybe twenty times.'

I relax against him and we sit in silence until the voices and laughter fade into the distance. I need to confide in him. Tell him my worries.

'There are things I need to tell you, Mitch. Things that are making me scared.'

He looks concerned. 'What things?'

'Something happened at school the other day and then again today. I didn't tell you before as I thought you'd think I was being stupid.'

'I wouldn't think that. Anyway, Izzy told me. Some kid called Sophie a baby.'

I shake my head. 'It's not that. It's something else. While I was taking the girls in, I think someone moved Noah's pram.'

Mitch frowns, confused. 'What do you mean moved it?'

'I'm sure I parked it outside their classroom, just under the covered porch, but when I got back, it had been moved.' I don't mention the locket. I don't want Freya to infect our lives.

'Where had it been moved to?'

'The porchway of the classroom next door.'

He bursts out laughing. 'There you are then. It's a no-brainer. You mistook one for the other.'

'It's not a joke, Mitch. And today, when I came out of the newsagent's, the brake was off the pram. I always put on the brake when I park it.'

'You didn't the other day when we were at the playground. I had to do it for you.'

'I know but—'

'Look, Kel. You're tired. We both are. It's easy to make mistakes… imagine things.'

I look at him coldly. 'Don't patronise me. You don't know what tired is. It's me who gets up for Noah when he cries in the night, remember.'

Mitch looks away. 'Because you never let me. A proper family is all I've ever wanted, but you just push me out – do everything yourself. I just wish I knew what was up with you. Lately, you've been so distant. So distracted.'

I turn on him, eyes blazing. 'For Christ's sake, Mitch. I had a baby three months ago. What do you expect? I tell you I'm worried for his safety and you just sweep it aside as though it's nothing.'

He shakes his head. 'That's what you say, but I know that something else is eating away at you. Something from your past… this thing with your mum. If you tell me, maybe we can work it out together. Please, Kelly.'

'There's nothing to tell,' I say. 'Don't ask me again.'

Taking Noah from him, I get up and leave the room. When I reach the hall, I hear the thump of Mitch's fist as it makes contact with the wall.

CHAPTER TWENTY-SIX

September 6th

Thought you might like to see this photo I took last week. She didn't want it taken as she hates the uniform, but I think the blue suits her. You know what they're like at this age – so fashion conscious! I would have taken a picture of both of them, but a tummy bug is doing the rounds and we didn't think it fair to spread the germs. Don't worry, she's fine. We used to be concerned whenever she so much as caught a cold, but she's a lot tougher now.

All the best

CHAPTER TWENTY-SEVEN
Kelly Before

A few weeks back, when her dad was out and her mother asleep, Kelly had watched one of their DVDs. It was called *Groundhog Day*, a film about a man who has the same day over and over again. It's this she's thinking of as she stands in the shadows of the hallway, waiting for her mum to open the front door. She's done this many times before; not just with the ones she can visualise: Jade, Mason, Charlene and Jasmine, but also others when she was too young to remember.

And there was Freya, of course. The girl with the pale eyes and translucent skin. The Gemini girl who, like her birth sign, had blown hot and cold, confusing her eight-year-old self. Fascinating and repelling her in equal measures.

Her mum and dad are standing in the doorway so she can't see properly, but Kelly's been down this road so many times before, she can picture it anyway: a girl or boy clinging to the hand of the social worker who's brought them here. Their expression one of bravado or else betraying their distress with a lowered head and a trembling lip.

'I can't tell you how happy we are.' There are tears in her mother's eyes. 'Come in. Come in.'

'We thought of you first.' The woman's voice has a London accent. 'We are so happy you agreed and after our meeting the other day, we knew this was undoubtedly the best decision.'

Kelly looks at her dad. He's standing behind her mother, his face expressionless. She knows him well enough to guess this was not his idea. It's something he'll go along with, just as long as he doesn't have to participate.

'Kelly, put the kettle on, would you, darling?'

Her mum's term of endearment is so alien that at first Kelly doesn't realise it's her she's talking to. She doesn't want to leave the hall. She wants to stay and see the next child who'll sleep in the meadow bedroom. But she has no choice. Going into the kitchen, she takes the kettle over to the tap and fills it. The front door closes and she hears them go into the living room.

There's a cake on a plate in the middle of the kitchen table. It's chocolate, the icing thick and fudge-like. It looks expensive, nothing like the cheap cake she'd had all those years ago on her eighth birthday. The word *welcome* is piped in white chocolate across the top as fine as a snail-trail. Bile rises up Kelly's throat as she remembers the glistening thread the snail had left on Freya's hand before she'd dropped it to the ground and hovered her foot over it.

Pulling herself together, she reaches into the cupboard above her head and gets out five plates, which she puts on a tray along with matching cups and saucers and the bone china teapot. Adding the cake to the tray, she walks carefully into the hall.

It's the social worker Kelly hears first as she nears the living room. This one sounds older than the others, her strident voice carrying easily.

'You have all the recent notes we sent?'

Her mum says something back that she can't hear.

'And this time we're looking longer term.' There's a pause. 'You were pleased with the decision, weren't you, dear?'

'Yes.' It's a girl's voice. That's good. She's missed having a sister.

Wondering if they'll get on, Kelly pushes open the door with her shoulder. Walking to the table, she puts the tray down and takes her first look at the new arrival.

The first thing she notices about the girl is her height. Even sitting down, she's nearly a head taller than her mum, her hair scragged back in a rough ponytail. But despite the unbecoming hairstyle, the bone structure of her face is arresting – the cheekbones high and sculpted like a model's. It's not her cheekbones Kelly's looking at, though, or the delicate mouth with its smile all for her. It's not even the row of silver studs that follow the curve of her ear or the one that adorns her nose. No, it's none of those things. What makes Kelly catch her breath are the pale blue eyes. Eyes she knows only too well.

Eyes that belong to Freya.

She drops a teaspoon and it clatters onto one of the saucers.

'For goodness' sake, Kelly,' her mum says. 'Whatever's got into you?'

Realising she's staring stupidly, she busies herself with pouring out the tea, feeling tongue-tied and stupid. Unable to process her feelings at this new development in her life. For six years she's wondered what had happened to Freya and now here she is – sitting at their dining room table as though she's never been away. This girl and her terrible secret.

'Where did you go?' It's all she can think of to say.

Freya says nothing, just puts her fingers to her lips and smiles. She doesn't seem surprised to be here. In fact, she looks very much at home.

'Don't bother Freya now, Kelly. She's only just arrived. Let her enjoy her tea.'

Her mother's cheeks are flushed with pleasure. Taking the knife, she cuts a slice from the cake and puts it on one of the plates. The fudge icing oozes and Kelly has to look away.

'You'll have a piece, won't you?' Her mother says, offering the plate to Freya.

'Of course, Mrs Harding. It looks delicious.' Taking the plate, she lifts the piece of cake with difficulty and takes a bite. 'Hmm. It tastes it too.'

'Mrs Harding?' Her mum looks at her in mock horror. 'Please…
it's Karen. It isn't as though we're not acquainted, after all. I'm
glad you like the cake. It's only shop-bought, I'm afraid. I would
have made one, but I'm a bit out of practice.'

Freya places her hand over Kelly's mum's. 'I wouldn't have
expected you to.'

'That's very kind of you. I just know that we're all going to get
along brilliantly. What do you say, Andrew?'

Kelly glances across at her dad, ready to share a conspiratorial
look, but instead, he gives Freya a warm smile. 'I'm sure we shall.'

They make a pleasing tableau – Freya at the head of the table,
flanked by her mum and dad. Hovering beside the table, Kelly
feels awkward and out of place. Unsure of where to sit. What to
do. In the end, she takes a seat beside the social worker.

Her mum turns to her. 'Isn't it wonderful that Freya's returning
to us after all this time?'

Realising it's not a rhetorical question and that it requires an
answer, Kelly mumbles that of course it is.

The social worker is speaking now. 'We'll give her a day or two
to settle down and then she'll be joining you at your school. Isn't
that exciting?'

Kelly can't stand it any longer. 'How long for?'

'I'm sorry?' the woman says. 'How long is what for?'

'How long is she… Freya, I mean, staying this time?'

She sees the social worker's eyes slide over to her mum's. 'It's
not possible to say for certain, Kelly. We'll just see what happens,
shall we?'

Like they did last time, she thinks. Never telling her anything.
Always so vague. Just when she was getting used to the idea that
Freya would be staying, she'd left and never come back – until
now, that is.

Why hadn't they told her Freya was coming back? Why did
they think it wasn't important for her to know? But why would

they? It wasn't as if they'd bothered to tell her anything the day Freya left. Explain why she'd gone.

She wants to sweep the stupid tea and the vile cake onto the floor. Watch their faces as Ben licks the chocolate icing from the carpet, treading tea and crumbs into the pile. But she doesn't, of course. She just bites the inside of her cheek and waits.

'Are you not having any cake?' Her mum's frowning.

'No, thank you. I'm not hungry.' So as not to appear rude, she pours herself some tea and drinks it as quickly as the hot liquid will allow. She wants to be on her own – not in this living room where everyone's focus is on Freya. She needs space to work out how she feels about what's happening. There's no escaping, though, so she remains where she is until at last her mother fixes her eyes on her.

'Why don't you take Freya up to her room, Kelly? Show her where everything is.' She flashes a smile at the social worker, who is dabbing at her mouth with the serviette she's been given. 'I went out and bought her a few bits and bobs. I wasn't sure what she'd be bringing.'

Kelly glances over at Freya. She's wearing a pair of very worn denim dungarees that look too big for her, the legs rolled up over her delicate ankles. Underneath is a simple sleeveless white T-shirt. Nobody she knows would be seen dead in dungarees, but on Freya they look good – like she's stepped out of the pages of a magazine where the photographs have been shot on a ranch in California. Her skin is still as pale as it ever was, but the sun they've had recently has brought out a sprinkling of freckles on her white shoulders.

She meets Kelly's eye. 'Shall we go?'

'If you want.' Without waiting for her, Kelly leaves the room and walks across the hallway to the stairs. Her mum's voice follows her.

'I do apologise for my daughter. She can be difficult sometimes.'

Kelly climbs the stairs, digging her nails into her palm until the desire to cry passes. How can she say that, when all she ever does is try to please them in the hope that they might love her just a little bit? It's never been about her. About what *she* wants. For all they care, she might just as well have not been born.

'Hey, slow down.' Freya is behind her, pulling at her sleeve. 'What's your problem?'

Yanking her arm away, Kelly shoves open the door to Freya's room. 'I don't have a problem.'

'Then why are you being so weird? I thought you might actually be pleased to see me.'

Is she pleased? She can't decide. It's all too much of a shock. Kelly goes over to the window and rests her elbows on the sill. She looks out at the meadow where they played all those years ago. 'It's all happened so suddenly, that's all.'

Freya remains in the doorway, her slim body leaning against the frame. 'What do you mean? Surely you knew I was coming?'

'No.'

'Why not? They've known for ages.'

Kelly turns her head to look at her, trying to hold back the tears. 'They don't tell me anything. They're more likely to tell Ben than they are me.'

Freya regards her for a moment. 'I think that's pretty shit.'

'I do too.' Although her eyes are still shiny with tears, Kelly manages a smile. There's something about this exchange that's cut through the resentment she's been feeling. Going over to the wardrobe, she opens it and takes out a pair of pink pedal pushers.

'Look.'

Freya takes the stretchy material between her fingers. 'Fuck me! Your mum doesn't expect me to wear those, does she?'

'Pretty hideous, aren't they?' She doesn't want to admit that she likes them. That she'd thought about hiding them at the bottom of her own clothes drawer and hoping her mum wouldn't remember she'd bought them for Freya.

'About as hideous as this,' Freya says, unhooking a turquoise spaghetti-strapped top and holding it up to her.

Kelly thinks she looks cool – like Zoe Ball – but says nothing.

'So, what's been going on while I've been away?' The way Freya says it, it sounds as if she'd just popped to the shops for a couple of hours, rather than out of her life for six years.

'Not a lot.'

'What do you do? For fun, I mean.'

'I run. Cross-country, mostly. I'm a junior in the athletics club.'

Freya looks her up and down. 'That figures. What else do you do?'

'Swim… at the sports centre.'

'I never swim.'

Her arms fold across her stomach and Kelly's taken back to that day in the changing rooms. A discarded sock on the windowsill, a plaster under the bench. A swathe of shiny puckered skin. She shivers and changes the subject. 'What year will you be in when you start at my school?'

'Year twelve. What year are you in?'

'Ten.'

Freya studies her. 'You're pretty tall for your age, aren't you? Is that why you're a good runner?'

Kelly shrugs. 'Maybe.'

'I remember when I was here before, how I wished I could be strong and healthy like you. You always had so much energy.' She sighs. 'I find it's an effort just to stay alive.'

Kelly looks up, shocked. 'What do you mean?'

'I don't mean anything. Just that life can be a drag sometimes.' She pokes Kelly in the ribs. 'Don't look at me like that. It's just an expression. I've probably read too much Sylvia Plath. I think I should have been born in a different age when it was fashionable to be melancholy.'

Not wanting to admit she doesn't know who Sylvia Plath is, Kelly just smiles, but there's something she has to ask. Something that's been eating away at her.

'Where did you go?'

Freya's back is to her now. She's sliding the hangers along the rail in the wardrobe, looking at the dresses and trousers that are hanging there. Muttering under her breath when she sees something particularly bad. 'When?'

'Before. When you were ten.'

Freya's hand pauses for a second and then the metal hooks slide again. 'Here and there. Let's not talk about it. It's boring.'

'But nobody—'

Kelly jumps as the wardrobe door slams. She thinks she's angered Freya, but when the girl turns, she's looking pleased with herself. 'I got you a present.'

'A present?'

'Yes.' Freya gives an exaggerated sigh. 'Surely you don't need me to explain what a present is?'

Dipping her hand into the pocket of her dungarees, she brings out a thin square of tissue paper and hands it to Kelly. 'Go on then, open it.'

Carefully, Kelly unfolds the tissue, gasping when she sees what's inside.

'It's a locket!'

'Of course it's a locket and it took bloody ages to find one the same as mine. See what's inside.'

Sliding her thumbnails down the join, Kelly unclasps it and sees her own face looking back at her. In the other side, is a picture of Freya. The pictures were taken when they were both children.

'You can thank me if you like.'

'I'm sorry. Thank you. It's lovely.' Her face flushes. No one's given her a present in friendship before… or love.

Downstairs her mum is calling them and Freya frowns. 'Jesus, what do they want now?'

Kelly glances nervously at the door. 'I suppose we'd better go down, or they'll wonder what we're doing. The woman you came with will want to know you're okay.'

'What, nosy cow Lawson? She couldn't give a shit about me. None of them do. She'll just be glad to be shot of me.'

'You don't mean that?'

'Don't I? What would you know? With your precious mum and dad. Living in your lovely house in its chocolate-bloody-box village. Never having to worry about where you'll be going next. Not knowing if there'll be some stupid girl asking her bloody stupid questions.'

The atmosphere has changed. Freya's fingers have formed into fists, her skin stretching white where the points of her knuckles press.

Kelly stares. The outburst is shocking. 'I... I didn't mean—'

'Of course you didn't. Little miss goody two shoes.'

The injustice of what Freya's said, brings stinging tears to her eyes. Freya's sudden changes in mood are no different to when they were children. She's still able to turn things around to make like it's Kelly who's in the wrong. But what does Freya know about her life? What does she know about living with parents who don't want her? She catches her breath as a thought occurs to her. But of course, she does know. If not, why would she be in foster care?

In different ways, they are living the same life.

It's like time has turned back. She is eight and Freya is ten. They are both lonely. Sliding her hand across the bed until their little fingers touch, she waits. Neither of them speaks. After what seems like an age, she feels her foster-sister's fingers wrap around her own and, when they do, Kelly knows, just as she did all those years before, that things are going to be all right.

CHAPTER TWENTY-EIGHT

Kelly Now

'Mum! Mum! Charlie's been sick.' Isabella's voice carries up the stairs, a mixture of fascination and revulsion. 'It's all over the floor and his bed and it's yucky. That's not all. Come and see.'

I quickly pull the tabs of Noah's disposable nappy across and stick them down. Picking him up from the change mat on the floor, I put him back into his cot and hurry out of the bedroom, not caring that he's started to cry again.

'Don't touch anything, Izzy,' I say, running down the stairs. 'I'm coming. Where is he?'

'He's under the table,' she calls back. 'Sophie's with him.'

When I get to the kitchen, I stop. The smell is atrocious. 'Come away from there.'

Next to Charlie's bed is a pool of vomit and by the back door is a puddle of urine. I must have been so tired that I didn't hear him bark. On the floor, next to the worktop, are the remains of the box of chocolate truffles I bought for Maddie.

I feel the blood drain from my head, leaving me light-headed, and I can't think what to do. Charlie is under the table as Isabella had said. He's lying on his side, panting loudly and Sophie is next to him, her arm around his belly.

My phone is on charge on the worktop and I snatch it up, punching in Mitch's number. He left early, without even saying goodbye and wouldn't have been into the kitchen.

'Yes?' He sounds off with me.

'It's Charlie,' I say, knowing my voice is rising hysterically. 'He's eaten the chocolates I bought for Saturday. He's been sick. Oh, God. What if he dies?'

'Calm down, Kelly. I can't hear what you're saying properly. There's a frigging bulldozer working right outside the office.'

From under the table, I hear a whimper and Sophie throws her arms around the dog's neck. I've got to keep myself together for the children's sake. Taking a deep breath, I repeat what I told him.

'Shit. Have you phoned the vet?'

'No,' I say, realising how stupid I've been. 'I phoned you straightaway.'

'I'll get off the phone and you can call them. They're bound to have some sort of out of hours emergency cover.'

From under the table, I can hear Sophie crying, the sound muffled by Charlie's fur. Suddenly, I'm overwhelmed with panic – as helpless as a child. 'I can't cope with this,' I say, my voice cracking. 'Not as well as the baby and the kids.'

I can hear Mitch moving around the Portakabin. 'Ring the vet. I'll come straight home.'

'Thank you.'

Pulling myself together, I make the phone call. The emergency vet asks me some questions: how much chocolate Charlie's eaten and what his symptoms are. He says he'll open up the practice, and as soon as Mitch gets home, he can take him in.

Crouching down, I reach under the table to stroke Charlie's head. He doesn't move, just lies looking at me, his dark eyes sad.

Isabella has left her vigil of the dog's basket and is tugging at my dressing gown.

'Is Charlie going to die?'

'No,' I say quickly. 'Of course he isn't.'

'But that's what you said would happen if we left our chocolate out.'

It's true. When Isabella had left her chocolate egg on the coffee table last Easter, from the way I'd reacted you'd have thought she'd committed a crime worse than murder.

'I know I did but… well, the vet's going to make him better.' I pray that it's true.

From under the table, Sophie looks at me with eyes filled with tears. 'Why did you leave the chocolates out, Mummy?'

It's a question I haven't considered. I remember thinking I must put the box of truffles in the cupboard where we keep the cereal, making a mental note to remember to take them when we left for Maddie's at the weekend. But thinking it is the only part I remember.

Upstairs, I can hear Noah crying and my head starts to pound. Instead of going straight to him, I flop down onto one of the kitchen chairs and massage my temples. Did I? Did I put them in the cupboard? I'm usually so careful about things like this. Reminding the children not to leave sweets around in case Charlie spots an opportunity. It's not like me at all.

I stare at Charlie in dismay, trying to replay my actions.

I'd thought I'd put the truffles away, but now, I'm not so sure.

CHAPTER TWENTY-NINE
Kelly Before

It's another mild day and Kelly and Freya are sitting on the playing field. They've finished reading their horoscopes in the copy of *Cosmopolitan* Freya bought and are now eating the lunch her mum has made them. Coronation chicken and salad on thick, fluffy bread from the bakery at the end of their road. She knows people are looking, wondering who the strange new girl is, but she doesn't care. For once she's not on her own. She has someone to talk to.

Kelly takes a bite of her sandwich. 'So how did it go?'

'How did what go?'

'Your first morning.'

Freya shrugs. 'It was okay. Why wouldn't it be?'

'I don't know. Because you're new.' She remembers back to her first day at Millcroft Comprehensive. The sea of faces she couldn't distinguish between, the confusing corridors, the teachers who all seemed to expect her to know more than she did.

'So I'm new. So what?'

Kelly unwraps a chocolate bar. 'I don't know. I just thought it might be hard. Some of the boys can get a bit stupid around new girls.'

'Acting like pricks, you mean? Yeh, I've had a lot of that.' She sounds amused.

'And you don't mind?'

'If I don't like it, I just tell them to piss off.' Freya leans back on her elbows, stretching her long legs out in front of her. The skirt her mum bought for her is too short, but either she doesn't notice or doesn't care. Kelly studies her. She's pulled her fine blonde hair into a tiny tight bun at the back of her head and, in profile, could be a ballerina or Gwyneth Paltrow at the Oscars. Since Kelly last saw her at the age of ten, she's certainly blossomed from an ugly duckling into a swan. In contrast, Kelly feels babyish and frumpy.

Over by the football post she can see Ethan and his friends. They're taking it in turns to see who can keep the football off the ground the longest. He hasn't spoken to her since the day Mr Seymore called her out to the front of the maths class, and she's disappointed. Not that she was expecting him to. After all, why would he when she's in a class two years below him?

Freya shields her eyes from the sun. 'What are you looking at?'

'Nothing.' Kelly lowers her eyes and pulls a daisy from the grass.

'It didn't look like nothing to me.' Sitting up, she wraps her arms around her knees and studies Kelly. 'Your eyes were nearly popping out on stalks. Which one do you like?'

Kelly feels her cheeks begin to burn. 'I don't like any of them.'

'Could have fooled me.' Freya lies back down and closes her eyes, blocking out the sun. 'Not that I'd say no to the cute fair one given half a chance. He's in my English class.'

Praying that there are other boys with fair hair, Kelly glances over at them. They've formed two lines and are taking it in turns to get the ball past the goalkeeper. It's as she knew it would be: they are all dark-haired except for Ethan and one other boy.

Her heart sinks and she turns back to Freya. 'Have you ever… you know?'

Freya opens one eye. 'Have I what?'

Kelly blushes furiously, wishing she hadn't asked.

'Are you asking me if I've had sex? Gone all the way? Fucked?' She raises her arms above her head and arches her back. 'No, but I shall... very soon. I wanted to do it before I was legal, but I never found anyone who I could imagine sticking their dick in me. They were either too ugly or too boring.'

Kelly's hand shoots to her mouth. Although Carly and her old friends are always on about boys, she's never heard any of them talking in the way that Freya just has. She's appalled, but at the same time, doesn't want her to stop.

'What about you?' Freya folds her slim arms across her eyes. 'Got a boyfriend?'

'No.'

'Want one?'

'Not really.' She hopes Freya can't see she's lying.

'That's the way to be. They'll only leave when they can't take the heat. My dad left my mum. Did you know that?'

It's the first real piece of information Freya's told Kelly since she told her her secret. 'No.'

'Well, he did. Anyway, I don't want to talk about him. He's a piece of shit. What's your dad like? I don't remember much about him from when I was here before, but he seems okay.'

'He's not there much. He works all the time and I hardly see him.' She realises she's not mentioned the word love. It's hard to love someone who hardly looks at you.

'Well, last night, after he got home, he helped me with my maths homework, so he can't be that bad.'

A kernel of jealousy lodges in Kelly's stomach. 'He did?'

'Yeh. I came down after you were in bed and he was in the kitchen. He looked... I don't know... bored and fed up. I asked him if he'd help with my homework and he seemed pleased.'

'Where was my mum?'

'She'd gone to bed with a headache.'

A bell rings from somewhere inside the school. All around them, people are getting up, dusting grass off their clothes and lifting bags onto their shoulders. No one hurries. Everyone would rather be out here in the sunshine.

'What have you got next?' Kelly puts her lunch box in her bag and zips it up.

'Maths, I think.'

Kelly pulls a face. 'Good luck. Mr Seymore's a bastard.'

'A bastard?' Freya's eyes widen, the mascara she's put on her lashes making them seem even paler than usual. Like glass. 'Sounds interesting.'

'It's really not. You'll be in there.' She points to one of the prefab huts at the edge of the field.

'Thanks.' Picking up her bag, Freya walks away, her long legs in the short skirt making heads turn. The boys might like it, but Kelly knows the girls won't. She's already overheard some of their bitchy comments.

Her next lesson is in the main building and she joins the queue of others waiting to go in the main doors. As she waits, she looks to see if Freya has gone to the right hut. Mr Seymore is leaning against the open classroom door, his back against the frosted glass windows. At first, she thinks he has a cigarette in his hand, but it's only a board marker. With his black shirt and tie he looks more like a bouncer in a nightclub than a maths teacher.

Freya's got to the hut now and Kelly wonders if she'll be the next one to do the walk of shame. Being new won't make her an exception. She's walking past Mr Seymore now and he stops her. All around her, girls and boys are pushing their way inside, but Kelly wants to watch. Will he give Freya that supercilious look of his? Will he lay down the law before she even gets inside?

She waits with bated breath but none of these things happen. Instead, Mr Seymore says something to her and she hears Freya laugh in reply. He says something else and then they turn and go into the hut. The door closes behind them.

'Decided not to bother with afternoon lessons then?'

Kelly turns to see Ethan and her heart skips a beat. He's waiting to get by. 'Oh, no, sorry. I was miles away.'

'Looks like it. I meant to tell you, I'm thinking of joining the athletics club. I've always liked running and fancy giving it a go. What days do you train?'

Her heart gives another jolt and she feels her mouth dry, but it's not the time to get tongue-tied. 'It's Tuesdays and Thursdays. Five until seven. Once the evenings get darker, we train at weekends instead.'

'Will you be there tomorrow?'

She tries to keep her voice neutral when what she really wants to do is shout *Yes! Yes! Of course I'll be there!* Instead, she says, 'I expect so.'

'Great. Maybe see you there then.'

She moves aside to let him go by, then leans against the wall, wondering if it's possible to expire with happiness.

CHAPTER THIRTY

Kelly Now

'How's Charlie today?' Mrs Allen asks as I go into the classroom to collect Sophie. For the last few days my daughter has refused to line up with the others and I'm relieved that Mrs Allen isn't forcing her to.

'He's much better, thank you. He came home yesterday.'

I still feel sick at the thought that we might have lost him. The vet had kept him in for monitoring and fluid therapy and thankfully he'd recovered well.

'What about Sophie? Has she been any better?' The girls are in the reading corner and I see that, as usual, it's Isabella who is choosing what books Sophie will read.

Mrs Allen leans against her desk. 'Sophie's better when our classroom assistant, Miss King, is here. She's new to the school but is utterly brilliant and Sophie adores her.'

I have a momentary pang of jealousy at the possibility that Sophie might like someone as much as me but force it away. 'I'm pleased.'

'She sits with your daughter and encourages her to engage,' Mrs Allen continues. 'She's a bright little girl and is doing some good work. We're working on the alphabet and high frequency words and she recognises most of the ones we've covered so far.'

My spirits lift a little. 'And is she speaking yet?'

A picture comes into my head of Freya, standing on our doorstep the day she arrived. Pale and silent. I don't want my daughter to be like this.

Mrs Allen shakes her head. 'Only to Isabella or Miss King. We try to encourage her to join in during show and tell time, but she prefers to just listen. The other thing is, this past week, Isabella's been complaining that she can't hear me properly. It could be why she gets a little distracted. I've moved her to a table closer to the front, but it might be worth getting the doctor to have her hearing checked.'

I press a finger to the skin of my forehead between my eyes, willing myself to concentrate on what she's saying, but it's near impossible. Mitch and I have been tiptoeing around each other, finding reasons not to be in the same room, and I can't remember the last time I had an unbroken night's sleep. But that's not the real reason my nerves are jangling. Whatever I'm doing, wherever I am, I can't stop thinking about the unsettling things that have been happening recently… or push away the feeling that something worse will follow.

'Are you feeling all right, Mrs Thirsk?' Mrs Allen's voice is concerned.

'Yes. Sorry.' I stand straighter in the hope that it will make me feel better. 'I'm just tired, that's all. Noah still wakes a lot at night and Sophie's taken to coming into our bed.'

I'd hoped it would be a one-off, but ever since she started school, Mitch and I have woken to find Sophie sandwiched between us, her thumb in her mouth and her skin clammy. At first, I wondered if she was coming down with something, but now I realise she's just scared. Scared of the noisy classroom, scared of the playground with its play equipment, scared of being away from me.

'So what do you think,' Mrs Allen continues, 'about taking Isabella to have her hearing checked?'

For a minute I'd lost track of what we were talking about. 'Oh, yes. Of course. If you think it might be affecting her work.'

I look over at Sophie who's sitting in the reading corner, a picture book on her lap. Despite what Mrs Allen's said about Isabella's hearing, it's still her I worry about. It can't be right for a child to look so anxious all the time.

'Do you think I should be concerned about Sophie?'

'It's early days. I didn't mean to worry you. Sophie, do you want to show Mummy the picture you drew today? I put it in your book bag.'

I pick up the blue bag from the table and am about to open it when I see Sophie shake her head. She's never liked sharing things in public.

'You can see mine.' Isabella thrusts a rather creased picture into my hand. 'It's a spider eating a zombie. It's better than Sophie's boring one.'

I hold out Isabella's coat to her. 'I shall be the judge of that. Now come on both of you. I'm sure Mrs Allen has better things to do than talk to us.'

'Not at all.' She pushes herself off the desk. 'I'll see you tomorrow, girls. Oh, and there's just one other thing, I'm sure it's nothing to worry about, but it's something the head wants parents to be aware of. The notice is in the girls' book bags.'

'What's it about?'

'It's about Stranger Danger. The local community officer has been in this morning to advise us that there have been reports of someone acting suspiciously around one of the local schools in the Whitehawk area. He wants parents and teachers to be extra vigilant and talk to their children about not talking to strangers.'

My hand flies to my mouth. 'Oh, my goodness. Is it a man or a woman?'

'They're not sure. A van's been spotted a few times, parked in the same place near St Joseph's Primary. It doesn't appear to belong to one of the parents. No one thought to take the number, but now the police are aware, it shouldn't be long before they find out who owns it. We just need to be observant until that happens.'

'Of course. I'll read the notice and talk to the children. They know not to speak to anyone they don't know, but it doesn't hurt to tell them again.'

Going over to the book corner, I tell Sophie it's time to go. She puts down her book, then stands and takes my hand.

As we walk home, I listen to Isabella's chatter about a girl called Adele who can't button up her own coat and a rhyme that Mrs Allen has taught them about numbers. But even as I'm replying to her, I can't shake the horrible feeling inside me. I can't lie – I'm unnerved. With all the unsettling things that have been happening recently, I don't like the thought that somewhere out there, there might be someone watching our children.

CHAPTER THIRTY-ONE
Kelly before

The next day, when Kelly arrives at the athletics club, she tells herself that it doesn't matter to her if Ethan is going to be there or not. The hall is already full of young people dressed in tracksuit bottoms or running shorts. They're standing in groups, chatting about their day at school, but she doesn't join them – just takes herself off to the other end of the hall as always to do some stretches. As she presses her hands against the wall and reaches her left leg out behind her, feeling the muscles tighten, she tries to ignore the door that keeps opening as new people arrive.

Peter Alcock, their coach, is gathering everyone together, looking at his clipboard and ticking off names. It won't be a long run today, as the evenings are drawing in, and instead of the path that leads to the top of the downs, they'll be taking the lower route through the woods.

Ethan still hasn't arrived, and Kelly tries to ignore the ache of disappointment in her chest, reminding herself that she's not bothered if he comes or not. It's only as they're leaving the hall that she sees him getting out of his dad's car. Her stomach does a turn. He's already in his running gear and jogs over to the coach who nods and writes something on his board.

Trying not to think about him, Kelly joins the others and starts to run, taking it slow and steady as she's been taught. Across the cricket ground, along the road for a bit and then up through the trees by the waymark. At first, they are bunched together, but as they start to climb, the gap between each runner widens. Kelly's run this route many times and, as she begins the ascent through the trees, she leans into the slope, rising on her toes and letting her arms swing naturally. As she concentrates on the rhythm of her steps, Kelly waits for her mind to empty as it always does. It's the part of running she likes the most. The only time in the week when she can forget her mother and father.

It's not happening today, though. As Kelly's feet pound the chalky path, and the trees pass by in a blur of white trunks and green leaves, she can't get Freya out of her head. It's as if she's never been away, but whenever they are together, there is still the elephant in the room. The thing she told her when she was eight and Freya ten, as they'd played in the woods beneath the Gemini tree – for that is how she thinks of it now. In all the time that's passed, she hasn't been back to the clearing. Not once. Except, in her nightmares.

'Hey, slow down.' Ethan has caught up with her. His running shirt is sticking to his chest and his cheeks are red, but the nearness of him, as he runs alongside her, causes butterflies to dance in her stomach.

It's hard to talk when they're running, so they don't try, but it's good to have someone next to her. Someone to keep stride with. The fronts of her thighs have turned pink and she know her hair looks awful pulled back from her face in a band. She's sweaty too, but for some strange reason, it doesn't bother her. Everyone's the same. Out here, away from school, no one cares what they look like. What matters is the feel of the wind on their skin. The blood pumping through their veins.

They run companionably for another thirty minutes and then they are back at the cricket field where Peter is waiting with his stopwatch. As each runner passes him, he logs their time on his board.

'Good run today, Kelly,' he calls after her. 'Five minutes off your previous time.'

Kelly slows. 'Really?'

'So the stopwatch says. How do you feel?'

'Good,' she says and it's true. There are no muscle cramps and she feels relaxed.

'And you?' He's looking at Ethan who is bent at the waist, his hands on his knees, getting his breathing back to normal. 'Think you'll come again? The next session's Thursday.'

Ethan looks up, his face red and his hair stuck to his forehead. 'You bet. It was fun.'

Kelly hugs his words to her. Since Freya came back, she hasn't been going to the running club as much, but now she wouldn't miss Thursday for anything.

All the way home, Kelly is buzzing. Trying to remember how it felt to have Ethan running next to her – the powerful motion of his tanned arms, the stride that had kept in time with her own, the rhythm of his breathing. He didn't have to run with her, but he'd chosen to. At school, when she next sees him, she will view him differently. He will no longer be just the boy all the girls fancy. And he will see she is different too. He'll look beyond her shyness and her odd family and see only what they have in common. A shared love of running that will make her stand out from the other girls.

She's nearly home now and the light is going, becoming darker as she reaches the lane that leads to their house. The street lights become fewer as the lane narrows, each pool of light picking out the potholed path and the leaves of the hedgerow that darken again once she's run past.

The lane bends to the left and there it is, the long, thatched roof of the house, its windows hidden behind drawn curtains. She's sweaty and hungry and can't wait to grab something to eat and run herself a bath. When she reaches the front door, she realises she's forgotten her key. Not wanting to make her mum cross, she goes round to the back of the house. She opens the shed door and reaches up on tiptoe, feeling along the top of the door frame until her fingers meet the spare key. As she opens the back door and lets herself in, she sees her mum at the kitchen table, her head in her hands, her fingers laced through her hair.

'Are you all right, Mum?'

Wondering where Freya is, Kelly pulls up a chair and sits down, noticing as she does, the two empty plates on the side.

'What time do you call this?' Her mum looks up, her face white and pinched. 'Your supper's ruined.'

There's an edge to her voice that Kelly recognises. One that tells all her senses to be on red alert.

'It's Tuesday, Mum. Athletics club. Did you forget?'

The slap comes before she can stop it. A hot sting on her cheek. 'Don't be cheeky.'

Raising her hand to her face, Kelly tries to think of something to say to make it better. 'I'm sorry. I should have reminded you.'

'You think sorry is a magic word? That it will make everything all right?' When Kelly says nothing, she grabs her arm, her fingers pressing into the flesh. 'Well, do you?'

'No… I don't know.' She's near to tears. 'Mum, you're hurting me.'

'You're no better than your father,' she says, dropping her hand and turning away from her. 'No better.'

Kelly wants to ask why her dad isn't home, but when her mum's in one of these moods, it's better not to ask. Instead, she asks where Freya is.

'She's upstairs waiting for you. I don't know how you can live with yourself and your selfishness.'

Her selfishness? She searches her memory for a clue. Something that she might have forgotten. Had she told Freya that she would spend the evening with her? She doesn't think she had.

'I'll go up and see her.'

'You do that.' Her mum sucks in her cheeks. 'You see if you can repair the damage you've done because I'm telling you, young lady, if you ruin this for me, I will never forgive you.'

She turns away, her knuckles to her lips and Kelly stares at her, wondering what it is she's meant to have done. Not just this day but every day since she can remember.

When her mum says nothing more, she climbs the stairs, her cheeks burning, not just from the slap but from the injustice. Why does everything have to be her fault? She always goes to the athletics club on a Tuesday and she's done her best to be nice to Freya since she's been back. She can't help it if her dad prefers his office to this miserable house. She'd leave it too if she had anywhere to go.

Freya's door is closed and Kelly knocks and waits. She's dying to tell her about Ethan. Tell her how her heart had squeezed when he smiled at her. Tell her that she thinks he might actually like her.

When there's no answer, she turns the handle and opens the door a crack. The room is in darkness.

'Freya?'

'Go away.'

The curtains are drawn, but there's no light on. Freya is under the rose-patterned duvet, her pale hair just visible in the dim light.

'What's the matter? Are you ill?' Darts of anxiety shoot through her. What if the same thing's happening again? What if she's unwell? What if she leaves?

Freya's face is turned away from her. Walking over to the bed, Kelly switches on the bedside light and is shocked to see her face is wet with tears. For a moment, she looks just like the frail girl from six years ago.

Reaching out a hand, she touches her shoulder through the duvet. 'What is it?'

'You left me.' Her voice is small like a child's and Kelly doesn't know what to say or do. She's not sure what she means. When did she leave her?

'I was at the athletics club.' She's sick of saying it – as though she's done something wrong. 'It's on every Tuesday and I haven't been for ages.'

Freya turns towards her. 'I thought sisters were supposed to be there for each other.'

The air in Freya's room is hot and stuffy, the radiator on even though it's only September. She wants to throw open a window – let some fresh air in – but Freya has her arms wrapped around her as though she's cold. There must be something she can do to make amends.

'Ethan came running today.'

Freya raises an eyebrow. 'Ethan Jackson?'

'I think he likes me.' It's not something she knows for certain, but she's sure it's something that will impress Freya.

Freya pats the bed next to her and grins. 'I think you should tell me everything about it.'

Kelly looks at the bed, then at Freya. Her change of mood is disconcerting. A minute ago, she'd been feeling sorry for the girl – guilt running through her for having gone out and left her – and now this. She doesn't know how to be with her. If she can be trusted.

Freya holds out her hand to her. 'I've always wanted someone to share things with. Haven't you?'

A wave of self-pity washes over her. Of course she has. Needing no more persuading, Kelly climbs onto the bed next to Freya and leans her back against the headboard.

As she starts to tell her about Ethan – about the way his hair falls across his face, the sound of his laugh and the way he makes her stomach do somersaults – she feels Freya's body press against hers. The encouraging squeeze of her fingers. Ethan's the first boy she's had a crush on and the words come tumbling out in her excitement. When she was younger, she'd tried to confide in her mum about things, but her mum had cut her off, calling her needy. It didn't take long to realise it was better to keep her thoughts to herself. Or tell them to Ben. Sharing her innermost feelings with Freya makes her feel like she belongs to someone at last and the relief is indescribable.

When her mum knocks on the door to ask them what they're doing, it's Freya who calls out.

'We're fine, Karen. I'm just helping Kelly with her homework.'

'Good girl,' her mother says. 'You're such a good girl.'

They hear her footsteps going back along the landing and collapse into giggles, tears rolling down their faces.

Freya stares at the door, her face a picture of distaste. 'I know she's your mum, but she's such a fucking loser.'

'Freya!' There's something deliciously disloyal in what Freya's just said. 'You can't say that.'

'I just did, didn't I? That woman is suffocating me. At my last place, they weren't that bothered about me, but at least I had space to breathe.'

Kelly leans up on her elbow. 'What do you mean?'

'She can't do enough for me... you'd think I was about five not sixteen. It's always *How was school? What would you like for your dinner? Would you like me to serve you grapes on a silver platter?*'

Despite herself, Kelly can't help laughing. 'I don't think she's even got a silver platter.'

'Maybe not, but you don't know the half of it. I've caught her at night watching me from the doorway when she thinks I'm asleep. Is that creepy or what?'

'It is a bit.'

She can't tell Freya that there's nothing she'd like better than a mother who looked in on her when she was sleeping. A guardian angel watching over her in the night. Kelly tries to imagine what it must be like but can't. Her mum likes her to keep her bedroom door firmly closed after she's gone to bed and if she gets up at night, she has to make sure she steps over the creaky floorboard on the landing so as not to wake her. The person Freya's describing is like someone she's never met.

'And as for your dad,' Freya continues. 'Can't she even see what's going on under her own nose? I thought lipstick on a collar was just something you read about in trashy novels but looks like I was wrong. Still, he's not too bad when you get to know him and at least he's good for maths revision.'

Kelly's feeling ill at ease now. She doesn't like the way the conversation has turned. She knows what she thinks of her father, how his absence adds to her loneliness, but it's different when someone else is saying it.

'I heard Karen give him a piece of her mind the last time he helped me. She thought I'd gone upstairs, but I was listening at the door. What's her problem?'

Freya turns off the bedside lamp and bends her arms behind her head. In the darkness, her face is a pale globe. 'Anyway, who needs the crazy woman when we've got each other.'

The uncomfortable feeling melts away and Kelly's body is filled with a new warmth. It's the first time she's had someone to laugh about her mother with. To tell secrets to.

Someone to be normal with.

'I know,' Freya says. 'Let's see what your horoscope says. Maybe it will tell you that you'll meet a fit runner called Ethan.'

Reaching under her pillow, Freya pulls out a *Cosmopolitan*, then switches on the bedside light again. Finding the page with the horoscopes, she runs her finger down it until she comes to Leo.

'*This is not the time to sit back and let the grass grow,*' Freya reads in a grave voice. '*Grab the bull by the horns and take matters into your own hands.*'

They collapse onto the pillow in a fit of giggles and Kelly can't help wishing time would stand still.

Yes, Freya is the best friend she's ever had.

A true sister.

CHAPTER THIRTY-TWO

Kelly Now

There are eight of us seated around the large table in Maddie's kitchen, the detritus of the meal we've just eaten littering the waxed cloth with its print of bright red strawberries. A box of After Eights is being passed around the table, but I don't take one – it's a reminder of the truffles we should have brought. The ones Charlie ate.

My own dessert lies barely touched in the bowl in front of me, the meringue and lemon curd congealing, the pastry turning soft. I stare at it, wondering how long it will be before we can collect Noah, who's asleep in his pram in the living room, and go home. For the first time since I've had him, he's slept longer than three hours and it's also the first time that I wish he hadn't. Leaning back in my chair, I strain to hear the slightest sound from him, but there's nothing. Maybe I can use our neighbour, Stephanie, as an excuse to leave – she kindly offered to babysit which meant we didn't have to bring the girls. Sneaking a quick look at my watch, I see it's not yet eleven and the dinner party shows no signs of winding down. I expect the night is still young for the others seated around the table, but on a Saturday, I'm usually in bed by ten. Exhausted from a day of keeping the twins entertained, trying to settle Noah and keeping on top of the housework while Mitch is at the site.

The kitchen is warm, hot even – the shiny blue Aga, where Maddie cooked our vegetable lasagne, still pumping out its heat.

It's noisy too. Voices talking over each other in a bid to be heard. The other guests are all people Mitch knew from his life before he met me. Part of his old gang who he hasn't seen in a while. There's also a thin young man, with a goatee beard, who I gather is Maddie's latest interest. I've forgotten his name already, but I remember she said he was a musician. During the meal he's said almost as little as me, preferring to look at his phone.

Maddie sits at the head of the table, looking beautiful in a vintage velvet dress, its emerald colour setting off her blonde hair perfectly. Self-consciously, I raise my hand to my own lank hair. I was going to wash it before we came out, but just as I'd turned on the shower, Noah had decided it was time for another feed. There's a stain of baby milk on my shoulder that I hadn't noticed before we came out. I bristle. Why hadn't Mitch told me?

I hear his laughter from the other end of the table. He's seated on Maddie's left-hand side and has clearly found something she's said hilarious. I can't take my eyes off them, and as she bends her head to him and whispers something, eliciting another bark of laughter, my insides twist. They look so comfortable together.

My eyelids are heavy, tiredness threatening to pull them closed. I long to be in bed, to fall into the oblivion of sleep, not be here amongst these people I barely know.

Around me, the conversation ebbs and flows, but I can't bring myself to participate in it. I know how I must look: bored and dull. A mother of young children with nothing of interest to say. How surprised they'd be if they knew what really sets us apart. The loss I've felt. The feelings that have been coming back – the ones that overwhelm me every time I think about the locket in the jewellery box on my bedside table and how it's found its way back to me. Most of all, though, I'd like to see the look on their faces if they knew the hideous thing I saw in the woods when I was fourteen and the guilt that's been with me all these years.

'It's been a great evening, hasn't it? Maddie's such a wonderful cook.'

A woman's voice brings me back to the present. It's Jackie, who's sitting beside me. I've found out she works in a shop in the lanes that sells crystals, angel jewellery and other holistic items. Surprisingly, her husband, who is on my other side, works for the council and has already talked at me about bin collection days and the state of the local roads. They're nice enough, but we have nothing in common.

Turning my attention to Jackie, I force myself to look enthusiastic. 'Yes, she is, but I suppose she has the time. What I mean is,' I hurry on, scared I've sounded catty, 'it's easier to cook when you don't have a child pulling at your top asking where their silver unicorn is or a baby throwing up on your shoulder.'

'You can say that again.' She pulls a face and I remember that, over our starter of feta and pine nut tart, she'd told me in no uncertain terms that she and her husband didn't ever want children. Seeing her eyes alight on the milk stain on my dress, I turn away, mortified.

Mitch laughs again and I look over at him, even though I don't want to. The wine glass in front of him is full. The last time I'd looked, it had been almost empty. *Just one*, he'd said before we'd left. *It's different now. I know when to stop.* Maddie's slim fingers are playing with the label on the wine bottle, scraping at the edges with her blackberry nail polish while she talks. Did she top his wineglass up or did Mitch help himself? Anger flares. Maddie must know that Mitch has been trying to cut down.

Over the course of the evening, the talk has moved from music to the state of the building industry and now there is an animated discussion on Brexit. It's only myself and Maddie's date who aren't joining in. Mitch doesn't usually like to discuss politics, preferring to keep his opinions to himself, but now he's leaning back in his chair pointing a finger at Carl, a large man with a beard, who used to be the landlord of the pub he and Maddie frequented a few years back.

'Didn't know you were an outie, you bastard.' It's said with a smile, but his words are starting to slur. I'm worried. He's not a good drunk.

'Mitch,' I call across the table.

He looks away from Carl and our eyes meet. But it's not just *his* eyes that are on me, the others are looking too. It's almost as if they'd forgotten I was there. Maddie has a half-smile on her face and her cheeks are flushed a delicate pink. She's tipsy too. I don't like the way she's sitting so close to him. Her fingers, with their chunky silver rings, dangerously near his. I will my husband to see how unhappy I am, how desperate to leave, but he looks away again. Lifting the bottle from Maddie's hand, he refills his glass and then hers.

'To old times,' he says, raising his glass to the table. 'Can't beat 'em.'

I watch the red liquid slosh over the rim of the glass and run down the stem as he takes a gulp and places it clumsily back on the table, leaving a circle of red on the cloth. How much has he had? I kick myself for not keeping check. Beneath the heavy waxed tablecloth my hands twist at my napkin. I wish now I hadn't suggested we walk Noah here in the pram to get him to sleep. If Mitch had driven, this wouldn't be happening.

'I think we ought to be going. I said eleven to Stephanie.'

From the other end of the table, Mitch frowns at me. 'She'll be fine for another half hour or so. What's the hurry?'

'I'm tired, Mitch.' I hate that we're having this conversation in front of the others.

Maddie is smiling at me. 'Stay for coffee at least.'

'Our babysitter. She's—'

Mitch cuts me off. 'It's ages since we've been out. You go if you like, but I'm enjoying myself.'

All eyes are on me, wondering what I'll do. There's a hollow feeling in my stomach. Mitch is my rock, the one who supports me, but tonight he seems different. The drinking… making himself the life and soul of the party… flirting with Maddie. It's got something to do with the argument we had the other evening about the letter from my mother. My refusal to see her. Why does he care so much? It's not as if he's seen his own mother since he was a boy. My face aches as I try not to cry. Standing up, I place my napkin on the table.

'I'm sorry, Maddie, but I really must go. Before Noah wakes.'

I go out into the hall and push open the door to the living room. The room is dark, the curtains closed. In the light from the hall, I see him stir and hear his small mewl. When I wheel him out, Jackie is already at the front door, holding it open. I can hardly see her through my tears.

'I'll get Kevin to walk you back.' She sounds embarrassed.

'There's no need.' I'm humiliated enough without having someone else's husband walk me home. Manoeuvring the pram down the step, I set off along the dark street, feeling as though my life is unravelling.

It's quiet tonight, the only sound the shush of the pram wheels on the pavement. As I walk, I count under my breath, keeping my steps even. There are seventeen steps between each lamp post, but how many lamp posts in the street? If there are more than twenty, Mitch will come after me. If there are less, he won't.

I've almost reached the end of the road when I sense someone behind me.

With relief I turn, ready to forgive him, but there's no one there.

The street is empty.

CHAPTER THIRTY-THREE

Kelly Before

It's the weekend and Kelly has spent most of the day in her room looking at her clothes. Ethan was at the athletics club again on Thursday and had run next to her like he had before. The following day at school he'd said he and his mates would be at the skateboard park at the bottom of the cricket field on Saturday afternoon. Maybe he'd see her around. *See her around.* In the hours since he'd said it, she'd worked herself into a state trying to work out his meaning. Was he hinting he wanted her to go there to watch him? Or was it just a throwaway comment?

Whatever he meant, there's nothing in her wardrobe that would make him look twice at her, just plain T-shirts and jeans, jumpers with roll-necks and shoes with heels no higher than she had when she was a child. If she had a weekend job, it would be different – she'd be able to catch the bus into Churchill Square and buy the things the other girls had. But her mum won't let her, saying she needs her in the house. Not that she ever takes any notice of her when she's there.

'What are you doing?'

Freya is leaning over the bed. In her hand is a pink blouse with ruffles down the front. 'What in God's name is this?'

Cheeks burning with embarrassment, Kelly takes it from her and throws it into the corner where it joins a pile of equally hideous things. 'I know. It's awful, isn't it? I'm sorting things out for the charity shop.'

Freya stares at the clothes in the wardrobe. And pulls a face. 'I'd get rid of the lot if I was you.'

'Then I'd have nothing to wear.'

'Oh, poor little Cinderella.'

Freya gets up and puts an arm around Kelly, pulling her close to her side. 'Don't look like that, darling. I was only joking. Next week, we'll take the bus into town. I can buy you something. Treat you.'

She kisses her cheek and Kelly's grateful. It's something her mum never does. In fact, she suspects she wouldn't look at her at all if she could help it.

'You'd do that? What about money?'

But Kelly knows Freya has money – she keeps it in a sock in her drawer and it's what her mum pays her for cleaning the house. She does it on a Saturday morning and it's certainly made the house nicer. There are no longer dead bluebottles on the windowsills or dirty footprints where Ben has walked across the tiles after being in the garden. The only room she's not allowed to clean is the small one at the back of the house which Kelly's dad uses as his office. But she does it anyway – Kelly's seen her coming out.

Her dad's home a lot more now than he used to be. As she sits in her bedroom, struggling with her homework or daydreaming about Ethan, the music her father loves will rise up to her from his office: the strains of a violin, followed by the mournful bass notes of a bassoon. It's comforting.

'Do you want to go or don't you?'

'Of course. Thank you.'

Kelly slips an arm around her foster-sister's waist to hug her but instead of the soft indentation above the waistband of her jeans, she feels something hard.

'What's that?'

'Ta da!' Freya lifts her sweatshirt and whips out the bottle of vodka that's wedged between the material and her skin.

'Where did you get that?' It looks like one from her dad's drinks cabinet.

'Where do you think?' She grins. 'He won't find out, and even if he does, he won't mind. Your dad's a big softie when you get to know him.'

Kelly turns away. It's as if Freya has no idea how her thoughtless words are killing her. 'You should put it back.'

'Don't be a spoilsport. I thought we could take it with us to the rifle range.'

Kelly stares at her. 'The rifle range?'

'Yes – at the other end of the meadow. Don't tell me you've never been there.'

She hasn't. The thought of the place makes Kelly shudder. Even on a Saturday afternoon, it sounds sinister – conjuring up images of bullets ricocheting off metal targets. And anyway, she'd wanted to go to the cricket field to see if Ethan was there. 'Will anyone else be there?'

Freya shrugs. 'Why? Isn't my company good enough? Maybe you'd rather go with lover-boy.'

Kelly cringes at the name. Over the last couple of days, Freya's been asking about him, helping her to come up with a plan to get him interested. It's the first time, since she told her, that she's been like this. Could she be jealous?

'Don't be silly. I don't want to go with *anyone*, all right?'

If the people at school are to be believed, the place is littered with broken glass and stinks of piss. Ivy growing unchecked up the crumbling walls. She imagines the wind that whistles up the length of the markers' gallery and howls through the derelict target stores. The rain that darkens the graffiti-covered walls. The damp. The decay. But, more than this, she can't get the phantom sound of rifle shots out of her head.

Freya is grinning at her, holding the bottle up. 'Well? Are you coming or are you chicken?'

Kelly sighs and closes the wardrobe door. 'All right, I'll come.'

They go downstairs and, through the kitchen door, they see Kelly's mum. Freya knocks and pokes her head round the door. 'We're just going to take Ben for a walk, Karen. We won't be long.'

The sickly-sweet way she's said it makes Kelly cringe, but her mum has clearly not registered the sarcasm in her voice. She looks up from the potatoes she's peeling. 'Thank you, love.'

As they close the back door behind them and clip Ben's lead to his collar, Freya shakes her head in despair. 'She's pathetic. She makes it sound as if I'm doing her a favour. At one of the places I was at, they made me a timetable for chores. There were three of us there, me and their own kids, and we all had to do our bit. Even the nine-year-old.'

'Did you mind?'

She shrugs. 'I found ways of making the others do mine. When I was found out, you'd have thought, from the fuss they made, I'd spiked their Ribena or stolen their pocket money. When my foster-parents took their side, I told them that the making of timetables was symbolic of a totalitarian state and that my foster-mother was no better than a dictator. It didn't go down too well, as you can imagine. In fact, they used it as an excuse to get rid of me. Said I was taking advantage of the younger ones. A bad influence. Your mother might be unhinged, but at least she appreciates me.'

'I don't think you should talk about my mum like that.' Kelly's not sure why she's defending her but, as her only daughter, it seems the right thing to do.

Freya looks at her coldly. 'Oh, sorry, miss high and mighty. I forgot you've got a *real* mum whereas I have to make do with what social services give me.'

She marches ahead, pulling Ben by his collar, and Kelly walks quicker to keep up with her long strides.

'I didn't mean it like that. I just think that maybe you should be a bit more grateful that she's taken you in.'

Freya wheels round and she almost bumps into her. 'You think you're so special, don't you? So much better than me. What do you know about anything, stuck up in that bedroom, scared to say boo to a goose in case it upsets anyone? Though what you've got to be worried about, I don't know. You've got it all: a mum, a dad… and a bloody dog. You even live in a thatched house that backs onto a meadow, for fuck's sake. It's like living in *Little House on the Prairie*.'

Kelly knows there's no point in arguing with Freya when she's in one of her moods. It's easier to let it pass. 'I don't know what you want me to say.'

Freya glares at Kelly for a moment, then her face breaks into a smile. 'You don't have to say anything. Ignore me. I'm just a jealous cow. Friends?'

Freya's changes of mood are doing her head in. Could it only be yesterday that they were sitting on the school field, giggling at Mr Seymores' trainers? Agreeing he only wore them because the year elevens and twelves had lost a protest to make them part of the school uniform. It seems a lifetime ago but, despite her irritation, Kelly knows nothing's altered. She wants Freya's friendship as desperately as she did when she was eight.

'Of course we're still friends. The best.'

'Then what the fuck are we waiting for?' Freya leads the way down the stony track, Kelly following, and when they get to the stile, they let Ben off the lead. He runs through the gap at the side, happy to have his freedom.

The meadow is empty. At this time of year, it's lost its colour – the green and butter-yellow heads of the grasses flattened by the rain and the feet of walkers. It looks sad and neglected. Waiting for the new year to bring it back to life.

Walking in silence, they follow the path that will take them to the rifle range, but as they near it and the brick wall of the markers' gallery comes into sight, Kelly holds back.

'Can't we just sit there?' Kelly points to the grassy slope on their right. At the side of the path, giving a view of the meadow, is a bench. No one is on it.

Freya looks at her as though she's stupid. 'Why on earth would we do that? The bench will be wet and every dog walker in the area will see us. Anyway, I love the rifle range – the graffiti especially. There's an edginess to it that helps me forget I'm living in some godforsaken backwater.'

They've reached the end of the valley and in front of them is the stile that separates the meadow from the disused range. Ben has already pushed underneath it and is sniffing at the undergrowth that has grown up around the brick wall.

Freya climbs over and Kelly follows. There's not much to see at first, just the wall stretching away from them, its surface covered in blue and yellow graffiti. On the other side, forming a narrow corridor, is another wall – this one part of a derelict outhouse. It smells damp and the air is colder than it had been in the meadow.

'I can't believe you've never been here.' Freya touches a finger to the pregnant blue letter of a tag and looks at her, her pale eyes giving nothing away.

Kelly's heard the rumours. Knows that groups of older kids from her school come here to party. To drink and do drugs. It scares and thrills her to think of it. What does Freya know about it, though? Has she been creeping out when they've all been asleep?

Without waiting for Kelly to answer, Freya rounds the corner of the wall and stops, her hands in the back pocket of her jeans. 'This is the markers' gallery where they raised and lowered the targets. Cool, isn't it.'

Kelly stands next to her and looks where she's pointing. Stretching away from them is a long area of wall overhung by a narrow roof. This wall too is covered in pictures and tags, the common vocabulary of some of the kids at school: *slag, minge, tosser.*

She looks away, turning instead to the eight rusted-metal target frames in their brick and concrete pits that run parallel to the wall. The carriages that once held the targets are still there and she stands, for a moment, imagining the clank of the wheel that's attached to the top. The one that would have hoisted the targets above the wall.

She can almost hear the crack of the guns and the whistle of the bullets.

Freya is sitting on the ground, her back resting against the yellow belly of a giant Homer Simpson – her long legs stretched out in front of her. With long slim fingers, she unscrews the lid from the bottle of vodka, puts it to her lips and takes a mouthful. Wiping her mouth with the back of her hand, she looks sideways at Kelly and holds the bottle for her to take.

'Here, have some.'

Kelly hesitates. She's tried alcohol before, just red wine one Christmas, but she hadn't liked it. Not wanting to look stupid, though, she holds out her hand for the bottle and takes a sip. It tastes disgusting, but she can feel it as it goes down her. Warm and comforting.

'Like it?'

She nods, trying not to pull a face. 'It's okay.'

Freya's delving into her bag again. This time it's a can of spray paint she brings out.

'What are you going to do with that?'

'What do you think?' Standing up, Freya pulls off the plastic lid. She turns to the wall and positions the nozzle close to the brickwork. Crouching, she presses down with her index finger and sprays a vertical line of green paint across the rough surface. She repeats with another close to it, then finishes it with a horizontal arc top and bottom. At first Kelly isn't sure what she's drawing, but then she recognises it.

She's seen that symbol in the horoscope column of the magazine they were looking at the other day.

Gemini.

Freya stands back to admire her work. 'What do you think?'

'I don't know.' There's something about the look of it that gives her the creeps and she knows what it is. The two vertical lines Freya has drawn remind her of the horrible trunks of the Gemini tree. She glances to her right. Where the long concrete gallery ends, she can just see the top of the hill with its line of trees. It's where the Gemini tree is waiting. She feels its pull and gives an involuntary shudder.

She takes another swig of the vodka and closes her eyes, allowing the alcohol to warm her. She's starting to feel different. Looser. More at ease with her surroundings. Everywhere she looks there are words and symbols. They are large, overlapping, fighting for prominence. A sea of colour contrasting with the stark brown metalwork of the target frames, their rusting skeletons never to be used again. Freya's graffiti stands out against the rest, its paint wet and vivid.

From her pocket, Freya produces a rather battered packet of Marlboro and a yellow, plastic lighter. Lighting a cigarette, she tips back her blonde head and draws the smoke into her lungs. As she exhales, she looks at Kelly through half-closed eyes.

'I suppose you haven't smoked either.'

'Of course I have.' Kelly holds out her first two fingers and accepts the offered cigarette. Taking a drag of it, she tries to make it look as if it's something she does every day. Knowing that if she inhales too deeply, she'll cough.

They sit for a while in silence, but there are things Kelly wants to know. Questions she's been dying to ask Freya since she came back to them but hasn't had the courage. Now, the drink is making her brave.

'That thing you told me. When we were children. Was it true?'

Freya blows out a plume of smoke. 'What thing?'

Kelly's scared now that she'll say the wrong thing. That the fragile bond between them will be broken. She's no longer sure she wants to be alone with her in this place. Freya's older now, her actions more impulsive.

'About your sister.' She swallows, making herself continue. 'What you did.'

She waits, not daring to look at Freya. Wanting, yet not wanting, to know. Vainly, she tries to imagine what it must be like to carry around a secret such as hers. One that has hovered like a spectre between them since Freya returned. There but ignored.

The wind picks up, ruffling what's left of the silver birch leaves behind the target frames and blowing an empty cigarette packet across the concrete where they're sitting. There are empty cans too and the dead butts of cigarettes. She hadn't noticed them before.

'Why would I lie?' Freya leans in towards her, her eyes narrowed, and Kelly edges away.

Over by the entrance to the range, Ben is investigating one of the empty buildings, his yellow tail thumping against the wall as he finds something illicit to eat. Kelly wishes he would come over to them. Wants to feel his soft fur beneath her fingers.

'Because…' She licks her dry lips. 'Because it's such a dreadful thing to say.'

Freya doesn't reply and Kelly wants to ask more: *What did you do? Who else knows?* But she's scared of hearing the answer. Instead, she tries another tack.

'Why did it take so long for you to come back here?'

Flicking her cigarette butt into the depression that houses the machinery, Freya taps her temple. 'They were sorting out my head.'

Kelly giggles, the vodka having its effect.

'You think it's funny? You think *this* is funny.' Freya pushes up the sleeve of her coat and Kelly sees the fine trail of silvery scar tissue that criss-crosses it. A silvery snail-trail. She stops laughing.

'Did you do that?'

'Who do you think did it? The other do-gooder foster carers? Though I wouldn't blame them, I can be difficult.' The words are spoken parrot-fashion as though she's repeating what someone has told her.

'No, of course not. It's just that I can't imagine...' She touches a finger to the inside of her wrist, scattering ash across her jeans, and tries to imagine the drag of a sharp object across it. The pain as the skin splits apart. The fine line beading with blood.

'If you tell anyone, I will do more than that.'

That threat again. That horrible image that Kelly's been trying to tell herself was just the ravings of a strange and damaged child. The awful rope that hangs from the Gemini tree. Is it even there still?

Freya draws up her knees and leans back against the wall again. Her arms crossed around her body. Her fingers stroking her side.

Mimicking her action, Kelly imagines the feel of the strange shiny skin beneath her top.

'Were you in a fire? Is that how your sister died?' She blurts out the words, shocking herself.

Kelly hears it before she sees it, the sound of breaking glass as the vodka bottle hits the rusting iron skeleton in front of them. Shards of glass litter the concrete.

'I'm going to count to twenty,' Freya hisses. 'And if you're not out of my sight before then, you will regret it forever. Go on. Take your stupid dog and fuck off!'

The broken neck of the bottle is within Freya's reach. Kelly can see her eyes on it. Throwing down her cigarette, she gets to her feet, swaying slightly from the effects of the alcohol.

'I didn't mean anything...'

'I said, fuck off! One. Two...'

Calling to Ben, Kelly runs back along the concrete walkway, scraping her hand on the brickwork as she throws herself around the corner. Behind her, she can hear Freya counting. She's reached seven.

The stile is difficult, her legs like jelly, but she makes it over. Then she and Ben are running across the meadow. She's not sure what she's afraid of, knows she can outrun Freya, but there's something she'd seen in the girl's eyes that scares her.

As she ploughs through the naked stalks of grass, it's she who's counting now, not Freya.

Fifteen. Sixteen.

If she sees the thatched roof of her house before she's reached twenty, everything will be all right. If not…

She turns her head and sees Freya emerging from the rifle range. As she turns back, her foot catches in a bramble and she pitches to the ground.

She's reached twenty, but the house is still not in sight.

CHAPTER THIRTY-FOUR
Kelly Now

It's the morning after Maddie's dinner party. Reaching to the phone that's on my bedside table, I see it's nearly six. There's no sound from either Noah or the girls and I'm grateful. It gives me time to muster my thoughts. Decide what I'm going to do.

Mitch lies beside me on his back, the sheets pushed away from him. He's snoring loudly and I can smell last night's wine on his breath. See how his skin, normally so brown from working outdoors, looks sallow in the early morning light.

When he'd eventually come home the previous evening, smelling of wine and cigarettes, I'd pretended to be asleep. Watching him through half-closed eyes as he'd fumbled with the buttons of his shirt, his hand getting stuck in the sleeve where he'd forgotten to undo it, then losing his balance as he'd tried to take off his sock. I was too angry and upset to confront him then but now that it's morning, I'm surprised to find that all I want to do is lay my head on his chest and forget the evening ever happened.

He stirs and rolls over onto his side, his arm falling across my body. I run my hand down his bicep, noticing how the sun has joined up his freckles into larger clumps. Loving the feel of his skin. I want to hate him for what he did but am unable to. During the long night, I've been thinking about the past and how Mitch has saved me from it. My head is still crowded with images of my childhood: the procession of brothers and sisters on the wall of my mother's stairs, the window looking out onto the wild meadow.

Most of all, though, I've been thinking about Freya. In death, she's doing what she's always done. Getting between me and anyone I've ever really cared about – even if it's only in my head.

Mitch grunts and moves his head closer to mine until our foreheads are touching. Leaning in, I kiss his lips and, when his eyes flutter open, I see myself reflected in the pupils.

'Morning, beautiful,' he says, stretching.

'How's your head, Mitch?'

The sleepy smile falls away as he remembers.

'Christ, Kelly. I'm sorry.' He runs a hand down his face, his stubble rasping under his palm. His voice is strained. 'What an idiot. What a fucking idiot.'

Reaching out, I take his hand, lacing my fingers with his own. 'It's not just you, Mitch.'

He brings my hand to his mouth and kisses it. 'I'll never forgive myself for letting you walk home alone. How could I have done that? What if something had happened to you?'

'Nothing did,' I reply. But it's me I'm trying to convince, not him.

My eyes stray to the jewellery box on my dressing table. I picture Freya's locket, lying in its small, velvet compartment, the word *sister* scratched onto the back, and dread gathers in the pit of my stomach. The things that have been happening recently… are they a threat? Someone is reaching out to me, but I don't know who.

I want to tell Mitch about the feeling I'd had, how I'd thought someone was behind me last night, but stop myself. He's beating himself up enough without my help.

'What happened?' I ask.

He drops my hand. 'Nothing happened, Kelly. I swear.'

I'm confused by his answer, then, with a shock, I realise he's talking about Maddie. It wasn't what I was asking; it had never occurred to me that they might go further than a bit of harmless flirtation, believing that if anything was going to happen, it would have done so years ago before he met me. But now he's put the idea into my head.

'I didn't mean that, Mitch.'

Mitch looks away and I can see from his face that he's realised the significance of what he's said.

'Nothing happened,' he says again, quieter this time, and I hear the defensiveness in his voice. 'There was a time when you would have believed me.'

I shake my head. 'I never said I didn't.'

Suddenly, his face changes. Softens. 'Why are we arguing, Kel? We never used to argue.'

It's true. We've always been careful of each other's feelings, knowing that it's what helps us keep our tight-knit family together, but recently we seem to be unravelling.

'It's when you drink. It brings out a different side of you and I feel like you forget I'm there. You made a promise when Noah was born to cut down, but it didn't last long.'

Mitch rolls onto his back. He puffs out his cheeks, then exhales. 'I've tried, but I never seem to be able to stop at just one. I can't help it, but sometimes the past creeps up on me, and when it does, the easiest thing to do is have a drink. It stops me dwelling on stuff.'

I watch how the vertical lines between his brows deepen. It worries me. 'What sort of stuff?'

Mitch has always been the strong one. The one who anchors me... even when he's not in the same room. Or the same house. It's what I've always loved about him. His pragmatism. How he's ruled by his head, not his heart. The Mitch I see today is one I've never seen before. There's a vulnerability about his face that he usually keeps hidden.

'What sort of stuff?' I ask again. My voice quieter this time.

He turns his head to look at me and I can see he's thinking. Wondering what to say.

'The children's homes,' he continues. 'The foster carers who didn't give a damn about me. The things I did that I'm not proud of... just as I'm not proud of what I did last night. I need to tell you, Kelly, or I'm scared I'll become that boy again.'

His eyes are on mine as he waits for me to say something. I know that he was in and out of homes as a child, but I've never asked him for details. It might be because I'm scared of what he'll tell me. Or maybe, it's because if he does, I'll have an insight into what Freya's life might have been like before she came to stay with us in the thatched house. A knowledge that will fuel my guilt.

But this isn't about Freya, it's about me and Mitch. We both managed to pull ourselves out of our lonely childhoods to find each other and, despite not opening up about them, the things that happened when we were children have made us who we are now. It's also what keeps us close.

I take my husband's hand, the callouses on his palm rough against my skin, and trace the whorls of dried plaster that are ingrained on his fingertips. 'You can tell me.'

Mitch captures my fingers and gives them a gentle squeeze. He looks uncomfortable. 'Are you sure you want to know?'

I'm not, but I nod anyway. 'Yes.'

'All right.' He gives a small, tight smile. 'I've never told anyone this, but I broke into a house once – me and a couple of the older boys from the children's home.' He stares into the middle distance as if replaying the scene. 'They weren't really friends – just kids I hung around with because there was no one else.'

When he pauses, I know it's because he needs my encouragement to continue.

'What happened?'

'By this time, I'd been in a good few months and had learnt to toughen up. Built an armoured shell around me so people would think I was tough, even though I wasn't. Inside I was still the same frightened little boy I'd been when I first got there.'

I soften my words with a smile. 'Go on.'

'I was the smallest, so they made me climb through the window and let them in. We took stuff – junk really but precious to the person who lived there.'

His voice is heavy with regret, his eyes wandering. The desire to drop the conversation is written across his face.

'I didn't know,' I say, trying not to sound shocked.

Mitch stares at me, his eyes anguished. 'Christ, Kelly. I can still hear the old woman's voice calling down the stairs. *Who's there? Who is it?*

He curls his hand into a fist and beats his forehead. Once. Twice. 'She was someone's mother. Someone's grandmother probably. What was I thinking of?'

I try to keep my voice steady. 'We've all done things we're not proud of. Especially when we were young. You were just a kid.'

He rolls over to face me again. 'But don't you see? I could have said no. They were older, tougher, but there would have been ways. I could have told someone at the home, but I didn't, and I have to live with that… every day of my sodding life. I've pushed these memories down so deep that sometimes I can almost convince myself it happened to someone else. When I first moved here, it was Maddie who helped me through the rough times, and last night reminded me of that. I just wanted to have some fun. To grab back some of the old me.'

My heart clenches. 'The one you were before you got married and had children, you mean.'

Mitch takes my hand again and his eyes travel across my face as if trying to read it better. 'I didn't mean it like that, and I know it makes me sound like a whinging loser. You and the kids… you're everything to me. I just wish that you'd open up more yourself. Talk to me. Maybe then I can understand why you're so adamant you won't go to your dad's funeral.'

'I'm not going because he means nothing to me.' But even as I'm saying the words, I feel a tear trickle down my cheek. Once, he meant everything to me.

Mitch pulls me to him. 'Kelly?'

I can't speak. Just bury my face in his shoulder.

'I know you hate the place, but if you go back there, Kel, it might give you some sort of closure. Put an end to all this… this stuff that's going on in your head. The worries about the baby.' His eyes are pleading. 'I never knew my dad, he knocked my mum up, then pissed off, but you knew yours. And, whatever you may think of him now, that stands for something. Will you go to his funeral… for me?'

I stare at my husband as if he's mad, but he brushes my hair from my face, his eyes pleading. 'Please, Kelly. I don't expect you to understand it, but I think it's important to make your peace. Say your goodbyes. You don't ever have to go there again.'

I want to tell him no. Make him see that it's the last thing I want to do, but I stop myself. I owe him something for opening up to me. If I go to the funeral, I can sit at the back. I don't need to talk to my mother; I can slip away without being noticed. And maybe Mitch is right. Maybe if I go, things can go back to how they were before. Maybe it will help get our marriage back on track.

Taking a deep breath, I make myself say the words.

'All right. I'll go.'

Mitch takes me in his arms and I feel how solid he is. How safe he makes me feel. We'll put yesterday's horrid evening behind us and start again. Mitch loves me and I love him.

That's all that matters.

CHAPTER THIRTY-FIVE
Kelly Before

'Anything wrong, Kelly?' Peter's standing over her, tapping his pencil against his front teeth.

Kelly finishes tying her running shoe and twists her head to look at him. 'No. Everything's fine.'

She doesn't want to tell him that she has the start of a headache and that she's shivering despite the layers she's wearing. If she does, he'll send her home.

'That's good then. It's just that you've been tying that shoelace for a good few minutes and, if I didn't know any better, I'd say you were playing for time.' He smiles and puts his pencil behind his ear. 'Waiting for someone, are you?'

Feeling herself blush, Kelly stands and zips up her running top. 'No.'

'Then you need to get going. There won't be much daylight left if you hang around here. You're the last to go and I'd be happier if you caught up with the others. It's the last evening we'll be running. Next week, we'll leave the cross-country until the weekend when it's lighter.'

He notes down the time on the clipboard and she sprints away from him, wondering if he's guessed it's Ethan she's waiting for. She'd hoped he'd be training this evening, but it's clear he isn't. The disappointment is immense. Over the last couple of weeks, she's let herself believe that they might, just might, be more than just running partners. That he actually likes her. Each night in bed, she's imagined what it would be like to kiss him – telling herself she hasn't imagined the way he looks at her.

She knows he isn't ill. She'd seen him and Freya walking out of the English room at break earlier that day. They were in front of her in the corridor and Freya's head was close to his, her hand cupped around his ear. He'd stopped in his tracks at something she'd said, his face registering surprise, staring after her as she'd walked away. Then, after a few moments, he'd run to catch up with his mates, leaping onto the nearest one's back, looking excited.

Kelly feels uneasy remembering it.

She'd ask Freya what was going on, only she isn't talking to her. Since that afternoon at the rifle range, she's tried to avoid her as much as possible. Despising herself for having been scared of her. It's just that she's sick of never knowing which Freya she's going to get from one moment to the next: the one who tries to be her mother's best friend or the one who's slagging her off. Whatever role she's playing, the perfect sister, the perfect daughter, she plays it to perfection. Pretending to be so flawless when nothing could be further from the truth. In the last couple of weeks, her dad's been around more at the weekends, having breakfast with them and coming home earlier from work. There must be something he sees in Freya that he never saw in *her*. Something that makes him want to be a proper father.

As Kelly starts the ascent up the hill, her legs are heavy and her throat feels tight. If it wasn't for the thought of seeing Ethan, she would have given tonight's session a miss, but she didn't want to lose her chance to be with him on her own. She's got used to him running beside her as she's tried to orchestrate a seemingly accidental touch of hands when they reach a narrow section of path. Now she's running on her own, the others way out of sight, and she doesn't like it.

The circuit they're running today climbs high above the village, following the horseshoe-shaped ridge before descending to the town on the other side of the valley. She's halfway up the ascent and struggling already – her chest tight, her lungs finding it hard to pull in enough air. By the time she's reached the top, she's fallen behind the others. Even if she finishes, her time will be way short of her target. As she's been running, the sun has disappeared behind the hills and the air has grown colder. What had at first been a general ache in her legs has now turned into needles of pain running from thigh to ankle. Her head is throbbing too.

At the next waymark, Kelly stops, her body bent at the waist, her fists pressed into her sides, trying to get her breathing back to normal. Far ahead, she can see the snake of runners as they cut down the grassy slope on the other side of the small valley. If she carries on after them, it will be dark before she gets back, and she'll never hear the last of it from Peter.

She looks at the footpath sign. There's nothing for it; she'll have to take the shortcut back to the village. A path she hasn't run before. She's avoided it because it passes close to the disused rifle range – the short woodland descent opening out onto a ridge above the markers' gallery, before joining up with a track that will take her back to the village. But she has no choice. Not if she wants to get back before it's dark. The path is steeper than the one she should be taking, but it will mean she should be back around the same time as the others.

She begins to run, taking the right-hand fork through the trees, thankful that the path is dry and reasonably clear of brambles. It's only when she starts her descent, leaving the main path behind, that it occurs to her that no one will know she's gone this way. She slows to a jog – the last thing she needs is to fall and twist her ankle. Everything is aching. Her legs, her head… even her back. She longs to be home in her warm bed with a mug of Lemsip. It was stupid to think she'd be able to run today and it's not even as if Ethan is here to spur her on.

She's walking now, forcing one foot in front of the other, her teeth chattering even though it's not that cold. Pulling up her hood, she makes herself carry on and is relieved when she's out of the trees, the valley stretching out before her towards the village.

Below her is the rifle range and she knows that if she looks between the silver branches of the birch trees that cling to the edge of the slope, she'll see the rusty target frames rising from their concrete holdings. She doesn't want to look, though. She's had enough of that place.

The sound, when it comes, is like someone in pain. Kelly freezes. The blood draining from her face.

It comes again. The same noise. It's deep, guttural and this time she thinks it must be an animal. Fear squeezes her stomach. What is it? It's coming from below her. From the markers' gallery. Too scared to see what it is, she hurries on, trying not to make any sound. The path arcs round and she follows it, then, without warning, the trees clear.

A gasp escapes her, for directly below her is the graffiti-covered wall she was sitting against the other day, Homer Simpson's giant belly nudging up against the Gemini symbol Freya had sprayed on its surface. But it's not that she's looking at. It's something worse. So much worse.

She knows now what she heard. The animal sounds she couldn't place.

Freya is up against the wall, her face pressed against the brickwork, and someone is pushed up against her, his trousers around his ankles, his pale buttocks moving in a frantic rhythm. Again and again. With each thrust, he lets out a grunt, but Freya is silent. Her eyes closed. Her face impassive.

Kelly's rooted to the spot. Horrified at what she's witnessing, yet unable to make herself move away. In the growing darkness, she can't see clearly, but there's something that's draped over one of the target frames that makes her want the earth to open up and swallow her.

Ethan's leather jacket.

CHAPTER THIRTY-SIX

October 20th

It's funny how everyone just automatically presumed they'd get on – even you, I expect. Now they're older, though, their differences are becoming more obvious. I'm sure things will blow over, but at the moment, it's not the easiest of relationships. Unequal, I'd say. I'd love your opinion, but as we both know, that's 'not allowed'.

All the best

CHAPTER THIRTY-SEVEN
Kelly Before

When Kelly gets back, all she wants to do is go to bed and never wake up. Everything is ruined. Freya has taken away everything that she's ever wanted.

The shivers are coming in spasms now and a bone-chilling coldness has wormed its way under her skin. She knows she must have a temperature, but the paracetamol is in the cupboard above the microwave and her mother is in the kitchen. She doesn't want to have to answer her questions or let her see her red eyes or her tear-stained face.

She's just climbing the stairs when her mum calls out. 'Kelly, is that you?'

Kelly hangs her head. Scared to ignore her but not wanting to answer.

'Kelly, come in here. I've something important to tell you.'

Reluctantly, Kelly retraces her steps, stopping at the hall mirror to wipe away the mascara that's pooled under her eyes.

'What is it, Mum?'

She's at the kitchen table, her laptop open and a pile of leaflets beside her. Picking up one, she waves it at Kelly. 'I have some wonderful news. I was going to tell you when your dad got home but,' she glances at the clock on the wall and then back down, 'I'm just too excited to wait.'

'What is it?' Kelly's head feels like it's stuffed with cotton wool. Pulling up a chair, she lays her head on her crossed arms and closes her eyes, but not before she's seen the freshly washed floor, the worktops that have been cleared of clutter and the smell of baking bread. She didn't even know her mother knew how to make bread. Freya's return to the fold has worked wonders.

Her mum's voice is sharp. 'I've something important to tell you and the least you could do is have the decency to give me your attention.'

With great effort, Kelly raises her head. 'I'm not feeling well.'

Ignoring her, her mother takes Kelly's hands and squeezes them between her own. She's smiling and her eyes are shining, just like they were the day Freya first arrived all those years ago. 'Your father and I have decided that we're going to start adoption proceedings.'

Adoption proceedings? She wants to ask but is scared of what she might be told.

'Freya will be your sister,' her mother cuts in. 'Isn't it just perfect!'

Kelly pulls her hands away, placing them over her ears as the enormity of what she's just been told sinks in, but it's too late to block out her mother's monstrous words. 'But you can't. Please, Mum, don't do it.'

The smile drops from her mother's face and she stiffens. 'Don't be ridiculous. I'm fed up with your jealousy. It's taken me a long time to find someone your father loves as much as I do. Why can't you just be happy?'

'Because you've got me. You shouldn't need anyone else.'

With a scrape of wood on tile, her mother pushes back her chair. 'I won't hear any more of your nonsense. It's happening and I won't let you spoil it for me.' Getting up, she grabs her mobile from the table and looks at it before throwing it down again. 'Where the hell is your father?'

Lowering her head onto her arms again, Kelly's thoughts race. There must be something she can do to stop this awful thing happening. Images gather in her head. Ethan's white buttocks… the gross sounds he was making… Freya's empty expression.

Maybe there *is* something she can do after all. Something that will get rid of her for good.

'Freya's been having sex with a teacher,' she blurts out. 'I've seen them in the maths hut after school and they're up at the rifle range now.'

CHAPTER THIRTY-EIGHT

Kelly Now

'I don't know if I can do this, Mitch.' I smooth down the lapel of my black jacket and check how I look in the long mirror that hangs on the inside of the wardrobe. I haven't worn the trousers that go with it since before my pregnancy and the waistband is too tight. It's the only thing I have that is suitable, though.

The children are downstairs playing and Noah is in his bouncy chair, crying.

'Are you sure you can manage?' I think of the bottles of expressed milk in the fridge and the instructions I've left. My breasts are sore from the pump. 'I don't have to go.'

Mitch puts his hands on my shoulders and looks me in the eye. 'Stop worrying. Of course I can manage.' Bending to Noah, he lifts his little top and blows a raspberry on his stomach. 'Once the girls are at school, it will be all boys together. Won't it, mate.'

'Are you sure?'

He looks up at me from his crouched position, his head shining in the overhead light. 'We'll cope and so will you.'

'Will I?'

I think of the village, the school where I'd not exactly excelled, the long walk home down the dark and rutted lane. Alone. Always alone… apart from a few short weeks. Getting by as best I could. Trying to find a way to be like everyone else. To be normal. I don't want to go back. After all that's happened recently, I've become more anxious – like a cord stretched too tight that's beginning to fray. I'm scared that if I see my mother, I might somehow turn back into the person I was then. The one who lied. The one who made terrible things happen. What if she tries to find out more about my life? Will I give away the fact I have children? The thought of my mother infiltrating my life again makes my stomach give a fearful twist. When I'd packed my things and left my parents' house for the last time, I'd vowed I'd never go back.

But it's not just that. I'm scared to leave the children. Fearful that it's only me who can protect them. What if I'm right and someone is watching us? What if it's not my imagination?

Mitch smiles. 'It's only a few hours and one day you'll look back on today and be glad you went.'

I wonder.

If I go to the funeral, I can see for myself that my father is dead. That my mother is living her normal life rather than trying to infiltrate mine. That the past is where it should be... in the past.

'Maybe you're right.' Forcing a brave face, I look at my watch. 'Make sure you leave plenty of time to get the kids to school. It takes longer than you think to get Noah ready and sometimes Sophie needs a lot of coaxing to go into class. Oh, and don't forget their book bags.'

'Bloody Nora. I'm not a complete idiot.'

'I'm sorry. I know you're not. It's just that it's the first time I've left them all day and it's not even as if I want to go. You can't blame me for being a bit on edge.'

I think of the girls downstairs in the kitchen, fighting over the breakfast cereal. Needing me to go and sort it out. It's my job to make them feel cared for. Loved. It's been my job since I gave birth to them – it's all that matters. In a minute, Isabella will call up the stairs, needing to know where we are. They'll be waiting for us to come down so they can start their breakfast. Without warning, I'm back in my mother's house. When I lived there, it was like I was always waiting for something: for people to tell me what was going on; for my mother to wake up to how miserable I was; for a new foster-child to arrive; for my father to come home.

But I wasn't just waiting – I was wishing. Wishing the man whose funeral I'm going to could be like the other girls' dads. One who'd sit and watch TV with them. Joke with them. Help them with their homework.

That wish came true… but the girl he did that for wasn't me. However much I hoped the parents who raised me would love me – choose me over any other child that stayed with us – I wasn't the one to wave that magic wand.

Mitch stands behind me and puts his arms around my waist.

'Tell me what it is you're worried about. Is it seeing your mum, or is it something else?'

'It's everything. It's facing my childhood.'

He rests his chin on the top of my head. His voice is thoughtful. 'Do you think there's a chance any of the kids they fostered will be there?'

'I don't know.' It's not something I'd thought of.

'It's possible, don't you think? But, then again, how would they know… about your dad dying, I mean.'

I imagine them lined up in one of the church pews, but however hard I try, I can't capture what they would look like now. They're locked in my memory at the age they once were. Mason as a ginger freckle-faced boy. Jade with her pierced tongue and her sulky face. Freya…

I go cold.

Freya is in my head as clear as if she was standing in front of me. It's an image I've tried to push back, but this time I can't. It's sickening. Horrible. And, now that it's with me, I know I won't be able to get her out of my head again.

CHAPTER THIRTY-NINE
Kelly Before

Kelly's running through the trees, but it's not Ethan who's beside her; it's Mr Seymore. Liar, he says. Fucking liar. She knows she's dreaming, but she can't wake up. They've reached the rifle range, and instead of Homer Simpson, Ethan's face is sprayed onto the wall in blue paint. Freya is trying to scrub it off, but when Kelly tries to help her, she pushes her away. With every reach of Freya's arm, the running top she's wearing exposes the shiny puckered skin on her stomach. Frantically, she tugs at the hem, turning to Kelly with a face streaked with tears of green paint. You told my secret. I'll never forgive you. Kelly wants to tell her she didn't, that she's never told, but when she tries to speak, the razor blades in her throat slice and tear.

Through her dreams, Kelly hears sobbing. A voice pleading. Another door slams – this time the front door. Is she asleep or awake? There's something important she needs to do, but she doesn't know what it is. Come with me, Freya is saying. Let's play together by the Gemini tree. She doesn't want to go. The tree is evil. Then I'll go by myself, Freya says. Thick, hairy vines are sprouting from the scar tissue, twisting around her body, twining around her neck. Her veins stand out. Her eyes start to bulge. Kelly tries to pull the vines away, but they're tightening. Tightening.

Kelly wakes. Her forehead bathed in sweat. Her pyjamas are stuck to her and the room is swaying. As she lies there, she thinks about what she heard before she went to sleep. Her parents had been shouting – the odd word from her mother coming to her from the kitchen below. *Disgusting. An abuse of trust.* Her dad's voice had been too low to hear. Later, it was Freya's voice she'd heard. *She's a fucking liar. What else has she told you?* A slammed door. Crying. Silence. Then her parents starting again. Their voices rising and falling. Fading in and out.

What has she done?

Kelly feels worse than she did earlier, her limbs aching, her shivering uncontrollable. If only she could take something to make it better. Forcing herself to sit up, she slides her legs out of the bed. The wooden floorboards feel cold against the hot skin of her feet. With difficulty, she makes her way across the landing and into her parents' bedroom. Her mum's sleeping tablets are always on the bedside table. If she just takes one, it might help her feel better. She's so desperate she'll try anything.

Popping one out of its silver blister, she swallows it down with some of the water that's in a glass beside her mum's bed. Then she goes back to her room and waits to feel better. Her head is burning. The yellow digits are too bright – projecting out at her like in a 3D film. There's a strange lethargy to her limbs but sleep still seems a million miles away.

Pushing back the covers, she forces her legs to move. The room lurches and a rush of nausea hits her. The dream is still with her and she knows what Freya did, but despite her fear and resentment, she needs to know she's all right.

The landing is in darkness, the house so still you'd think it was empty. She can't think straight. Everything's muddled in her head. When she reaches Freya's door, it's closed and when she presses her ear to it, she hears nothing. Raising her hand, she pushes on the handle and opens the door just far enough to see in. The curtains are open, the room light enough to see that Freya's bed hasn't been slept in.

What if she's gone to the Gemini tree? What if she's gone to do what she's always threatened? Kelly knows she must find her. She loves her. She's made a mistake and should never have said what she did – made up that lie. It had been her jealousy that had made her do it.

It's like the scales have fallen from her eyes and she sees it as it really was. Ethan never saw her as anything more than a running partner; she'd made up the rest. Stumbling back to her own room, Kelly pulls on her jeans, losing balance as she tries to get her leg through the hole. Her T-shirt is next and the sweatshirt she'd worn while she was out running.

Holding the banister for support, she tiptoes downstairs, feeling disembodied. Like her legs don't belong to her. In the kitchen, Ben looks up from his bed. Scared he might bark, she unscrews the lid from his jar of treats and gives him one. The clock on the kitchen wall says ten past four.

She puts on her raincoat, then picks up the flashlight from the hook by the back door. Flicking it on, she steps outside, watching the light bounce off the fence in front of her, then switches it off again, scared it might be seen. Instead, she feels her way to the gate in the darkness, not turning the torch back on until she's safely outside.

It's cold in the lane, the wind funnelling between the trees, flapping her raincoat against her body. It's starting to rain too, but beneath Kelly's clothes her skin is burning – her jeans chafing like sandpaper. As she stumbles down the lane, the light from the torch swings wildly and she stops, forcing back a wave of nausea before making herself move on again. She's seen the silver tracks on Freya's wrists. Knows what she's capable of. She must stop her. Tell her that she'll always be there for her.

Kelly weaves through the meadow grass, the clumps of wet stems soaking through her jeans. Her limbs heavy. Ahead, the black whale-like humps of the downs are almost indistinguishable from the night sky. She's climbing the hill towards the dark band of trees, taking the path they took when they were children. It's where Freya's gone. She knows it.

When she reaches the wood, Kelly has no idea how she's got there. Time has expanded and contracted, and it seems only a few moments ago she was in her bed. Her hair is plastered to her face, her jeans wet and cold against her legs. The musty smell from the earth is intoxicating. As she walks, her torch picks out the colours of the decomposing leaves, the copper and gold merging as she struggles to focus. Thunder rolls above her head and the lightning that brightens the sky above the canopy of leaves is her own personal light show.

Stopping, she rests her forehead against the rough, wet bark of a tree to cool it, wrapping her arms around the trunk. Leaning into it. But then she remembers why she's come here. Freya is in trouble. She must find her.

As she carries on deeper into the wood, it becomes increasingly difficult to stop her feet slipping and sliding on the wet leaves and twice she stumbles over roots that are hidden beneath them. The rain is falling harder, blurring the edges of everything. The colours that were so bright in the torch's beam when she first passed through the kissing gate, now fading. In the distance, the thunder rolls across the downs.

Kelly's aches are worsening and she's consumed with a paralysing fear, but it's too late to turn back. She's already at the place where the trees start to thin. Opening up to reveal the clearing.

The Gemini tree towers over her, dark and deeply rooted. It stretches upwards – its skeletal branches twisted. Kelly puts her hands to her heavy, pounding head. She hears Freya's voice in her head. *I'm going to count to twenty and if you're not out of my sight before then, you will regret it forever.*

She doesn't want to be here.

Kelly tries to run but finds she can't. Her limbs are so heavy it's as if she too is anchored into the sodden earth. A sudden flash of lightning brightens the clearing, picking out the contours of the tree. It illuminates the two ugly trunks and also the body that swings from the rope attached to its lower branch.

A crack of thunder makes her drop her torch and she's in darkness. As if released from a spell, Kelly screams and steps back.

Freya's done what she threatened to do.

CHAPTER FORTY

Kelly Now

My knees buckle. It's as if the blood has drained from my body. Mitch manages to catch me before I fall.

'Jesus, Kelly. What just happened?'

I lean against him, my body shaking. Unable to answer.

I can still see Freya's staring eyes. Her lifeless body swinging from the rope attached to the creaking branch. The idea of going back home, to the place where it happened, must be affecting me more than I thought.

'Are you ill?' Mitch helps me onto the bed and stands awkwardly beside me, unsure of what to do. 'Shall I phone the surgery?'

I shake my head. What would I tell him? That I'm scared my past is coming back to haunt me? That I've come to believe my mother has decided it's payback time for Freya's death and wants me to know it? I doubt that Mitch would understand my fear that her obsession has grown in the years since it happened and she's waiting for the chance to take something from me in her turn. My baby.

'I'll be fine,' I say, closing my eyes and breathing deeply. 'Just give me a moment.'

Slowly, I count back from twenty. When I get to one, I will stand up and walk down the stairs. I will kiss my children goodbye and leave my house. I'll go to the funeral and look my mother in the eye. Tell her to leave my family alone. Nothing will happen to me because I'll have made it so. The numbers will have worked their magic.

'Seven, six, five…'

'Kelly, stop it!' My shoulders are being shaken and, when I open my eyes, Mitch's face is in front of me. 'What are you doing?'

With a shock, I realise I've been counting aloud. My stress levels are still sky high. I haven't finished. He's made me stop and now I can't remember where I got to. Sinking my head into my hands, a well of misery opens inside me.

'Look at me, Kelly. Talk to me.'

'It won't go away.' I stare up at Mitch with red-rimmed eyes. 'I keep thinking it will get better, but it doesn't.'

'What, Kel? What won't go away? You've got to tell me.'

I look at my husband. For years, I've kept it to myself, but I know that I can't do it any more. If I don't tell someone, I'm scared I'll go mad.

'I had a sister,' I begin. 'A foster-sister called Freya.'

'There were lots of foster-children, weren't there? Why is this one so different?'

I pause, digging deep for the strength to continue. Hoping that by telling my husband, the dreadful picture in my head will go away. 'She died. Committed suicide.'

'Shit.' Mitch sits heavily on the bed and rubs his cheek. 'I wasn't expecting that. How old were you when this happened?'

There's a knot in my stomach as I tell him. 'I was fourteen and she was sixteen. It happened one night after an argument with my parents.'

'What was it about?'

I hadn't been meaning to tell him so much, but now I've started, it all comes flooding out.

'When we were just kids, she told me something. Something terrible. She said if I ever told anyone, she'd kill herself. The night she died, she thought I'd told her secret to my mum and dad.'

'And had you?'

'No.'

I can see from his face that Mitch is trying to keep up. 'And what was this thing she told you?'

The knot pulls tighter. 'That she'd killed her sister.'

Mitch looks at me in disbelief. 'What do you mean? Wouldn't she have been in prison?'

'She was just a young child when it happened. I think everyone thought it was an accident, but it wasn't.'

'And you know this because?'

The knot eases a little, the space it leaves replaced by irritation. 'I said already, Mitch. She told me.'

'And you believed her?'

'Why wouldn't I?'

Mitch sighs. 'Kids make up all sorts of things for attention. Especially kids who have had their lives mucked up big time. Christ, I should know. I did it all the time. Told the kids in the home that I was the son of a racing driver just because I thought it might give me a bit of kudos. And what about Isabella? She told her teacher that we lived in a house with a swimming pool, for Christ's sake.'

I clutch at his arm. 'It doesn't matter if it was true or not. What mattered to her was that she thought I'd told. She trusted me and when she thought I'd let her down, she hung herself from a tree.'

'Jesus.'

I feel my throat constrict. 'And I'll always feel guilty for that.'

'And you say you never told your parents this secret of hers?'

'No. I never did.' What I don't say is that the thing I told my parents was something worse. Something that could have wrecked someone else's life if I'd been believed.

'There's something else.' I get up and go to the jewellery box on my dressing table. Sliding out the drawer at the front, I lift out the locket I found in Noah's pram and hold it out for Mitch to see. The delicate chain shivers and I realise my hand's shaking.

'It's your locket. Why are you showing it to me?'

'It's not my locket.' Reaching inside my blouse, I take out my own.

'Well, it looks pretty much identical.'

I can hardly bear to say it. 'It's Freya's, Mitch. My mum bought her one when she was first with us and then, when we were older, Freya bought me one the same. I found it in Noah's pram on the twins' first day at school. Someone must have put it there.'

Mitch scratches his head. 'How can you know it's hers? It could be anyone's.'

I want to cry with frustration. 'It's Freya's, I know it. Look… she wrote *sister* on the back.'

Taking it from me, Mitch turns the locket over in his large hand. 'Where? Where does it say sister?'

'There. Look.' I point to the back of the locket.

'It doesn't say sister. It's just a scratch.'

I take the locket from him. I haven't looked at it since that day at the school – feeling that, somehow, it might bring bad luck. Now, I study the marks on the silver and realise he's right. It's exactly what he's said… just a scratch. Yet I'd been so sure.

Mitch folds his arms. 'Are you sure you haven't had that locket all the time? Maybe you just forgot where you put it.'

'You're not listening, Mitch. Freya was wearing it the day she died, and I haven't seen it since that day. I didn't just "forget where I'd put it" as you say – it was in Noah's pram. Someone put it there – don't you understand!' I know my voice is rising, that I'm sounding hysterical, but I can't help it.

Mitch looks worried. He glances at the bedside clock, then takes my hand. 'You were concerned about the girls, tired after not sleeping. There's a simple explanation I'm sure, Kel. But you need to hurry or you're going to be late. We can talk more about this when you get home if you want. Come downstairs with me now and have a coffee before you go. It will steady your nerves.'

Feeling numb, I follow Mitch downstairs. When I reach the hall, I see the children's book bags. They've been placed by the front door with their lunch boxes, ready to be collected on the way out.

Mitch sees me looking and grins. 'See. I can be pretty organised when I want to be.'

Sophie's reading book is on the hall table. I pick it up and manage a smile. 'Oh, yes?'

With an exaggerated sigh, he peels open the Velcro flap of Sophie's book bag to put it in. 'Even superman had to have a day off sometimes. What's this?'

He pulls out a piece of folded paper and holds it out to me. It's a picture Sophie's drawn. Through the kitchen door, I see my daughter chasing Coco Pops around a bowl of chocolatey milk.

'What did you draw for me then, sweetie?'

She looks at me and shrugs. I can tell from her face that she's unhappy I'm not taking her to school today.

The picture is folded in half and I open it up. I'm expecting to see a drawing of Rapunzel, with her long hair, or maybe a face that she'll say is me or her sister. It's neither of these things, though.

On the white page, Sophie has drawn a tree. It's fat and brown with blobs of green for leaves. And it looks just like the one from my nightmares.

CHAPTER FORTY-ONE

Kelly Now

I sit at the back of the church, my eyes fixed on the large photograph of my father that's been placed on the stone windowsill below the stained-glass window. It's an old photo. He's in profile, laughing at something away from the camera and he's just as I remember him. The sandy hair, the aquiline nose, the thin face. I try and remember that once I loved that face.

The place is half-full and I recognise some of the people. A couple of his business friends and their wives, looking the same but a little greyer, a little older. Carly Freeman's parents are there too and someone who looks like she could be Tabby's mum or Ava's. Dad was an only child, and his parents died when I was young, so the only person he has here who still cares for him is the woman who used to be his wife.

My mother doesn't know I'm here. I deliberately left it late to come in so that I wouldn't have to speak to anyone and could lose myself in the row of people at the back. It's only twenty minutes, I tell myself. Only twenty minutes, then I can confront my mother and be gone.

While the service is going on, I stare at the back of my mother's head. Her hair, which is mostly grey now, is still long and wild, and when she lifts her hymn book, I see how the rings cut into her fleshy fingers. She's weeping openly, blowing her nose into a cotton handkerchief. From the way she is, you wouldn't know that my father left her years ago.

As the service ends, I realise I've hardly heard anything the vicar's said. Just the odd word or two: *family man. Attentive father. Sadly missed.* That's because my mind has been elsewhere. Slipping back to a time and place I've tried to lock away – a field of waving grass, the graffiti-covered walls of the firing range, the Gemini tree that I've never been back to but that my daughter's painting has put uppermost in my thoughts.

Phantom places of my childhood.

That's not all, though. On the drive to the village a thought had come to me that I still can't shift. All those years ago, I'd promised Freya I wouldn't tell anyone her secret. Until this morning I hadn't, but now Mitch knows, and I can't get rid of the nagging worry that now I've told him, something bad will happen.

Music is playing, a classical piece I remember my father listening to in his study. It's a cue for people to get up and put on their coats. I'd wanted to challenge my mother about the things that have been happening but now the opportunity is here, I find I can no longer face it. I don't want to be in this place where someone might recognise me. Question me. Dredge up the past.

My mother's letter said there was to be no wake and I'm glad. I've done my bit and can't wait to get back in the car and drive home. I'm not going to speak to her after all. Mitch thought by coming to my father's funeral it might help me come to terms with my past, but he's wrong. If anything, it's just confirmed what I've always known – that I was right to leave it all behind.

Taking out my phone, I send a quick text to Mitch. *Service over. Leaving soon.* His reply comes back almost immediately. *Hope you survived. Me and the little man are watching Loose Women.* I want to laugh, but I don't, not wanting to bring attention to myself. Instead, I put my bag over my shoulder and stand.

As soon as I start to move out of the pew, I know I've timed it badly. My mother is walking down the central aisle, her arm linked with that of a woman I recognise as one of the social workers who once came to the house. I stop where I am, my fingers gripping the back of the pew in front. There's no way I'm going to be able to avoid her seeing me.

As she reaches me, she stops, her face giving nothing away and I feel paralysed. 'You came then.' She turns to the woman beside her. 'Leave us a minute, will you, Mary?'

She waits until the woman has walked away, then buttons her black coat. It's one I remember seeing her wear when I used to live here. It came out every time a foster-child left and went back to their family. It's only now I understand the significance. She was grieving for them – just like she is now for my father.

'I want you to come back to the house with me. It's important.' It's said bluntly, without warmth, and I realise that the years have done nothing to soften her.

While she's been speaking, I've been counting the number of tiles between the pews. 'No. I can't do that. I have to get back.'

'There's something I want to tell you. I should have done it earlier, but the time was never right.'

The church is empty now, the sun shining through the stained-glass window above my mother's head. It's a modern design showing a hill, circled by a crown of trees. It spills green geometric patterns onto the floor and I look away.

'There's nothing I want to hear.'

'Maybe not, but I'd like to tell you all the same.'

My fingernails dig into the soft flesh of my palm and I'm filled with a sense of foreboding. I want to run from this place. Away from *her*. But there's something in the force of my mother's stare that makes me stand mute and waiting for whatever it is she's about to tell me. Despite the years that have gone by, nothing has changed. A part of me still wants to please her.

At last I find my voice. 'It's about Freya, isn't it?'

I watch the colour drain from her face at the mention of her name. 'No,' she says. 'It's not.'

In the years since I've seen her, her plump skin has slackened around her jaw and the eyes are empty. It's hard to reconcile this woman with the one from my childhood – the one whose eyes lit with feverish excitement whenever a new brother or sister was arriving. She's hurting, and despite myself, I can't help but feel sorry for her. In trying to create the perfect family, she sacrificed her own flesh and blood. She's ended up with nothing and now the man she did it for is dead.

'All right. I'll come back, but I can't be long.'

She nods and takes out her car keys. 'I'll see you there.'

I get to the house before my mother does and park in the narrow lane outside. The place hasn't changed. If anything, it seems larger than in my memory. It looks sad. Lost. The small-paned windows mean and black. The thatch heavy and damp-looking.

By the time my mum's old Fiesta pulls into the small standing space at the side of the house, I've almost persuaded myself that I won't go in, but she comes over to the car and knocks on the window. With a sigh, I get out and follow her to the door, standing back to let her open it. Her hand trembles as she tries to fit the key in the lock.

'Here. Give it to me.' Taking the key from her, I unlock the door and push it open to reveal the dark hallway I haven't seen in years. As I step inside, I notice that the wallpaper is the same as when I lived here, if a little more faded. There are two darker patches either side of the door where small hands once rested as shoes were taken off.

'I'll put the kettle on. Make yourself at home.'

Make yourself at home. The way she's said it, you'd think I was a distant relative or acquaintance – not her daughter. Even as a child, I struggled to feel at home in this house. Always felt as though I shouldn't be here. It's the same now. Going into the living room,

I sit gingerly on the edge of the settee. It's where Freya lay the day she got ill, before she left us the first time. I can still see the way she smiled as she slipped my twisted blanket around my doll's neck and held it above her head.

'Tea or coffee?' my mother calls from the kitchen. It's followed by a sigh, as though I'm causing her inconvenience.

'Tea,' I say, a lump coming to my throat as I realise how sad it is that she doesn't know. There are so many things she doesn't know about me.

I try to keep my memories at bay as I wait, craning my neck round to look through the window at the garden where I used to play. Beyond the fence at the back, is the field of wild grass. It can be seen only from the room the foster-children used to sleep in and I get a sudden urge to see it. Watch the seed heads bending against the wind.

I don't move, though. Just wait.

'I didn't know if you took sugar.' My mother places a tray on the coffee table and sits opposite me. As she holds out my cup to me, the teaspoon rattles on the saucer, and I fight to keep my heart hardened to her.

'Are you all right?' I ask.

She looks at me blankly. 'You never expect someone you love to die.'

As I take the cup from her, I wonder if she's thinking about Freya as well as my father. If things had been different, she'd be surrounded by people who loved her. Me, Mitch and the kids… her family. Sophie and Isabella would have made cards to cheer her up and we'd give her Noah to hold, hoping the feel of his little body in her arms would give her comfort.

Instead, there's just me.

'Why do you hate me so much?' I don't mean it to come out. I expect her to look shocked, but she merely looks surprised.

'I don't hate you.' She takes a sip of tea. 'I don't feel anything.'

A wave of self-pity floods through me. 'But why? I tried so hard to please you both, but I could never do anything right. You loved the foster-children more than me.' With a shock, I realise I'm crying. Tears running down the neck of my blouse. Pulling a tissue out of my sleeve, I blow my nose, hating that I've shown this woman my weakness.

She shakes her head sadly. 'It's what I need to explain to you. Why I asked you to come here today. I would have been in contact before, but I thought it might cause trouble.'

'Trouble?'

'It doesn't matter.'

We don't speak. The only sound is the tick of the clock on the mantelpiece. I see that she's moved the photographs that once followed the line of the staircase, onto a table by the window. To my surprise, I see there's a photo of me there too.

'The problem was, I loved my husband too much and had to prove it to him every day. You know there were other women?'

I say nothing in reply. It doesn't surprise me.

'He never particularly wanted to have children, but I thought that if I could just provide him with a child he loved, he'd change his mind. Wouldn't leave me. When you arrived, I was overjoyed.'

The words hang in the air between us and I know what she's telling me. 'I guess my dad wasn't then.'

'No, he thought I'd tricked him, gone behind his back, but by then, it was too late. After you, he was even more distant, refused to share a bed with me. I thought it was because you cried too much… had all the attention… didn't have his eyes. But it didn't put me off – it just made me more determined to provide him with the perfect family.'

If I wasn't hearing it with my own ears, I wouldn't believe it. Can it really be that my mother stopped loving me because my father couldn't?

'But what about me? I was just a child. You can't know how terrible it was not to be loved.'

Her face falls. 'Oh, I know all right. I just thought that if I could find the one child he could love too, everything would work out. But it didn't. It wasn't the happy ending I'd prayed for. Instead, it all went wrong.'

A sob bursts from her, and with a sting of certainty, I know that Freya was that one. Maybe I always knew.

I get up to leave, not wanting to hear any more, but as I'm picking up my coat, a thought occurs to me. 'Why are you telling me all this now?'

She stands and clutches my shoulders with her swollen fingers. 'Because you have what I never had. A husband who loves you and three perfect children. I want to be part of that. A part of your family.'

I stop, my arm half in my coat sleeve. 'What do you mean? What do you know about my family?'

She drops her hands. 'It doesn't matter.'

But I know she's lying. I can see it in her eyes. 'Tell me, Mum. Or I swear I will never come here again. You'll be as good as dead to me.'

'If I do. You mustn't think badly. It was done for the best.'

I sit heavily on the settee. 'I don't understand.'

I watch as she goes over to the sideboard and pulls open one of the drawers. Her hand hovers for a moment and then she takes something out. It's a bundle of letters and photographs. With a sigh she hands them to me.

'I'm sure he meant well, but every letter, every photograph, was like a dagger to my heart.'

With a shock, I see that the photograph on the top is one of Sophie, she's standing beside a border full of tulips, so fair and tiny that she looks like a flower fairy. I remember taking it while we were at the park. The next one is of both the twins. It was the one I took the day they started school, standing stiffly to attention in their uniform, by the front door. There are other photos too.

Ones of them when they were babies and a couple of Noah in his bouncy chair.

'Where did you get these?' My voice is cold. Expressionless. For I know the answer already.

Pulling a letter from the pile, I read it and recognise the handwriting immediately.

Mitch.

CHAPTER FORTY-TWO

Kelly Now

I stand in the doorway of the living room. I haven't even taken off my coat or shoes.

'Why did you do it?'

Mitch knows what I'm talking about. I can see it in his eyes – the seconds of confusion followed swiftly by the certainty. I wonder whether he'll try to deny it or make excuses, but he does neither. Instead, he crouches down beside the play mat and lays Noah on his back beneath his activity gym. Without looking at me, he taps at a red-maned padded lion that hangs from the frame, and watches it swing.

'I take it you're talking about the letters.'

I'd been hoping that the drive home would calm me, but it hasn't. 'Of course, I mean the letters. What else would I be talking about? Unless you mean the photographs you've been sending my mother for the last five years. Five fucking years! How could you, Mitch?' I'm seething with anger. 'I'm just wondering if there's anything else you haven't told me – that you've taken the girls round for tea or asked her to be godmother to the baby.'

'Don't be ridiculous.'

I stare at him wide-eyed, throwing my handbag onto the settee. 'I find out that my husband has been sending letters and photographs to my estranged mother and somehow it's me who's being ridiculous? You shared with her the details of my children's lives – their first day at school, their arguments, their haircuts. You even put in some of Sophie's hair! What were you thinking of?'

'Our children.'

'What?'

'They're *our* children.'

I glare at him. 'That doesn't give you the right to go behind my back. Tell her things that don't concern her.' The room is too hot. My anger making my face glow with a film of sweat. Shrugging off my coat, I sink my head into my hands.

'How could you, Mitch? How could you do this behind my back? Lie to me.'

'I didn't lie to you. I just didn't tell you. I'm sorry, Kelly, but I did it for the best.'

I lower my hands and stare at him. 'The best? For whom, Mitch? Certainly not for me or the children. For all I know, she could have been creeping round our house spying on us.' A coldness pierces through the red anger. 'But of course, this isn't about us at all. It's about you, isn't it?'

I see from his expression that I've hit the nail on the head. He looks at me with eyes dark with pain. 'They're my children too, Kelly. Whatever you might think, everyone has a right to know their family. I know you didn't want your mother to meet them, but I thought if she could just see their photographs. See how great they are—'

'Yes? What then? What did you think was going to happen? That we'd all live happily ever after? Did you really think that what you did would change what happened to you as a boy? My mother is dangerous, Mitch. She ruined my life once before, who's to say she won't do it again.'

Mitch gets up. He stands awkwardly, his arms hanging heavily by his sides. 'I don't know what I thought.'

'No. You never do. You didn't have a proper family, but that doesn't mean you can foist one on our kids. You know nothing about my mother or what she was like.'

Bored with watching the swinging lion, Noah has started to cry. I go over to him and pick him up, trying not to give in to the tears that are stinging my eyes. The smell from his nappy hits me and I stare at Mitch accusingly.

'He's only just done it… honestly. I'll change him.'

Ignoring him, I grab the muslin cloth that's draped over the back of the chair and leave the room. As I go upstairs, I hold my baby close to my chest. My mother knows where we live. It was a long time ago, but I remember, only too well, the lengths to which she would go to have the perfect child.

'Let's at least talk about it, Kelly.'

I don't want to talk about it. Don't want to hear his excuses and explanations. I want to hold my anger to me. Scared that if I look at Mitch it'll melt away as it always does. This time he's stepped over the line.

'I'm going to change Noah,' I shout down at him. 'Then I'm going to collect the girls from school. You do what you want.'

Mitch follows me up the stairs and reaches out to me, but I bat his hand away. He looks hurt.

'Don't be like this, Kelly.'

'How do you expect me to be?' Turning my back on him, I lay Noah on his change mat.

He stands helplessly and watches as I pop open the legs of Noah's little trousers. 'You haven't even told me what happened at your dad's funeral.'

I don't answer. Even if I'd wanted to, I can't form the words to tell him that the man he's talking about never wanted me.

'Well, I'll be out of your way this evening.' His guilt has made his voice belligerent, like a child's. 'I'm going back to work, then straight to the pub. I said I'd meet Maddie.'

It's said as a challenge and I stop what I'm doing.

Without saying anything else, Mitch leaves the room and I hear his heavy footsteps on the stairs. The front door slams. I think of Maddie with her willow-thin body and her dimpled smile. Despite what he told me, I know he's been seeing a lot more of her recently. It bothers me that once I would have been invited too. In the last few weeks Mitch and I have been talking less and I wonder if it's because he's said all there is to say to *her*. I lift Noah's legs and take the soiled nappy from him, then drop it into the yellow plastic bin on the floor.

What does he tell her? Does he talk about our marriage? Our family? And do they laugh at the wife who's slowly going crazy?

Sinking onto the bed, I take a deep breath and try to relax, counting slowly from one to twenty. Something tells me that I need to hold things together if I'm to protect my family.

CHAPTER FORTY-THREE

Kelly Now

The children have been at school for almost two months now and I'm relieved that Sophie has been less reluctant to go into the classroom in the mornings. I've just come back from collecting them and Isabella is sitting cross-legged on the hall floor, her book bag emptied out in front of her. I stare at the scraps of paper, half-finished drawings and sweet wrappers in despair. Even the bookmark, that holds her place in her reading book, looks like it's seen better days.

'Oh, Izzy. You really need to sort that bag out.'

I unclip Noah from his pram and place him on my hip, his little feet kicking at my side. He's grizzling as usual and I force myself not to give in to the frustration that's pushing up through me. I'd hoped that by now he'd have become less demanding, but it hasn't been the case. He still isn't sleeping through the night and although he'll smile and gurgle when the girls play with him, it doesn't take long for the smiles to turn into cries of pain. I look at him now, with his red cheeks, his wet chin causing a rash to develop, and wonder if he's teething.

'You don't need all that rubbish in there, Isabella,' I say wearily.

I open my hand and my daughter empties an assortment of sweet wrappers into it.

'There you are, Mummy.'

'Where did you get all these anyway? You shouldn't be eating sweets at school.'

She looks at me through dark lashes. 'Jack gave them to me. He's my best friend.'

I frown. 'Isn't Jack the one who was mean to Sophie?'

'Yep.'

'Then I don't think he's the greatest choice for a best friend. It would be nicer if you spent more time with your sister in the playground. Try to include her in your games.'

Through the glass rectangles in the living room door, I can see Sophie. Her thumb is in her mouth and she's watching a cartoon. She looks up when Isabella kicks off one of her shoes and it hits the door, then back at the screen again.

'She doesn't need anyone to play with her,' Isabella says. 'She's got Miss King.'

I glance again at Sophie. So fair. So quiet. 'What do you mean?'

'Jack says she's a teacher's pet and she is.'

Taking off the other shoe, Isabella tosses it into the corner. 'It's not fair. She gets to have indoor time when I have to be outside in the cold.'

'I didn't know that.' I make a mental note to ask Mrs Allen about it. 'It's probably because she needs a bit more time to get used to the other children.'

'She's had lots of time. We've been there ages.'

It might seem like ages to them, but it hasn't been all that long really. They've been uneasy weeks, with Mitch and I edging around each other. After the children have gone to bed and it's just the two of us, our dinners have been eaten in near silence. Once it would have been companionable, but now it's awkward. I used to look forward to that time when we could be a couple again. We'd chat about Mitch's building project, our plans for the future or how the girls were getting on at school. We'd laugh at the memory of Isabella's impression of Mrs Allen trying to rap the alphabet or would try to think of ways to make Sophie's classroom experience easier.

But that was before I knew what Mitch had done. Before he'd betrayed my trust. I hate how the bonds that once held us so tight are loosening, but I haven't the strength to tighten them again. Scared of what he might tell my mother next, I've begun to close myself off. I hardly go out at all now, isolating myself from others like I did when I was younger and, apart from when they're at school, I make sure I never leave the children with anyone else. Not now that the one person who can destroy my family is trying to get back into my life.

One of the pieces of paper that's come out of Isabella's bag is a letter from the teacher. I open it and read it. 'That's nice. It says here that next week at school you'll be making lanterns. Mrs Allen wants everyone to design some lovely ones at home.'

'Can we take them with us when we go trick-or-treating?'

I answer without thinking. 'We won't be going trick-or-treating this year, Izzy.'

Isabella stands up, her face outraged. 'Daddy said we could go. We always go.'

'Maybe we'll do something else instead.'

I can't tell her that the thought of the children wandering the streets, knocking on people's doors, unnerves me. Yesterday another *Argus* came through our door. Checking to see that no one was watching, I'd turned to the horoscope page, expecting to see a mark. A sign. But there'd been nothing. My own horoscope had been innocuous enough, something to do with making small changes in my life, but it had been the one for Gemini that had caught my eye. *Reject an impulse for revenge. You may not be seeing things from the same perspective.*

Even if I'd wanted to show it to Mitch, he'd have just said that whoever had put the paper through the letter box that first time had obviously got the wrong house again. He's probably right, but still I can't push the creeping fingers of unease away.

'I don't want to go somewhere else.' Isabella's shaking my arm. 'I want to go trick-or-treating. You're mean. You're the worst mean mummy in the world and the universe and I hate you.'

Through the glass door of the living room, I see Sophie cover her ears.

'Don't shout, Izzy. I'll talk to Daddy about it later.'

Isabella folds her arms and sticks out her lower lip, but at least she's quiet. I'm still worrying how I'm going to address the subject with a husband who I'm barely talking to, when there's a ring on the doorbell.

Moving aside Isabella's book bag, I go to open it, but my daughter gets there before me. Pushing the door wide, she stands back in awe.

'Mummy, it's a policeman.'

There are in fact two: one male, one female. They introduce themselves and I stare at them, my heart pounding, trying to work out why they might be here. My thoughts race haphazardly – is it something from my past that's catching up with me? Freya's secret? My mother? The lie I told?

'Mrs Thirsk, is your husband in?' It's the female officer who speaks. Her face giving nothing away.

'My husband?' I stare at her in confusion. 'No. He's at the building site where he works. I'm not expecting him home for a while.'

'We've just come from there. The foreman said he hasn't seen him since three. Any idea where he might have gone?'

'Has he done something wrong?' I fold my arms, numbers racing round my head. If I count to twenty quickly before she speaks again, whatever it is will be a misunderstanding.

I only get to five.

'May we come in?'

I stand back, the number five stuck in my head. My anxiety high. 'Yes, of course. Isabella, go into the living room and watch some TV with Sophie.'

'But I want to—'

'Now, Izzy!'

She slopes off into the other room and I shut the door behind her, then pick up Noah, his cheek wet against mine. 'Come into the kitchen. Would you like some tea?'

'No, thank you. We won't keep you long, but there are a couple of things we'd like to ask you.'

I place Noah in his bouncy chair, then pull out a wooden chair from behind the kitchen table and sit down. The officers remain standing, which unnerves me even more.

'What would you like to know?' I ask.

'Can you think of any reason why your husband would park his van outside St. Joseph's Primary?'

The school name sounds familiar, but I can't remember why. 'No. What's this all about?'

The policewoman exchanges a look with her colleague. 'A van with your husband's number plate has been seen on several occasions in various locations around the area of the school. Although he hasn't been formally identified, a man fitting his description was spotted hanging around outside.'

I go cold as I remember where I've heard the name of the school. It was in the letter from the headmistress the girls brought home. The one asking us to be vigilant and to talk to our children about the danger of speaking to strangers. To my shame, I realise I never got around to having that talk.

'You can't think that Mitch is doing anything wrong… You can't think…' I stop, nausea griping my stomach. 'Mitch is my husband. I know him.'

But do I? Do I really know the man who for five years sent letters to my mother behind my back? Once, I thought I'd known Freya too, but I never thought she'd do what she'd threatened to do, that night in the woods.

'Please don't upset yourself, Mrs Thirsk. We only want to talk to him.' She holds out a card. 'When he comes home, please ask him to ring this number or call in at the police station. No need to come to the door, we can see ourselves out.'

They leave me alone in the kitchen, my hands gripping the edge of the table. I stay that way until I hear the front door close. Soon after that, the living room door opens. I expected it to be Isabella, but it's Sophie who's standing there.

'Has Daddy done something wrong?' she asks.

'No, darling. Of course not.'

But I'm not sure I even believe that myself.

CHAPTER FORTY-FOUR

Kelly Now

The red tail lights of the police car disappear down the road and Mitch drops the curtain.

'They've gone,' he says.

When Mitch got home, I'd been waiting at the door with the sergeant's card in my hand. Thrusting it at his face as soon as he'd walked in. *For Christ's sake ring this number now, Mitch.*

They'd come round after the children were in bed and we'd gone into the kitchen, just as we had before. This time, though, Mitch was with us, trying to explain away what had happened. It had all been a misunderstanding. The Co-op on the corner was the place he bought his sandwiches from when he was on the way back from the builders' merchants. He'd park down the road to eat them and sometimes he'd get out and stretch his legs before driving back to the site. No, he hadn't given a thought to the fact that the primary school was right opposite.

When they left, they'd thanked Mitch for his cooperation and asked him to come to the station the next day to give a more detailed statement.

He smiles at me. 'Now we can get back to normal.'

My husband is clearly relieved, but I'm not convinced by his story. 'You need to tell me what's going on, Mitch?'

Mitch moves away from the window. 'You heard what I told them.'

'Yes, I heard, but now I want you to tell me the truth. What have you been doing?'

'I haven't been doing anything, for fuck's sake.' Throwing himself along the length of the settee, he rests his feet on the arm. Knowing it will annoy me as he hasn't taken his work boots off.

'Then why have people been making complaints? Given the number of your van?' I point to Isabella's book bag. 'They even brought a letter home about it!'

'You never said.'

'There are a lot of things I don't say. You're hardly ever here. You're either at Maddie's or hanging around schools.'

Pain pinches Mitch's face and I instantly regret the words. Swinging his legs off the arm, he points a finger at me accusingly. 'For your information, I've seen Maddie precisely twice in the last few weeks. Do you have a problem with that?'

I bite back my reply. This is not where the conversation should be going. 'I still don't understand what you were doing over in Whitehawk.'

'You heard what I told the police. It's just some busybody wanting to make trouble.'

I fold my arms. 'It's nowhere near the builders' merchants you use. You've always said the one on the trading estate near there was a rip-off.' I swallow. 'If you've done something, Mitch, I'd rather you told me.'

'There's nothing to tell.'

'It was right by the school.'

Mitch looks at me with naked horror. 'What are you trying to say?'

I'm confused – wanting to believe his version of events but not trusting my judgement. 'Just tell me why you were there, Mitch. The real reason.'

There's the sound of footsteps on the landing above our heads, the flush of a toilet and then more footsteps. One of the girls must have woken up. It's not long before Isabella appears in the doorway. She's taken off the clean pair of pyjamas I put her in and is wearing her favourite Bob the Builder ones from the dirty washing basket. Tucked under her arm, is the rather grubby grey rabbit she always sleeps with.

She scrubs at her eyes. 'I can't sleep. I want a cuddle.'

Usually, one of us would take her back to bed, but I'm surprised when Mitch holds out his arms. 'Come here.'

Isabella goes over to him, her rabbit swinging, his threadbare ear clutched in her fist. She climbs onto his lap, her dark hair falling around her face, and for one traitorous second, I wonder if I should take her from him.

I do nothing, though, watching as Mitch lowers his head to his daughter's, pressing his lips to her hair. Isabella's free hand reaches up to his cheek and pats it; she's always liked the feel of his stubble, and he rocks her back and forward as he used to when she was little. Slowly, her eyes close and his own eyes meet mine over the top of her head. It's then I see he's crying. Big, silent tears that trickle down his face into Isabella's hair.

'Mitch?'

I'm out of my chair, but Mitch shakes his head. When he swallows, his Adam's apple bounces. 'I'll take her back up, then we'll talk.'

When he comes back down, he's composed himself. He sits back on the settee and I wait for what he has to tell me, my heart thudding in my chest.

Mitch runs his hands down the front of his jeans. He stares at a photo of the twins on the mantelpiece, unable to look me in the eye. 'Sometimes I go back to the road where I used to live as a kid. Radnor Road it's called. Number ten.'

Seeing I'm about to interrupt, he stops me. 'I need to just tell you so I can get it straight in my own head. I park the van on the opposite side of the street from the school and stare at the house like I'm an idiot. The place hasn't changed much. They're the same old shabby semis, except that now half of them are pebble-dashed and have satellite dishes.'

'But why do you go there?'

'I don't know really. I think it's because of the letters I sent to your mum. It brought back memories of my own childhood and made me feel sad for the kid I was back then. Since we argued, I've found myself going there more often. Sometimes two or three times a week. Daft, isn't it?'

Unsure of how to answer, I get up and sit next to him, taking his hand in a bid to give him the strength to continue.

'I know that a lot of people have probably lived in that house since I did,' he continues, 'but I still think of it as my home and it's like a magnet pulling me. It's not just the house, it's the pavement where I once did wheelies and the grassy bank by the underpass me and my friends used to roll down. I suppose it's like if I go there, I can change the things that happened. Write a different ending. You see I never saw it coming – being taken into care. One day I was running around the estate as if I owned the place and the next...'

He pinches the bridge of his nose and I know it's to stop the tears that are glistening in his eyes from falling. I don't know what to say. Is this how I felt when I went back to my mum's house after the funeral? I'm not sure it is.

'I'm sorry, Mitch.'

But I can see it isn't sympathy he wants, he just needs to get it all out. As if by telling me about it, the dark hole of his childhood can be filled in.

'My mum used to sit on the doorstep, a fag in her hand. I'd watch her through the open front door, listen to her slurred words and see the tears slide down her face – wanting to wipe them away. Wondering how I could make it better. But of course, I couldn't. I was just a kid and she was a nineteen-year-old girl who didn't know how to cope with life.' He looks at me through tear-filled eyes. 'The woman who came to take me away was called Julie – I remember that. She told me she'd be taking me to a nice place while my mum got better and I believed her. It was a long time before I understood the significance of the tracks on my mum's arms and the baggy jumpers she wore with the sleeves pulled over her hands.'

The anger I felt when I learnt about the letters and photographs is being pushed aside by an unbearable sadness for that little boy. All the years we've been together, Mitch has never told me this. It's been pushed down inside him with the lid firmly closed, because he knows I hate to talk about the past.

But still I feel a niggle of unease. Too many things have been kept from me and I'm starting to feel I don't know my husband at all. 'What did you do when you went back there?'

'Nothing really, just looked. Sometimes I got out of the van and walked around. I hadn't thought about the fact that people would notice – that what I was doing might look weird.'

Getting up, I cross the room and part the curtains, seeing nothing but my face reflected back at me in the glass. Despite what he's told me, I'm disturbed by the urgency of his need to revisit the past. What else might there be that he's kept from me? And if there is anything, could it be something that would put my children in danger?

I turn back to him. 'I wish you'd told me. How long have you been going there?'

He clears his throat. 'A few months. Maybe more. The first time I went, it would have been my mum's birthday.'

'You know you can't go again, don't you?'

'I know.' He presses the heels of his hands into his eyes. 'Christ look at me. I'm being ridiculous.'

'No, you're not.'

'I just wish I'd tried to find her while I had the chance.'

'You still could.'

He shakes his head. 'My mum died when I was fifteen. I pretended not to know what had happened to her because the truth hurt too much.'

'Tomorrow you must tell the police the truth, Mitch. There's nothing to be ashamed of.'

'I suppose so.'

I can tell Mitch wants to talk more, but if he does, I'll have to tell him more about my past too. The lies I told to get rid of Freya, and how it led to her eventual death. It's not something I'm willing to do. Instead, I get up and walk to the door. 'It's late, Mitch. I'm tired.'

He stares at me. 'That's it, is it? I bare my soul and you're going up to bed?'

'Don't be like that. I just don't know how long it will be before Noah wakes up.'

My husband wants absolution for the things he's kept from me: his letters to my mother and now this. But I can't give it to him. After his confession, I should feel relief, but I don't. There are too many question marks hanging over our marriage and I can't shake the mistrust.

Switching off the table lamp, I leave Mitch on the settee and walk into the hall. When I reach the stairs, I hear him call after me.

'And you know what the worst of it is, Kelly?'

I stop, my hand resting on the bannister. 'No?'

There's a coolness to his voice that wasn't there before. 'That when the police were hinting at the reason my van was parked outside the school…' He pauses. 'Don't deny it. There was a moment, just a small one, when you believed them.'

CHAPTER FORTY-FIVE
Kelly Now

The following day, I try to get on with things as best I can, pushing thoughts of the previous day's revelations to the back of my mind. Trying not to care that Mitch spent the night on the settee. I've taken the children to school, changed the beds, done the washing and have just come back from a quick trip to the supermarket to get a few things before the afternoon school run.

Leaving the shopping bags in the hall, I push Charlie away from them.

'No, Charlie. There's nothing for you.'

Dragging Noah's change mat from behind the settee, I change his nappy. He starts to cry and my heart sinks. I'm too tired for this. As I pop up his trousers, I wonder how to entertain him, before remembering the baby bouncer we bought him a couple of weeks ago. He's only tried it out once but seemed to like it – bouncing in the doorway while I did the hoovering. I go and get it, then lay Noah on his back on the floor, slipping his legs into the striped canvas seat and making sure he's secure.

'There you are,' I say, lifting him up and fixing the metal clamp onto the top of the door frame. 'You can have a bounce while I unpack the shopping.'

As I take the food out of the bags and put it away, I can see Noah through the open door, bobbing in the doorway. For once he looks happy.

When I've finished, I pick up the empty Rice Krispies box and some other things destined for the recycling bin and fit the back-door key into the lock. I turn it and press down on the handle but am surprised when the door won't open. Frowning, I turn the key the other way and this time the handle presses down easily. I could have sworn I locked the door before I went out, but obviously I didn't.

I put the boxes in the recycling bin, then go back inside. Noah has managed to twist himself round on the bungee-like cord and the sight of it makes me suddenly nauseous. I'm remembering the wood and the Gemini tree. Freya's foot in the noose of the rope that hangs from its thick branch, her head tipped back. Spinning. Spinning. The rope getting tighter.

Noah gives a delighted squeal and I come back to the present. Fighting the instinct to take him out of the bouncer, I straighten him, then kneel and take his little hands in mine to help him bounce. He gurgles in delight. I've read it's not good to keep babies in bouncers for too long, but another five minutes won't hurt. I'm just glancing at the clock on the mantelpiece to check the time when something catches my eye.

The double glazing is misted as usual, the bottom running with water, but I'm used to that. What I'm not used to is seeing something drawn on the glass. Getting up, I go over to the window to take a closer look.

I stare at it and then my body starts to tremble.

Drawn in the condensation, about four centimetres in height, is a zodiac sign just like the one circled in the newspaper that was put through our door.

Gemini.

I hear my name being called and look up. I don't know how long I've been standing by the window, my forehead pressed to the glass.

It might only be minutes, but I suspect it's longer. For the first time in a long while, my counting hasn't worked and my limbs are frozen. I should be doing something, but I can't remember what it is. The only thing I know is what is in front of me.

Even when I hear the front door bang shut, I don't realise the significance. There are voices in the hall. Charlie barking. Noah crying. I hear it all as if from a distance. I'm not in my little terraced house in Brighton, I'm in the woods with Freya and she won't let me leave.

'Jesus, Kelly. I've been phoning you. Why didn't you pick up? I thought something had happened.'

I can see from Mitch's face that something's wrong, but my mind won't process what it is.

'Mummy! Mummy!' Isabella is behind him, trying to push past.

'Go upstairs, Izzy. Take Sophie with you and you can watch some TV in our room.'

'I don't want her to come, she's stupid.'

Taking Isabella by the shoulders, Mitch turns her around. 'Do as you're told before I change my mind.'

There's the sound of running feet on the stairs and then it's just Noah's crying I can hear.

'You didn't pick the children up. Where were you? When Mrs Allen couldn't get hold of you, she rang me at the site. Jesus Christ, I can't even get into the room.'

Noah is dangling in the striped bouncer that's attached to the top of the door frame. His face is red and angry, his fine hair plastered to his forehead. Only the tips of his toes touch the ground, and with each bounce, he spins around, his cries becoming louder.

'Kelly? Talk to me.'

I turn my head to look at my husband, watching as he crouches down in front of the baby. Gently, he rests him over his shoulder and pulls his legs out of the padded seat. Once released, Noah presses his face into Mitch's neck, covering him in tears and snot.

The crying stops, but the silence is crowded with all the things Mitch wants to say but is holding back.

'How long has he been in this thing?'

I look at Noah and the blood starts to return to my body. 'I'm not sure.'

'Not sure? What's wrong with you?'

Mitch walks up and down the room, his hand cradling Noah's head, and I can see he's trying to make sense of it. The baby's crying again, bumping his head against his shoulder.

'Does he need a feed?' he asks.

'I don't know. Maybe.'

'Do you want me to make up a bottle?' He's looking at me strangely and I can hear the effort it's taking for him to keep his voice normal.

I turn back to the window. 'I'll feed him in a minute.'

'Kelly. What's the matter? You've never forgotten the girls before. Has something happened?'

Without answering, I step back from the window, pointing a finger at the wet glass. 'Look.'

'What?'

'There.' My voice is rising in frustration. 'Can't you see it?'

Mitch leans forward and looks at what I'm showing him. Two horizontal lines separated by two vertical ones, like a roman pillar.

'You know what it is, don't you?'

He throws up his hands in exasperation. 'A gate? A tree trunk? Why are we playing guessing games when our kid's been screaming his head off?'

I jab my finger at the glass. 'It's a sign of the zodiac… Gemini.'

Mitch is looking at me as if I've totally lost it. 'Great. Brilliant. Hurray.'

As he moves away from the window, I grab his arm. I've got to make him understand. He's got to know I'm not making this up. 'I found it when I came back from shopping.'

'What are you trying to tell me? That someone came into our house and drew on our window. Something that could be absolutely anything.'

'It's not absolutely anything. It's a sign. Freya was a Gemini. She hung herself from a tree with two hideous trunks just like this.'

Mitch rubs the top of his head. 'Not this again. Jesus, the girl is dead, Kelly. Are you telling me you believe in ghosts now?' He gives a hollow laugh. 'Or is it just the ones that draw on windows.'

'No. Oh, I don't know. All I know for certain is it wasn't here when I went out, but it was here when I came home.' I'm blinking back tears. 'You have to believe me.'

He lets out a long breath. 'Did you lock the doors when you went out?'

'Of course, I did. I always do.'

'Then you must know that nobody has been in our house.'

But even as he's saying this, I remember how my turning of the key had locked the door, rather than unlocking it.

I grab at the sleeve of his sweatshirt. 'It was unlocked! I remember now.'

Mitch looks down at my hand, the fingers gripping the soft material. 'Are you sure? It wasn't what you said a second ago.'

I look up at him with wild eyes. 'It must have been my mother. She must have come in and...'

'And what, Kelly?' Carefully, he releases my fingers from his sleeve. 'She drives all the way here just to draw something on our window?' He runs a tentative hand down my arm, and I see the effort it takes to keep his voice gentle. Scared of how I might react to what he's going to say. 'Do you think you might have drawn it yourself?'

Upstairs, I can hear the children singing along to some cartoon or other. Noah's damp head is resting on Mitch's shoulder and there's an unmistakeable smell coming from his nappy. The realisation of what I've done is finally sinking in. I've been tired before, worried, but never have I been neglectful of my children.

I was so sure but now doubt is worming its way in. 'Why would I do that?'

'Because you're exhausted. Because your father has just died, and you've recently been back to the place where terrible things happened to you. It's brought it all back. Maybe you were just doodling.'

'Doodling?'

'Yes, like when you're on the phone. Come on. You've got to admit it's possible.'

'I suppose so.'

'But, Kelly, you have to snap out of it. Noah needs you. The girls need you. Maybe you should see a doctor?'

'I don't need a doctor. I just forgot the time. I…'

But there's nothing I can say that will make it better. We both know that what I did was inexcusable.

'Then take some time out. After you've fed the baby, I'll look after the kids and you can go for a run. The fresh air will do you good.' He's talking to me in the slow, patient voice he uses with the children and I know it's because he's unsure of what I'll say and do next.

I massage my temples. 'All right.'

'Good girl.'

Mitch hands Noah to me and looks relieved when I kiss his head.

'I'm sorry,' I whisper into my baby's hair. 'I'm so sorry.'

CHAPTER FORTY-SIX

Kelly Now

The tide is high and there's an ozone smell of sea spray as the waves rush up the beach and burst onto the breakwater. As I run, my blood pulses in my ears, each footfall keeping in time with my counting.

I'm relieved to be out of the house. Glad to be alone with my thoughts.

A vicious gust of wind whips my hair across my face and almost pushes me into the blue railings, but I don't care. Since I saw the Gemini symbol on my window, I've been numb, but the unforgiving weather is allowing me to feel again. Even if it's just the sting of salt on my lips and the bite of the wind on my cheeks.

My feet find their stride and I try to rationalise what happened earlier. I know Mitch must be right. The symbol couldn't have got there by itself, so it was clearly me who put it there. Stressed with Noah's crying, I must have run my finger down the pane while thinking of something else, not realising I was doing it. And it's no coincidence it was the Gemini sign I drew, for since the newspapers came through my door – the ones that were meant for someone else – I've found myself wandering into the newsagent's on my way home from dropping off the children. While June's been busy with customers, I've taken the local paper out of the stand and flicked to the back pages where the horoscope is. Reading both mine and Freya's as we used to all those years ago.

Pulling my sleeve over my hand, I scrub away the tears and carry on towards the West Pier, its naked metal framework bringing back memories of the target frames of the rifle range.

I stop and catch my breath, leaning my arms on the railing and watching the flock of starlings in their aerial show. Swooping and circling the pier, like a storm cloud, before settling to roost. I should turn around and go back but I'm scared to. My home used to be my place of security but now nowhere feels safe. The one thing I've always known for certain is that, in any circumstance, I would do the best for my children. Love and protect them. Today, that didn't happen, and although Mitch hasn't said anything, as I left the house, I read in his eyes what he was thinking. That I'm a bad mother. If he's right that I drew the Gemini sign myself, then I'm going crazy. If he's wrong…

I wrap my arms around my body as Freya used to do. The alternative doesn't bear thinking about.

The waves are turning on the beach, the horizon barely visible where the grey sky meets the sea. I remember the day I arrived in Brighton, desperate to move out of my parents' home but some inexplicable part of my brain preventing me from moving further than the next county. I took the first job I could get in a club under the King's Road arches and, almost immediately, the tension that I'd lived with for years, started to ease.

That first evening shift was a long one, not finishing until three in the morning. As I'd collected the last of the glasses and started to wipe the tables, I'd tried not to think about the fact that I had nowhere to stay. Nowhere to sleep that night. If one of the other girls hadn't taken pity on me, I might well have been joining the homeless in their sleeping bags beneath the pier. It was just a sofa bed in her small living room, and she'd made it clear it was only until I got myself sorted, but it was better than the alternative.

And it was certainly better than living at home in the weeks and months after Freya died. For, even when she was no longer there, the wheels kept turning and it became clear that the thing I told my parents the afternoon of her death was not going to go away. Of course, I feel bad about it now – know what harm I could have done if I'd been believed. However much I hated my maths teacher, he didn't deserve the hell I must have put him through.

The school was quick to act. Mr Seymore was questioned and had denied everything. The evening I'd said I'd seen the two of them at the rifle range he'd been at a departmental meeting. It was my mother who'd told me that. She said I was a liar and that everyone knew it. It was Ethan Jackson Freya had been with and now she was gone because of my jealousy.

From that day on, my mother talked to me only when she had to. Every day, I heard her crying behind her bedroom door and who could blame her. Her daughter was a liar and the child she'd loved the most was dead. Freya became a taboo subject and they never even told me when the funeral was. I didn't care; I just wanted to forget Freya had ever existed.

When I was moved to a new school, St Hilda's, I felt nothing but relief as, if I'd stayed where I was, I'd have been treated as a pariah. I'd sit in lessons, in my stiff uniform with its long, pleated blue skirt and blazer, and invent a better life for myself. Telling the girls I lived in a modern house on some smart estate. Foster-children didn't feature in my fantasy life and I had a mum and dad who loved me. I didn't care about the white lie as I was never going to be inviting them back.

Each day, after the bus dropped me back in town, I'd shut myself in my room and count down the months and years until I could escape. I might as well have been dead myself.

When my father left, a few months after Freya's death, I wasn't surprised. It was clear she'd been the only thing keeping him at home. But, for my mum, it was like being bereaved all over again and I'm ashamed to admit I was glad. Because now she'd know what it felt like to be unloved.

As soon as I was old enough, I left the miserable house with its low thatched roof and never went back… until Mitch decided to interfere in my life, that is.

It's getting dark now, the West Pier silhouetted against the indigo sky. It's beautiful, and in other circumstance I'd appreciate it more, but my head is too full of memories. I know I've not been coping well since giving birth to Noah and it's affected the way I've been thinking. Mitch isn't the only one who wants to help a lonely child come to terms with what happened. I'm beginning to think that the only way I'll be able to lay this ghost to rest is by going to see my mother again. I'll tell her the truth about what happened the night Freya died and, when she's heard me out, I'll confront her with the things that have been happening recently. Tell her she's to stay away from me and my family.

With a last look at the pier, I set off for home. When I reach the crossing and wait for the lights to change, I'm no longer looking for a flash of blonde hair through the windscreens of the waiting cars. It's as though a weight has lifted and that's because I've made a decision. The right decision.

Without looking back, I run the quickest way home. I'm eager to tell Mitch what I've decided, but when I reach the front door, I see him through the window. He's pacing the room, his mobile pressed to his ear. His face is like thunder.

As I let myself in, I hear Mitch's raised voice. He's stopped pacing now and is sitting on the arm of the chair, his mouth set.

'Sue me for what, for fuck's sake,' he shouts into the phone. 'If it wasn't for me, he wouldn't even have a job.'

'Daddy swore,' Isabela says, enjoying it immensely. 'He said the F-word.'

I shush her and, taking both girls by the hand, usher them into the kitchen where I fix them a drink. When Mitch is angry, having children in the room will not make him regulate his colourful vocabulary. While Isabella chats about her day and I put the kettle on, she climbs onto the worktop, even though she knows she's not allowed. By the time I've noticed, she's drawn a smiley face on the misted window.

'This is like the sticker Miss King gave Sophie. It's not fair – she has twenty million stickers on the chart and I've only got five.'

'I'm sure that's not true, Izzy. Anyway, you shouldn't be drawing on the windows, it will leave a mark.' I stare at the face she's drawn, remembering the symbol that I saw on the window of the living room. Maybe I have the answer to the riddle.

'Izzy, have you ever drawn something like this?' I draw two vertical lines down the window, adding a horizontal one top and bottom.

She looks at me as though I've asked her to wear something pink. 'Why would I do that, Mummy? It's stupid. It's not even a picture.'

Not wanting to be left out, Sophie clambers up too. Twisting round, she copies what I've drawn, then looks to me for approval. Now there are two Gemini signs side by side.

'What about you, Sophie? Did you draw this on the living room window?'

She shakes her blonde head, and in that small gesture my hope that it might have been one of the children melts away.

Pulling my sleeve over my hand, I quickly rub the pictures off, not wanting Mitch to see. I know he thinks I'm making things up and, with the mood he's clearly in tonight, I don't want to make things worse.

It isn't long before he comes into the kitchen and throws the mobile on the table.

'Little shit!'

'Mitch, don't,' I say, nodding towards the children.

'The bastard's only gone and injured himself.' He presses his fist against his forehead.

'Who? Who's injured themselves?'

'This new kid, Dale. I asked him to fix a loose hoarding. It's something even an idiot could do, but he fucked up. It fell on him and damn near knocked him out... or so he says. Threatening to sue me for compensation.' He sinks down on one of the kitchen chairs, the colour draining from his face. 'Christ, if that isn't all I need.'

He's looking at me, waiting for me to say something reassuring. But I don't.

All I can think about is going to my mother's tomorrow and what I'm going to say to her.

CHAPTER FORTY-SEVEN
Kelly Now

My mother's house is colder than I remember it being when I was a child. Reaching behind me, I feel the radiator, but it's not on and it occurs to me that, after my father left, she may very well have been short of money. It's not something that I would have known or even cared about but now I find that, just as I did on the day of the funeral, I'm feeling sorry for her.

Noah is asleep in his car seat on the settee beside me. I had to bring him as, even after what happened yesterday, I don't trust anyone else to look after my child. I hadn't wanted my mother to touch him, but when she'd been unable to hide her delight at seeing her grandson for the first time, I'd reluctantly given in and allowed her to hold him. As she'd walked up and down, whispering endearments, I'd had to close my eyes against the pain. Her loving voice was the one she'd saved for the foster-children. I don't remember her ever using that gentle tone with me.

My mother has made tea. The cups sit between us on the coffee table, but neither of us have drunk any. I haven't told her why I'm here yet and it's as if the quiet room is waiting.

'You wanted to talk to me.' It's a statement, not a question. Resting her hands on her plump knees, my mother waits for me to speak.

I fold my arms across my body, then unfold them again quickly as the action brings back memories of Freya. Even though she's the reason I've come here today, the image in my head of the frail child who I'd once longed to be my sister, is not going to help me with what I have to say.

I clear my throat, scared that the words I've been practising in the car will seem trite and heartless.

'I've been thinking about this for a while and there's something I need to tell you about Freya. About the night she...' I stop, unable to say the words.

'I see.' My mum looks away. It's impossible to know what she's thinking.

'What I wanted to say was that I wasn't honest about what happened that night.' I force my eyes to meet hers. 'I saw it all. I knew where she'd gone, and I followed her—'

'But you *did* say.'

I shake my head in frustration. 'Just hear me out, please. I thought if I could just get there in time, I could stop her.'

Freya's body hangs limp before my eyes. Her face mottled.

My mother's fingers tighten around the handle of her cup. 'But you didn't.'

'No. I didn't tell you at the time because I was too scared of what I'd seen. I was ill. Frightened. I didn't know what you'd do if I told you the truth.'

I hear again the raised voices, Freya screaming. See her empty bedroom.

My mother's face is impassive. 'You're not telling me anything new and I really don't see why you feel the need to bring this up now.'

I carry on as if I haven't heard her. 'She'd taunted me with it enough times. She was obsessed. To begin with, I thought she was crying wolf, but that night, I was in no doubt she'd do it. I think she wanted me to find her. To shock me. Later, I went back to bed and told myself that when I woke up, it would all have been a dream. But of course, it wasn't.'

My mother puts down her cup, some of the tea spilling into the saucer. Her hand hovers near her heart. 'Despite everything, I still miss her. If only things could have stayed as they were.' She looks away. 'The girl was troubled. I'm sorry you had to find her like that… with that boy.'

I close my eyes in frustration. 'I'm not talking about that. I'm talking about what she did later. It was all my fault. Freya wanted to punish me.'

My mother's eyes snap back to mine. 'Punish you? For what?'

I hesitate, wondering how much to tell her. 'When Freya was ten and I was eight, she told me a secret… about her sister. She made me promise I'd never tell anyone, but she thought I'd told you. It was why she did it.'

My mother shakes her head. 'It was no secret, Kelly. What happened to Freya's sister was common knowledge at the time.'

I can't believe what I'm hearing. 'You mean all the time she was living with us, you knew?'

'Of course I knew. We had several meetings about it, and it was in her notes. I would never have been allowed to foster her if I hadn't been fully informed. They chose us because they knew we were used to providing a home to the more difficult cases. That nothing could shock us.'

'You have to tell me, Mum. What did Freya do to her sister?'

With effort, my mother heaves herself out of her chair. She goes over to the photographs and picks up the one of Freya. I realise too late that she's heard the desperation in my voice.

'Will you bring the girls to see me?'

I don't want to bring them here. Don't want to subject them to my mother's twisted idea of love.

'Why would I do that after your pathetic attempts to scare me? Don't think I haven't worked it out.'

She traces Freya's image with her finger. 'I've no idea what you're talking about.'

Outside, the wind has picked up. It forces itself against the sash windows, making them rattle. It's like it's tired of pushing down the grasses in the meadow and wants to get in. It makes me shiver.

'You know what, Mum, don't tell me. I don't care any more. I'll take Noah home and you'll never see any of us again.'

My mother puts down the photograph and shrugs. 'Please yourself.'

I put on my coat and pick up Noah's car seat, but there's one last thing I need to tell her before I go. Something that's been on my conscience. 'You know, my only regret is that if I hadn't run away from that place, gone home and pretended to be asleep, I might have been able to save her.'

Even as I'm saying this, I know it's ridiculous. What could I have done to help her? What would I have used to cut her down?

I don't know what I'm expecting from my mother. Forgiveness? Absolution? I get none of these things. Instead, she's looking at me as though I'm mad.

'Why are you talking about Freya as if she's dead?'

I stare blankly at her, clutching Noah's car seat to my chest. She's still speaking, but her voice is phasing in and out like a radio that's not tuned in properly. I can't take in what she's saying. I try to answer, but numbers are filling my head and floating away again to leave the number twenty. Twenty. Twenty. Twenty.

At last, I find my voice. 'Because she is.'

She stares at me, her eyes unblinking. 'Whatever makes you think that, Kelly? Freya's very much alive.'

CHAPTER FORTY-EIGHT
Kelly Now

'I don't know what you mean.' I'm finding it hard to process what my mother has just told me. Freya is alive? How could she be? What sort of sick joke is this?

'Are you all right?' My mum starts towards me, then thinks better of it and sits down. Instead, she begins to talk again, and although I want to scream at her to stop, I don't. A little voice in my head is telling me it's important to hear what she's got to say.

'For many years, Freya was dead to me as well, but that's hardly surprising after what she did.'

As I put the car seat down, Noah opens his eyes, but I haven't the strength to pick him up. I can't take anything in. I feel numb. Stupid. Freya's alive and I don't know whether to laugh or cry. 'What did she do?'

'She wanted to have your father to herself, of course. Wanted him to love her more than he did me. I didn't know they would connect as well as they did, and I couldn't let that happen.'

'But you said that's what you wanted. You were going to adopt her.'

She looks at me, wild-eyed. 'Can't you see? When you told me you'd seen her at the rifle range with the teacher, I knew she had it in her power to take him away from me. She was someone who could break up families.'

I feel a flood of guilt for the lie I told. 'I'm sorry.'

My mother looks at me sadly. 'You don't need to be. I phoned social services and said I wanted her removed immediately. That I'd made a mistake and the placement wasn't working – though it nearly broke my heart to do it. Even when the truth came out, I knew in my heart what she was capable of. I'd wanted to believe she was a good girl... but they all turn out rotten.'

Noah is twisting in his seat, fighting the restraints, and I unclip the harness and place him on my lap, my heart thumping against his back. Freya's... alive. How could that be? I'm finding it hard to breathe.

My mother has got up – she's pacing the room, picking things up and putting them down again. 'When she knew she was leaving, she shouted and screamed, showed her true colours, but then she laughed in my face. Said I was a sad old cow and it was no wonder Andrew didn't love me. When she'd been cleaning, she'd snooped in his office and seen things she shouldn't have – knew about his indiscretions. I'd thought Freya would be the glue that bound your father to me, but I was wrong. In the end, she drove a wedge between us. The irony was, Freya turned out to be the child your father loved like his own after all and he never forgave me for making her leave. I lost him as well.'

I won't feel sorry for her. I can't. Because all the time I'd been living in that house too, wanting what little love they had to offer. 'And that's why she wasn't there in the morning. You said nothing. How could you not tell me you'd sent her away? Why was everything in our lives such a great secret?'

'I thought it would be easier for everyone.'

A pulse is leaping at the base of my throat. 'But I thought she was dead, for Christ's sake! How could anything be worse than that? And you wouldn't speak to me. Made me change schools.' Noah has started to cry. Lifting him from my lap, I carry him to the window.

'If you'd stayed in that school, you'd have been crucified for the lie you told. I had no choice.' She's joined me at the window, though there's nothing much to see – just the rain running down the glass and the leaden grey sky that sits heavily above the distant curve of the downs.

'I wondered if maybe I'd been wrong all these years putting my efforts into creating the perfect family. That if I just spent some quality time with your father, it might make a difference.' A tear trickles down the side of her nose and she wipes it away with the back of her hand. 'Of course it didn't and when he finally left me, it broke my heart.'

I hear the desperation in her voice. She wants me to understand and I realise, with a start, that we are not so very different. In our own ways we'd both been reaching out for a love that this man could never give us.

'She came back, you know,' she says, drawing her finger down the windowpane. 'I came home one day and found her sitting in the living room. It was a shock after all these years. She hadn't changed much – a little thinner maybe. I told her to leave. That she shouldn't be here.'

'What did she want?'

Noah is still grizzling. My mother reaches out her arms to take him and I don't stop her. She meets my gaze over his downy head. 'She wanted to see you.'

'Me?' A nub of fear lodges in my throat.

'Of course I told her you hadn't lived here for years. That I never saw you and had no idea where you were living now.'

My eyes dart around the room as though Freya might still be hiding in some corner. Where did she sit? Was it where I had been sitting?

My mother has asked me something and is waiting for my reply, but I haven't been listening. I'm counting in multiples of twenty. Over and over. It's okay, I tell myself. You're safe. Nothing will happen. I've reached my target and breathe deeply before asking her to repeat the question.

She's frowning. 'I was asking why you thought Freya was dead. You never told me.'

Her words hang between us and I don't know how to answer. I close my eyes, trying to remember that night. The rain that plastered my hair to my face. The lightning that turned the bare branches of the trees to negatives. The sleeping pill I took. The darkness that robbed me of one sense but heightened another, leaving my imagination to fill in the missing details. To create a story that could never have happened.

Another gust of wind rattles the window and whines down the chimney.

I bury my head in my hands remembering my anger. My jealousy. It had given me the courage to lie to my mother. Then, later, it overrode my ability to think rationally. My thoughts were wild. Skewed. My emotions overblown. I thought I knew where Freya had gone that night. That she was punishing me… but it was all in my head. I was never that important.

I remember how I'd gone in search of her – calling her name as I struggled up the slope towards the line of trees on the ridge. Clothes soaked. Breathing ragged. As the woodland had closed in around me, I'd stumbled along the path. The light from my torch picking out leaves and branches. Twigs catching at my hair. Unable to rid myself of the terror of being alone in the wood.

When the lightning had lit up the clearing, turning the swollen trunks of the Gemini tree white, I'd closed my eyes, then turned and vomited into the undergrowth.

I know now that there had been no body swinging from the rope that hung from its branch. In that flash of light, I'd imprinted what I wanted to see. It was just my imagination. My guilt.

'It wasn't real.' I lower my hands and look at my mother but of course she doesn't know what I'm talking about.

It wasn't real. These are the same words I say to Isabella when she makes up a story or to Sophie when she's woken from a nightmare. I want to believe that I've woken from a nightmare too, but I haven't. For I know that somewhere out there, Freya is alive.

She's been trying to get my attention.

She's seen my girls.

I see the imprint of her hands on Noah's buggy.

And it's like someone's walked over my grave.

CHAPTER FORTY-NINE
Kelly Now

I don't go straight home. Instead, I sit in my car and try to get my heart rate back to normal. Glad that Mitch has said he'll pick up the girls today in case I'm late back. Behind me, I can hear the jingle of Noah's giraffe rattle as he shakes it, then the sound of it hitting the floor as he loses his grip. In a minute, he'll start crying and I'm strung so tightly I don't think I can take it if he does.

Freya is alive. She's been back here, to this place where it all happened. Except it never did happen and that's what I'm trying to get my head around. Fifteen wasted years, living with the guilt of having not told anyone what I saw. Fifteen years spent hating myself for the lie that caused her death.

Was it Freya who put the locket in Noah's pram? It would explain a lot, but my mother swore she hadn't told her where we were living, and I believe her. I'd seen a look in her eyes when she spoke about Freya that I recognised. Fear. She knows as well as I do how unpredictable she was back then. What if she still is?

Switching on the engine, I pull away from the house. Through the rear-view mirror, I watch the thatched roof of my childhood home disappear around the bend in the road and relief washes over me. But it doesn't last long. Freya is out there somewhere, and she holds a grudge.

I drive on autopilot, my mind jerking from thought to thought. My knuckles white against my skin where I'm gripping the steering wheel too hard. Noah is quiet now and it doesn't seem any time at all before we've reached the outskirts of Brighton. While I've been driving, it's been getting dark, the street lights have come on and the roads are getting busier. I decide that the quickest way to get home is to leave the main road and drop down through the residential streets until I reach the seafront. It should only take a few minutes, but this evening the traffic is slow and, as I follow the line of traffic along the street, I realise why. I'd forgotten it was Halloween and families are out in force.

When I reach a pelican crossing, I stop to let a group of parents cross. One has a pushchair – a toddler dressed in a pumpkin outfit fighting his restraints. Another ushers a gaggle of witches and ghosts across the road, giving me a wave of thanks as the last one crosses. They're heading for the house on the other side where lanterns adorn the porch and a pumpkin grimaces from the window.

I carry on, relieved that I made the decision not to let the girls go trick-or-treating this evening. On a night like this, I want to know they're safely home with me.

At the seafront I turn left, but as I do, I realise my mistake. The cars are hardly moving. Not only that, the atmosphere has changed. The parents and young children I saw earlier have been replaced by teenagers. Some are walking purposefully along the promenade in the direction of the Palace Pier, but others have formed into large groups that spill onto the road. Instead of the devils and witches' costumes of the younger children, their outfits take on a more sinister note. One youth is dressed as Freddy Krueger. Another wears a bloodied apron, an imitation chainsaw in his hands. They barge against each other, jostling for position on the pavement, and from the sound of their loud voices and the bottles in their hands, it's clear they're in for a long evening of drinking.

As I get closer to the pier, the crowds thicken, and the traffic comes to a standstill. Someone wearing a clown outfit, his mouth a bloodied gash, jumps in front of the car and shouts an obscenity through the windscreen, shrieking with laughter at my shocked expression. His friend grabs him by his arm and pulls him away, but it leaves me shaken. I feel as though I'm in a house of horrors… only this one has no walls. It's unnerving and I don't want to be here.

And all the time, I'm searching for a face in the crowd. One that scares me more than any ghost or corpse bride.

I'm searching for a girl who's risen from the dead.

Searching for Freya.

CHAPTER FIFTY

Kelly Now

When I eventually get home, I'm surprised to find the house in darkness. Opening my bag, I rummage inside it but can't find my keys. I groan as I picture them in the dish on the hall table and ring the doorbell. There's no answer and I realise I'll have to get the spare front door key from the garden shed. Leaving Noah's car seat on the doorstep, I run round to get it, deciding, as I do, that there's no need to mention my forgetfulness to Mitch.

The house is silent when I let myself in. Putting Noah's car seat on the hall floor, I switch on the light.

'Mitch? Girls?'

When there's no answer, I go into the kitchen and try the back door. It's locked as it always is when we are all out. Where are they? It's as I'm going back to get Noah out of his car seat that I see the note on the kitchen worktop, my name scrawled in Mitch's untidy hand. I pick it up and read.

Taken the girls out trick-or-treating. I know you didn't want me to, but it didn't seem right when everyone in their class was going. We won't be late, and we'll bring you back some sweets if you're good.

Balling the note in my fist, I throw it across the room. How dare Mitch take them trick-or-treating when he knew full well how I felt about it? And how could he have been so stupid as to have fallen for Isabella's 'hard done by' story? But of course, Izzy would have known he would. Would have been waiting for her opportunity to coerce him the minute I wasn't there to say no.

Unbuckling Noah from his seat, I take him into the living room and lay him on his play mat. Then I go to the window and look out to see if Mitch and the girls are coming back. As I do, I can't stop my eyes from flicking to the mark that's still visible on the pane. The Gemini sign that won't completely disappear until I clean the glass properly. I'd allowed myself to be persuaded that it was me who drew it, but there's still a niggling doubt.

I turn back to the empty room. Without Mitch and the children, the house feels different. Empty. I think about checking the door again, then stop myself.

Picking up the television controller, I perch on the edge of the settee and flick thought the channels, but there's nothing I want to watch. The local news shows the seafront in Brighton where I've just been. It's packed with people wearing Halloween costumes, and as the reporter speaks to the camera, he's jostled and jeered at by the crowd. One reveller, in a hangman's outfit, dangles a noose in front of the reporter's face before running off.

With a shiver, I point the controller at the television and turn it off, then go into the kitchen to make myself a mug of coffee. As I wait for the kettle to boil, guessing how many seconds it will be until until the switch clicks up, I catch sight of my reflection in the rectangle of glass in the back door. For the first time, it occurs to me that anyone standing in the garden would see me too.

Moving over to the door, I double-check it's locked, and pull down the blind over the glass. Then I pull across a kitchen chair and do the same with the windows, checking each handle in turn to make sure they're locked. When I'm satisfied that everything is secure, I take my mug back into the living room and repeat the process with the windows in there, tugging at the curtains after I've closed them to make sure there are no gaps. All the while I'm doing this, something is bothering me, but I can't put my finger on what it is.

Outside in the street, life is going on without me: footsteps running along the pavement, a car's horn blaring, and every now and again, there's the shriek of an excited child. I've never liked Halloween – it reminds me too much of the films Freya made me watch when my parents were out. Nasty ones with 18 on the cover that gave me nightmares. I don't like the children being out there.

I look at my watch. It's only eight thirty, but the stress of the last few hours has taken its toll and I'm desperate for sleep. Deciding to take the opportunity to have a nap, I pick up Noah and carry him upstairs. When I've fed and changed him, I lay him in his cot and wind up his mobile to lull him to sleep.

I lie down on the quilt and close my eyes, but sleep won't come. Instead, I think about what my mother told me, wondering how Mitch will take the news. Will he reassure me, as he would have done once? Tell me Freya is no threat. Help me put it all into perspective. Or will he look at me the way he does when Isabella tells one of her tall tales? If I didn't know it to be true, I wouldn't blame him if it was the latter.

The Gemini symbol on the windowpane, the newspapers that came through the door with the horoscope circled, the locket that might or might not be Freya's. All of it sounds made up and when I tell Mitch Freya is no longer dead, I'm frightened he'll lose what little patience he has left.

Folding my arms over my eyes, I tell myself I'm being ridiculous. Every marriage goes through a rough patch and this is ours. We'll get through it. I just need to pull myself together. I've been stuck in the house with a baby too long – maybe it's time to consider going back to work.

*

I must have dozed off, as when I look at the clock again, it's almost nine. Mitch and the kids should have been back a long time ago. I've just started to message him when I hear the door slam. Relieved, I swing my legs off the bed and go downstairs. Maybe, once the children are in bed, I'll pour us both a glass of wine and tell Mitch that, despite everything, I really do love him.

Isabella meets me halfway up the stairs. Her zombie make-up smudged. The bottom of her costume edged in mud splatters.

'Goodness, Izzy. The state of you.'

She takes my hand and leads me down. 'We had the best time. We lost Sophie and Daddy had an argument with a man with a bullet through his head. I wasn't scared at all, was I, Daddy?'

She throws a look at Mitch who's standing below us in the hall, his hands in the pockets of his donkey jacket. Daring him to disagree.

My hand freezes on the banister. 'What do you mean, you lost Sophie?'

Resting one hand against the wall, Mitch takes off a shoe and places it neatly in the corner before taking off the other. Normally, he leaves them where they drop – just like the children. I take it as a sign of guilt.

'I asked you a question, Mitch.'

He looks up at me. 'It was nothing… You can see she's fine. It's not as bad as it sounds.'

'You took the children out when you knew I didn't want you to. You lost a child and then you say it's nothing?' My fear has been replaced by anger.

Isabella is watching us with interest, but Sophie's curled up on the settee, her face hidden behind her hands. The black cat costume she's wearing makes her look tiny. Her legs in their black tights birdlike. Going to her, I bend down and stroke her hair. 'No one's cross with you, Sophie. I just want to know what happened.'

Mitch follows me in. 'Look, she saw her teacher and thought she'd go and say hello. End of. It's no big deal. Nothing happened. She's here, isn't she?'

Isabella is tugging at my jumper. 'Daddy nearly hit the man with the hole in his head. And he swore at him. He thought he'd taken Sophie and put a bullet through her head too because he's a little shit and is trying to take Daddy to the dry cleaners. He wanted to have a fight with him.'

'Isabella! Ignore her, Kelly. She's just overtired.'

'I am not.' Isabella is seething with indignation. 'You said, "I'll fucking kill you." I heard him, Mummy. He really did say it.'

'That's enough!' Grabbing her arm, Mitch drags her up the stairs and I watch him in disbelief. He's never been rough with either of the children before.

Sophie is crying, leaving trails down her white face paint. I kiss away the tears. 'Don't cry, Sophie.'

Mitch comes back downstairs. He throws himself lengthways onto the settee and puts his feet on the arm. 'It was that little bastard, Dale. The one who's trying to fleece me. Told his solicitor he'd had concussion, but there was nothing bleeding wrong with him.'

I put my hands over Sophie's ears and Mitch grimaces. 'Stop mollycoddling her, Kelly. She should never have run off like that.'

I stare at him in disbelief. 'She's five. You should have been looking after her.'

'After yesterday, that's good coming from you. I only took my eyes off her for a second. Maddie was showing me…' He stops and fiddles with his wedding ring.

'Maddie? What was she doing there?'

'We bumped into her. Okay?'

'You just happen to bump into her and then you're so engrossed in what she has to say that you don't notice your daughter's gone.'

'You're being ridiculous.'

'*I'm* being ridiculous? That's your answer to everything. What is it about Maddie that's so fascinating, Mitch?' I hate the way I'm sounding, but I can't stop the words from spilling out. 'Is it her wonderful conversation or is it something more obvious than that?'

Mitch is on his feet again. 'You're unbelievable. You really think that me and Maddie—'

I glare at him. 'Don't tell me that in all these years you haven't thought about it.'

'If I told you I hadn't, would you believe me?' His voice is tight. Turning away from me, he goes into the hall. He yanks his coat back off the hook and puts it on.

Sophie struggles from my arms and runs to him, wrapping her arms around his legs. He looks down at her, then gently extricates himself. 'You go up to bed now, Soph. It's late.'

I force a smile. 'Yes, go up, poppet. I'll come and tuck you in in a minute.'

With a backward glance, she climbs the stairs and I watch her, glad that she always does as she's told. When she's out of earshot, I turn back to my husband.

'Where are you going?'

There's a challenge in his eyes. 'I'm going for a drink.'

I grab his sleeve. 'Don't, Mitch. Stay and we'll talk about it.'

His voice is frosty. 'Talk about what? How you don't trust me?'

Grabbing his keys from the pot by the door, he lets himself out.

'What time will you be back?' I call after him.

He doesn't reply.

CHAPTER FIFTY-ONE
Kelly Now

I wake at three, not knowing what's dragged me from my restless sleep. I thought I heard something, but now I'm sitting up listening, there's nothing. The house is silent, even though there are three sleeping children within its walls.

Mitch's side of the bed is empty. He hasn't come home and I feel as if someone has taken my insides and rung them out. It doesn't take a genius to work out where he is. Even though I know there'll be nothing there, I check my phone to make sure he hasn't sent me a message. He hasn't. The screen is blank.

I'm lonelier than I've ever felt before, without Mitch I feel untethered, but my greatest need is to see the children. Pushing back the duvet, I pad across the room and step out onto the landing. The twins' door is ajar, which is unusual as they like to have it closed – Isabella worrying that the zombies might get her if I leave it open. Pushing the door wider, I peer in. Isabella's bed is under the window and Sophie's is nearest the door. I go over to it, but in the soft glow of the nightlight, I see that it's empty.

I step back, my hands pressed to my mouth, my body tensing, but then I see what I didn't before. In the bed by the window are two little shapes, not one. Sophie must have crept into her sister's bed. The covers are thrown back and they're lying with their arms around each other, their foreheads touching. It takes me back to the night Freya came into my bed, the day after she was ill. I remember the press of her body against mine, how her heart beat against my chest.

I shiver.

Even though the valve on the radiator is turned to four, the room feels chilly. I stand looking at my children, one so dark, one so fair, and rub at my arms to warm myself. In my bedroom, Noah is sleeping too. It's just me awake and somewhere Mitch is sleeping in another woman's bed.

Needing to feel the warmth of someone's body, I tiptoe over to Isabella's bed and push back the cover further. I lift Isabella's arm from around her sister's body and scoop Sophie into my arms, burying my face in her hair. She moans, then wraps her arms around my neck and I cover her face in kisses soft enough not to wake her.

Outside the girls' room, the landing is in darkness. It's the first time I've spent the night alone with the children and I don't like it. Usually, if I get up, I hear Charlie's feet on the kitchen floor as he pads to his water bowl or the jangle of his collar as he shakes his head. Our body clocks in sync. Tonight, though, there's no sound from downstairs.

Sophie murmurs something in her sleep and, with a last kiss, I lay her in her own bed, pulling the covers up over her shoulders so that just the collar of her Dalmatian pyjamas is showing. They're the ones Mitch chose for her on one of his rare shopping trips. The overwhelming agony comes suddenly. Crippling my body. Doubling me up. What if Mitch doesn't come home? What if he leaves us?

Lying next to Sophie, I hold her close, no longer caring that I might wake her. Part of me wanting to. I've just started to count the rise and fall of her breathing, letting it soothe me, when I hear barking. It sounds as if it's coming from the back garden.

Getting up, I go to the window and look out. The security light is on and, running up and down the small paved patio, is Charlie, his sharp yaps surely waking everyone in the street. Unable to think why he's out there, I run downstairs, stopping when I reach the kitchen. It's freezing down here and, when I switch on the light, I see why. The door is wide open. Stepping outside into the cold night, I grab Charlie's collar and drag him back inside, before slamming the door shut.

I'm certain I locked the door after Mitch had left for the pub. Looking at the windowsill, I see the key with its green fob in the place I always leave it after locking up. I stare at it, as though it will give me the answer. Did I take it out and put it there without locking the door first?

Snatching up the key, I stab it into the lock and turn it, then stand with my back against the door. Charlie looks at me and whines, sniffing my hand as though I might have a treat in it. When he finds I haven't, he slinks off to his bed.

I want to text Mitch. Tell him that I'm scared and want him to come home. But I know what he'll say. He'll tell me I must have let Charlie out, then gone to bed and forgotten him. That's if he even answers his phone. I try to remember. Could this be what I did? I was certainly upset when Mitch left the house for the pub. But even if I did leave Charlie out there, wouldn't I have heard him earlier? And why was the door wide open?

A horrible thought occurs to me. What if someone broke in? What if they're still in here and I've locked them in with us? My heart starts to race. I know I should check, but I can't move. Instead, I slide down the door and crouch there with my arms around my knees. The clock on the wall says three fifteen. If I keep watching the minute hand until it reaches three twenty, everything will be all right.

It's where I still am when Isabella comes into the kitchen. She places a hand on my head. 'What are you doing, Mummy?'

Knowing I'm in danger of scaring her, I push myself up. 'I couldn't sleep, darling. Charlie was barking and I was just checking on him.'

She rubs her eyes with her fists. 'Can I have a drink?'

'Yes, of course you can. You go back to bed and I'll bring one up.'

'Can't Daddy sleep either?'

'No,' I say, feeling my heart ache at the mention of him. Will he be sleeping or will something else be keeping him awake? Or somebody.

Isabella goes back upstairs; the central heating has kicked in and the house is starting to feel normal again, but still I'm on edge. While I've been asleep, the back door of my house had been wide open. Anything could have happened. Anyone could have come in. Climbed the stairs. Looked in on my sleeping children. The extent of our vulnerability pushes my thoughts to Mitch. He left us alone when things got difficult. Blamed me for being suspicious, then found solace in that woman's bed. He put me last. He's no better than my mother.

Isabella's drink forgotten, I run upstairs and grab my mobile phone from the bedside table. Without stopping to think what I'm doing, I find Maddie's number, punch it in, then wait.

Eventually, Maddie answers, her voice groggy with sleep.

'Yeh?'

'I want you to tell me what you're playing at.'

'I'm sorry, I don't know what you—'

I hear a man's voice in the background. 'Who the fuck's calling at this hour?'

At first, I think it's Mitch but then I realise the voice is too high. Too young. I recognise the voice. It's the musician Maddie was with the night of her dinner party.

Maddie's speaking again. 'Is that you, Kelly?'

Cutting the call, I throw the phone onto the bed. Panic gripping me again. Not only do I not know how Charlie got to be outside, I now have no idea where Mitch is.

CHAPTER FIFTY-TWO
Kelly Now

When I wake the next morning, the radio that acts as my alarm is telling me it's going to be a cold day with a chance of showers. Feeling for my phone, I see it's nearly eight and as I put it back down, the enormity of the night before hits me. Mitch still hasn't come home, and I don't know where he is.

I want to bury myself in my duvet, block out the light and make everything go away, but I can't. I have Noah to feed and the girls to get to school. If we don't hurry, they're going to be late. From the other side of the room, I can hear Noah's mobile playing its tinkling tune. One of the girls must have wound it up for him. Grateful to whichever one it was, I get out of bed and slip on my dressing gown.

Noah is lying on his back, his comforter clutched in his fist and his eyes glued to the cars and buses that turn circles above his head. When he sees me, he smiles and waves his arms, waiting to be picked up.

'Good boy,' I say, lifting him out. 'You must be hungry.'

Trying not to let my worry about Mitch overwhelm me, I feed and change him, then go to see what the girls are doing. Their door is still closed. Pressing down on the handle, I open it to find them both asleep.

In my room, the mobile is still playing its tune. I look over my shoulder at the open door and then back at the twins. The curtains are thin, as Sophie doesn't like the dark, and there's enough light to see the gentle rise and fall of their little chests.

Blood drains away from my body and the tiny hairs on my arms raise. With no one to wind the mobile up, how is it possible that it's turning?

Holding Noah tightly to me, I carry him downstairs. The first thing I do is try the back door, but it's locked, the key on the windowsill where I left it in the early hours of the morning. The windows are locked too. Moving to the living room, I open the curtains and try the French windows, but they're also secured.

I don't like it. Upstairs the mobile is winding down, its tinny tune becoming distorted as it slows. I don't want to go back up there, but I have to wake the girls. I remember how when Freya had first come to us, I would wake to find her in my room, watching me. Her pinched face white and ghostly. I hadn't been scared but would pull back the duvet to let her in. I can still feel the tightness of her arms around me as I fell back into sleep. Had someone stood and watched me last night?

I might not have been scared then, but I am now. Things are happening which I can't explain, and Freya is no longer a child but an adult. One with a grudge.

I'm just wondering what I should do, when the sun moves from behind the cloud, flooding the living room with light. I hear voices from the girls' room, a burst of laughter, and my shoulders relax a little. I've got to keep a grasp on reality. Isabella will be telling Sophie about the trick she's played on me. How she'd tiptoed into my room, pulled up a chair and wound up Noah's mobile. Pretending to be asleep when I looked in on them. I'm just jittery from my disturbed night and my worry over Mitch. I've got to stop overreacting.

Leaning an arm over the banister, I call up the stairs. 'Isabella. Sophie. Time to get up.'

When I hear the thump that means they've got out of bed, I go back into the kitchen to make their breakfast. By the time they come downstairs, their hair messed and their cheeks pink with sleep, I've almost persuaded myself that the things that happened in the last few hours are the products of an imagination running overtime.

I'm just pouring milk onto the girls' cereal, when my phone rings. If I'd expected it to be Mitch, I'm disappointed. It's a number I don't recognise. The ringing stops, then starts again. I stare at it, too scared to answer. What if it's my mother calling me? Before I'd left her house, I'd given her my number, telling her she must call me if Freya tried to get back in contact. But after this morning, I've decided that if anything's happened, I don't want to know.

'Who is it?' Isabella asks, milk dripping from her spoon.

'Nobody. Just a wrong number.'

Trying to put everything that's happened in the last few hours to the back of my mind, I let the girls finish their breakfast, then take them upstairs to get dressed. As I pass my bedroom, I see Mitch's dressing gown slung on the back of the chair. I swallow down the lump that's formed in my throat. I've got to carry on as normal for the children. I close the door, thankful that his early starts at the building site mean they're used to not seeing him in the mornings.

We're just leaving the house when my phone vibrates in my pocket to let me know I have a message. I'm scared it's going to be from the unknown number, but it's not. It's a reminder to take Isabella for her ear appointment at the hospital. With a jolt, I realise I'd forgotten.

I bump the pushchair down the step and close the front door. When I turn back, I see someone standing at the gate. It's Mitch, and at the sight of him, a wave of mixed emotions floods through me: relief, love and anger at having put me through a night of worry. He looks tired and dishevelled, his clothes rumpled, and as the children run to him, I study his face for traces of guilt.

The girls fling their arms around his legs, asking why he's come home, but I hold back, waiting for him to speak. To apologise. But instead, he runs his hand over his head.

'Was it you who phoned Maddie?' he asks bluntly.

My face flushes with embarrassment as I remember my 3 a.m. call to her house phone. I want to deny it, but I've paused too long. It's all he needs to know it was me.

'I didn't know where you were.'

'So you presumed I was at Maddie's, even though I'd already told you there's nothing between us. Never has been. When she rang this morning to see if Sophie was all right after last night, she told me about the phone call. I guessed it was you.' He shoves his hands into his pockets. 'Why couldn't you have trusted me?'

'Because you didn't come home, Mitch. I was worried sick. Where were you?' There's a heartbeat's pause and I see him struggling with himself. I feel sick. My voice drops to a whisper. 'It wasn't Maddie, but you *were* with someone, weren't you? Christ, you smell of drink.'

Mitch looks meaningfully at the twins who are staring at us. 'This isn't the place to talk about it, Kelly.'

'Then where is?' I can't help the sarcasm creeping into my voice.

Mitch blanches. 'Don't be like that. I *was* with someone, but you've got the wrong idea. I was drunk and angry and there was this girl in the pub with her mates. She saw I was a bit down and asked what was wrong. She was interested in *me*, Kel – not some goddamn person from her past.'

'Go on.' With sickening certainty, I know where this is leading.

'We had a couple more drinks, and I'm not proud to admit it, but there was a moment when I was tempted by her offer to go back to her flat.'

His words are a blow to my heart. 'You were tempted?'

'Look. I didn't go, all right? When it came to it, I couldn't do it. I knew what it would do to you and the kids. It's you I want to be with, Kelly, but at the moment, you make it so bloody hard.' He rubs the small of his back. 'I slept in the site office and I think I've done my back in lying on those chairs. So you see, Kel, it wasn't what you were thinking.'

I don't want to hear any more. My heart is already breaking into a million pieces. 'You don't know what I'm thinking, Mitch. You never do, because you never ask.'

I push past him, the wheels of Noah's pushchair scraping against the gatepost in my haste to get away. 'Come on, girls, we're going to be late.'

'Wait, Kelly. Let's at least talk about it.'

Ignoring him, I carry on walking. There's nothing he can say that I want to hear.

CHAPTER FIFTY-THREE
Kelly Now

I don't look behind me but walk as quickly as I can, staring straight ahead to stop the tears from falling. A numbness has crept over me and I don't want it to go. Scared of what I will feel if it does.

Isabella's running alongside the buggy, complaining that her legs are aching, but Sophie has her hand on the white pram handle, as she always does. As she walks, she's reciting something under her breath. A rhyme, I think. I don't take much notice at first, too caught up in my own thoughts, but then the words filter into my consciousness.

I don't realise I've stopped walking until Isabella pulls on my sleeve. 'Why have we stopped?'

I collect myself, inhaling deeply, then bend down to Sophie. 'Where did you learn that rhyme, Sophie?'

She looks up at me, startled. Wondering if she's done something wrong.

'I know it too,' Isabella shouts, not wanting to be left out. 'Here's a tree in summer. Here's a tree in winter. Here's a bunch of flowers. Here's—'

I turn on her. 'Shut up!'

Isabella stops, shocked, and tears form in her eyes. Immediately, I hug her to me. 'I'm sorry. I'm sorry. I didn't mean to shout. It's just that I need to know where you've heard that rhyme.'

She looks up at me, her eyelashes wet with tears. 'Sophie taught it to me, and Miss King taught it to her.'

'Miss King?' I turn to Sophie. 'Wasn't it Mrs Allen you were with when you lost Daddy last night?'

Isabella answers for her. 'No, it was stupid Miss King.'

'Is that true, Soph? Did you leave Daddy to talk to her?'

Sophie nods miserably. 'She waved to me and I went to see her. You told us not to talk to strangers, but she's not a stranger. She's my teacher.'

It's with me again, the feeling of unease. 'It's all right, darling, I'm not cross, but I'd like to meet Miss King.'

Her face lights up. 'She helps me in the classroom. I like her.'

'I know you do, sweetie. Mrs Allen told me. But I've never met her. Maybe I'll pop in and have a chat with her when I drop you off. Find out how she thinks you're doing.'

Sophie nods her head vigorously. 'She's the best teacher in the school.'

Isabella looks at her in disgust. 'That's because you're a teacher's pet.'

'That's enough, Izzy.' We're nearing the school now and I'm thankful that we don't live too far away. There are usually cars parked outside in the street, but most of these are gone. We must be really late. Running the last of the way, we cross the playground and reach the classroom, breathless.

I push open the door and see that the children are all mostly in their seats. Leaving Noah directly under the window where I can see him, I usher the children in.

'I'm so sorry, Mrs Allen. It isn't the girls' fault we're late. We've had a few problems at home.'

Mrs Allen puts down the register and gives me a sympathetic smile. 'Please don't worry, Mrs Thirsk. These things happen. Is it anything I can help you with?'

'Not really, but I'd like to have a word with Miss King, if that's possible.'

She shakes her head. 'I'm afraid not. She's part-time and isn't in this morning. Is there something you'd like to ask me instead? Is it about Sophie?'

I feel a mixture of frustration and relief. 'No, don't worry. I can talk to her another time.'

'She's in this afternoon. You could come a little earlier and see her when you pick up Isabella later.' She flicks through her desk diary. 'I've got it down that you'll be picking her up at two. Is that right?'

'Yes, that's right.'

'Marvellous. I'll make sure she's ready.'

Blowing a kiss to the girls, I close the classroom door and go back to Noah. Before we leave, I check my phone. There are several missed calls from the number I saw earlier. I stand in the playground and stare at the screen, wondering whether I should ring back or not. Then, as if possessed, my finger presses the number.

My instincts were right. My mother answers straightaway and immediately she speaks, I can tell she's not well. She sounds strange. Breathless.

'Are you all right?'

I hear her forcing the breath into her lungs. 'I don't know. I'm finding it hard to breathe.'

'How long have you been like this?'

'Since last night.'

I look around me, wondering what I should do. 'I'm sorry, Mum. I'm at the school. Have you phoned the doctor?'

'I don't want to waste the doctor's time,' she gasps.

I press the phone to my ear, feeling the plastic case dig into my skin. Why has she rung me? Surely there's someone else she could have contacted. Friends. Neighbours. With a jolt, I remember Mrs Ringrose and her papery skin. The smell of roses. I don't even know if she's still alive.

My mother's coughing and I feel a pang of guilt. I make a snap decision.

'I'll be there as soon as I can.'

I end the call and text Mitch. *Please can you take Izzy to her appointment? My mother's not well and I think I should go and check on her.*

The reply comes back quickly. *Of course.*

I put my phone away and wheel Noah through the empty playground. I'll go to my mother's house, but it's not just because I need to know she's okay. It's because I know now what it is that's been bothering me. Something I should have asked her before.

CHAPTER FIFTY-FOUR

Kelly Now

The door opens on my first knock. My mother's standing in the hall. She has her outdoor coat on, and the buttons are straining over her stomach.

'What are you doing here? You're lucky to catch me as I've only just got in. Still, I suppose it's good of you to come. You haven't brought the baby today then?'

I shake my head. I'm not going to tell her how difficult it was for me to leave him. 'No, he's with my neighbour. I wasn't sure what I was going to find when I got here.'

She looks puzzled. 'What you were going to find?'

Stepping into the hallway, I close the door behind me. 'You're obviously feeling better, but I wish you'd let me know. It would have saved me a journey.'

My mother takes her coat off. She hangs it in the hall cupboard, then stands with her swollen hands on her hips.

'What was it you said you wanted?'

I feel my nails digging into my palms. 'It was you, Mum. You called me. You said you weren't well so, idiot that I am, I came to check on you. Though you look pretty okay to me.'

'Well, you're here now. I suppose you'll be expecting me to make you lunch or something.'

'I don't want lunch, Mum. I want to know what's going on. Why did you call me this morning if there's nothing wrong?'

My mother sighs. 'I didn't call you, Kelly.'

'You did.' Clicking the green phone symbol on my mobile, I find my recent calls and shove the phone under her nose. 'See, there it is.'

She takes the phone and looks at it. 'What time was this sent? I can't see without my reading glasses.'

'Earlier this morning and then again just after nine.'

She hands me back the phone. 'That would have been when I was having my bath and then, as I told you, I've been out.'

'And your phone. Where would that have been?'

'In my bag, I suppose.' Her brows draw together. 'Oh, no, I remember now. I left it downstairs to charge. Why are you asking me all these questions?'

'Because if it wasn't you who phoned me, it was someone else.'

My mother walks over to the window and looks out. 'That's not possible.'

But I'm becoming more certain that it is. The thing that's been worrying me – I have to ask her about it.

'That day you found Freya sitting in your living room. How did she get in?'

She turns to look at me. 'I don't know. I never thought to ask her.'

'Christ, Mum. Someone breaks into your house and you don't think to ask them how they did it?'

'She didn't break in. There was no forced entry.'

'Then how—?' But I know the answer already. So many times, when Freya and I were teenagers and my mother was knocked out on sleeping tablets, we'd have to let ourselves in using the spare key. 'Where do you keep it, Mum? The spare key. Is it still in the shed?'

'There was never any need to move it. It's useful if I go out and forget my handbag.'

'Freya knew where that key was. She'd used it enough times to let herself in after she climbed out of the window at night. But of course, you wouldn't have known that, would you? You were too busy thinking of her as the perfect daughter. Except, you forget, she wasn't your daughter, was she, Mum? I was.'

Mum's phone is on the side. A white charging cable lies beside it, one end plugged into the socket. The other end is no longer in the phone. 'It was Freya who rang me this morning. She let herself in, then made out she was you.' I remember the coughs and the rasping breathy voice she'd used to disguise her own. 'She wanted me to come here... but why?'

'I don't know.' My mother moves away from the window. It's the first time I've seen her look troubled. 'There *is* something, though. It's upstairs in the meadow room.'

'What sort of thing?'

She blinks. 'It's easier if I show you.'

Gesturing me to follow her, she leads me to the staircase. It's years since I've climbed these stairs and I'm not sure I want to. But I have to know. Maybe it will be a clue to where Freya is and what she's doing.

My mother pushes open the door to the room that used to belong to my foster-siblings. It looks the same as it did the last time I saw it, as though Freya has just popped out. It's as if my mother's kept it as a shrine and I shiver.

'It's this.' My mum points to the window. 'I came in to look for something and I noticed it.'

I look where my mum is pointing. Just like our windows at home, the glass is dappled with condensation and, in the middle of it, someone has drawn what looks like a letter M. 'You think Freya did this?'

She looks down at her hands. 'I think she might have.'

'But why a letter M?' I look at it again. On the right-hand side of the letter, an extra loop curls in on itself. I've seen this somewhere before, and as I remember where, the small hairs on my arms rise.

'I know what this is, Mum. It's the astrological sign for Virgo.'

She moves closer to see. 'Why would she draw that on the window?'

'Because she wanted me to see it. She drew something like it in my house and she knows I'll know what it is.' My fingers reach out to touch it, then jerk back again. The image is fresh. Freya must have been in this house recently, but if my fears are correct, she won't be here now.

'I don't understand.'

I don't answer her. My thoughts are running wild. My twins are Virgos and it's a message to me. Freya knows about them and she wants me to know it.

CHAPTER FIFTY-FIVE
Kelly Now

'She saw the photos of the girls Mitch sent to you, Mum, and read the letters too, I expect. I need to see them again.'

Leaving my mother standing in the empty bedroom, I run downstairs and into the living room. I pull the drawer completely out of the sideboard and empty the contents onto the floor, then kneeling beside it, spread them out until I find the ones I'm looking for. There is the photograph of the twins in their school uniform, the name of the school clearly written on the badge of their sweatshirt. Another shows them on the Palace Pier and there's even one of them on their scooters that's been taken outside our house. The number 27 almost, but not completely, obscured by the pyracantha that's growing beside the window.

A deep-rooted fear is taking hold. 'Oh, Mitch. What have you done?'

It wouldn't take an idiot to work out where we lived. What school the children went to. With heart-stopping clarity, I see myself taking the spare key from the top of the door frame in my garden shed. Why hadn't I chosen a different place to hide it? I know now I haven't been imagining it all. It isn't just my mother's house Freya's let herself into... it's mine.

Everything's starting to make sense now. The symbol on the window, Noah's mobile, the back door that had been left open. Putting the photograph down, I feel my panic rise, and as I hear my mum's footsteps on the stairs, I start to count. If I can get to twenty before she comes into the room, everything will be all right.

'Please tell me what's going on, Kelly. You're not making any sense.'

I've reached my goal and feel myself relax a little, but I haven't time to explain now. I need to go to the school and make sure the girls are okay. I won't be happy until I've seen them.

Leaving the letters and photographs on the floor, I run into the hall and pick up my coat. Checking my phone, I see there's a missed call from Mitch, but I haven't got time to ring him back. I can't focus on my husband right now; this is more important. In minutes, I'm in the car, retracing the journey I made only a short while earlier. As I drive, I think of my Sophie. So tiny. So fair. It would have been how Freya looked when she was that age. With certainty, I know that she's in danger.

At the roundabout, as I come off the A27, a car is slow to pull away and I press down hard on the horn, eliciting a black look from the passenger of the car on my right. 'For Christ's sake, get out of my way!'

I'm breaking the speed limit and just have to hope there are no police cars around at this time of day. Freya knows where my daughter is. She could have seen her in the classroom. She could have been waiting. Watching.

Either side of the road, the trees have started to lose their leaves. A rhyme comes into my head. *Here's a tree in winter. Here's a tree in—*

Bile rises to my throat. Miss King taught Sophie that rhyme. Miss King who I've never seen and who wasn't in school this morning. Is it possible? A worse thought hits me. Mrs Allen said she'd be coming in this afternoon. I press my foot on the accelerator, knowing I'm driving dangerously, but I can't help it. I have to get there as quickly as I can.

When I reach the school, I park the car on a yellow line outside the gates and run in. The playground is empty and I race across it, my bag thumping against my leg. Breathless, I arrive at the twins' classroom door and fling it open. Mrs Allen is in the reading corner, the children gathered around her. When she hears the bang of the door against the brickwork, she looks up, surprised.

'Mrs Thirsk. Isabella's already been collected. Your husband said you knew?'

'Yes, of course, but it isn't Isabella I want to see, it's Sophie.' Frantically, I scan the children but can't see her. Thirty-odd pairs of eyes stare up at me, but I'm too wired to care. 'Where is she? Where's Sophie?'

'Please calm down. Sophie's fine. She's with Miss King in the special needs room. She's helping her with her reading.'

'I need to see her. It's important.'

Mrs Allen looks unsure, but it's obvious I mean business. She points to the door that leads into the corridor. 'It's the first door on the right, Mrs Thirsk, but I can see you're upset. Why don't you wait here a while until you feel a bit calmer?'

I look at her as though she's mad. 'You don't understand. I need to see her now.'

Pushing past her, I open the door to the corridor. Along its length, classroom doors lead off it on both sides, but luckily, the room I'm looking for is clearly marked. As I barge in, I'm not sure what I'm expecting to find but it's not this: Sophie is sitting at a large table, her head bent to a reading book. She looks up and a smile lights up her face when she sees me.

'Mummy!'

'Sophie. Come with me now.' My voice is too loud, too high-pitched, but I don't care. I need to act fast.

Pushing back her chair, she runs over to me and flings her arms around my legs. 'Why are you here?'

I'm almost crying with relief. Bending my head, I kiss her hair. 'You're safe. Thank God.'

'Is everything all right?'

I'd been so relieved to see Sophie, I hadn't noticed the young woman at the other end of the room. She has a sheet of coloured stickers in her hand, which she replaces in the packet she's holding.

'This is my mum,' Sophie says, dragging me over to her.

'Delighted to meet you, Mrs Thirsk. I'm Miss King. Mrs Allen said you wanted to see me. I've just been giving Sophie a sticker for brilliant reading.'

The young woman who comes towards me with extended hand is petite with thick, dark hair tied back in a scrunchy. She can't be more than about twenty.

Suddenly, I want the room to open up and swallow me. How could I have been so mistaken? Jumped to the wrong conclusion. This girl couldn't be less like Freya if she wanted to be. I'd been so sure and now I'm not sure about anything.

Apologising for barging in, I leave. My face burning. There's nothing for me to do except go home.

As I walk along the corridor, I remember Mitch's call. Taking my phone out of my bag, I see he's left a voicemail.

Kelly, I've been held up. The shit's hit the fan. That kid, Dale, reported what I did to him and I need to get some legal advice. I managed to get an appointment at the solicitor's, but he's running late. Is there any way you can collect Isabella for her hearing test after all? If I don't hear back from you, I'm going to have to ask Maddie to collect her and drop her off to me at the solicitor's as it's on the way to the hospital.

I stare at my phone, then throw it back into my bag. I've heard the message too late. My day is going from bad to worse.

CHAPTER FIFTY-SIX

Kelly Now

I'm just passing reception on my way out, when Lorraine, the school secretary, calls to me.

'Mrs Thirsk. Could I have a word?'

'Of course. If it's about me barging into Mrs Allen's classroom, then I'm sorry but it was an emergency.'

Lorraine swivels her chair away from her computer and looks at me through the sliding glass panel. 'It isn't that. I just wanted to talk to you about our policy for picking children up from school.'

I'm not sure why it's me she wants to talk to. 'Yes, what about it?'

She takes off her glasses. 'It's just that, even with permission, we don't really like children being collected by adults they aren't familiar with.'

'I understand that.' Now, I'm very confused. 'But why are you telling me this?'

'Because of Isabella's ear appointment. Luckily, she's a confident little girl and didn't seem to mind being collected by someone she hadn't met before, but I expect it would have been a different story if it was Sophie. We do prefer it to be someone the children know who picks them up although, obviously, there will be times when—'

'No, it's fine,' I interrupt her. 'Maddie's a family friend. Isabella's known her for most of her life.'

'That's what your husband said when he rang to give permission, but Isabella looked a little unsure when she came to pick her up. Can you confirm her name is Maddie Parker?'

'Yes, that's right.'

'That's fine then. That was the name she gave.'

My phone's ringing again. Maddie's name flashes across the screen. I hope there's not a problem. 'Excuse me, do you mind?'

Lorraine shakes her head. 'Go ahead.'

As I answer, the memory of my embarrassing call last night presses down on me. 'Hello.'

'Oh, I'm glad I caught you, Kelly.'

'Why? Is something the matter?'

'Yes, there's been an accident on the A259. I'm stuck in a jam and nothing's moving. A police car went by about five minutes ago and I can see the lights of an ambulance behind me, so it doesn't look as if I'll be going anywhere for a while. I'm really sorry but I haven't even got to the school yet. I thought I should let you know.'

A sick feeling rises inside me and I grip the edge of the counter for support. 'You mean you haven't picked Izzy up?'

'No, I told you. I don't think I'm going to be able to get there. I'm really sorry.'

Jesus.

Ending the call without even saying goodbye, I bang on the glass of the receptionist's window. 'Are you sure Isabella's definitely been collected?'

Lorraine looks up and frowns. 'Yes, I'm certain. I saw her leave.'

I look out of the double glass doors that lead onto the playground. Desperate to be wrong. Scared to ask the question. 'What did this woman look like?'

'I thought you said you knew her,' she says pointedly.

'Please, just tell me.'

Lorraine closes her eyes as if trying to conjure up a picture. 'She was tall and quite thin, like a model actually. Very striking.'

'Her hair. What colour was her hair?'

'It was unusual. Very pale… almost white. She was wearing a black coat and a blue scarf. What is this all about, Mrs Thirsk?'

I don't answer. It's what the woman who gave me the tree survey leaflet was wearing, on the children's first day at school. The same day I found the locket in Noah's pram.

It's Freya.

Mitch mentioned Izzy's appointment at the hospital in one of his letters to my mother. It's how she knew. There's no doubt in my mind the woman who killed her own sister has my child. I slide down to the floor, my head cradled in my hands, and break down in tears.

'Mrs Thirsk. What's happened?' Lorraine is beside me, her hand on my shoulder.

I look up at her with wild eyes. 'Phone the police. Please hurry. My foster-sister has Isabella and I'm not sure what she's capable of.'

'And her name is Maddie?'

'No, Freya,' I shout at her, as though she's mad.

'Please sit down and I'll get you some water.' Taking my arm, she helps me to my feet. 'I'm sure it's just a misunderstanding.'

I brush off her hand in frustration. 'It's not a misunderstanding. She pretended to be Maddie to get to my child. She's unstable. Ring the police now. Please.'

Lorraine looks uncertain but goes back into the office and picks up the telephone. She watches me as she speaks.

'Yes, police please. It's Lorraine Jarvis from Longways Primary. I'd like to report a possible child abduction.'

CHAPTER FIFTY-SEVEN
Kelly Now

The police say they'll send someone straightaway to take a state-ment, but as the minutes go by, I become more agitated. Scenes from my past come back to me. Freya leaning with her back against the wall of the rifle range, her long legs stretched out in front of her, the vodka bottle between us. Freya up against that same wall, my first crush, Ethan, pressed against her. Freya telling me her awful secret.

The tea Lorraine has brought me sits untouched on the low table next to the chair I'm sitting on. This area is meant for visitors, not for mothers who have just lost a child. The head teacher has been to see me and is now talking to Mrs Allen and Miss King. Mitch is on his way. The police are on their way. Everyone is doing something except me.

I can't just sit here and do nothing when my child needs me. My guilt is like a physical pain. All these years I've worried about Sophie. Fussed over her. Loved her more than her robust sister because, in some strange way, she reminds me of the little lost girl who arrived at our door when I was just eight. My motherly instincts have been skewed by parents who didn't want me and by those few short weeks when Freya was my sister. When I needed someone to love me.

If it had been Sophie who'd had the ear appointment, she would never have gone off with a stranger. Her nervousness would have kept her safe. But Isabella, my feisty, fearless little daughter who will talk to anyone – of course, she was the perfect choice. And Freya would have known that. When Mitch had written his letters to my mother, full of those choice things he thought were safe to say, he wouldn't have known who else would read them. That one day these same words would put my daughter in danger.

Taking out my phone, I write a short message to Mitch, telling him where I'm going, then pick up my coat and hurry to the door. When I reach the car, and start the ignition, I wonder if I'm doing the right thing. Maybe I should wait for the police and try and explain, but if I do, it could be too late.

It's the second time I've driven this way in one day, but this time there's an urgency to my mission that wasn't there before. The only thing I can think about is getting back to my mother's house. It's where Freya will have taken her. I just know it.

It's getting dark by the time I arrive at the house, but there's a light on in the kitchen window. I see my mother at the sink and bang on the glass. She looks up, startled. Realising she can't see who it is who's banging, I go to the front door and call through the letter box.

'Mum, it's me, Kelly. Open the door. It's important.'

The door opens and I push past her. 'Where is she? Where's Isabella?'

She folds her arms. 'I don't know what you mean. Why would she be here? Without you?'

Every nerve in my body feels stretched to breaking point. 'Because Freya has her. I don't have time to tell you everything, but have you seen anything odd here at all? Any cars in the road you don't recognise?'

My mother shakes her head. 'No, but this came through the door earlier. I thought it rather strange.' She lifts a newspaper from the sideboard. 'I don't have my paper delivered, but someone pushed it through my letter box.'

I snatch it from her and tear at the pages, throwing them aside until I get to the one I want. The horoscope page has been marked, just as I knew it would be. The Gemini symbol circled in red ink.

The words themselves are innocuous, something to do with needing to be more assertive and being more capable than you realise, but it's the symbol itself that's the message.

'When we were teenagers, Freya spray-painted her sign of the zodiac on the wall of the rifle range. She's telling me where she is, Mum.' I think of the leaflet that was shoved at me the first day at school, the beech tree with its spreading branches. 'All this time, she's wanted me to know she's found me. She left me clues, but I let Mitch persuade me it was all in my head.'

'But why wait?' My mum sits heavily in the chair. 'Why not just come up to you? Speak to you directly?'

'I don't know. I think she was biding her time. Waiting until she could take my child. Where she's taken Izzy is important. She wants me to go after her.' Running to the back door, I unlock it. 'If Mitch comes, tell him where I am.'

The torch is on the shelf in the same place it's always been and I grab it, then let myself out, slamming the door behind me. My fingers fumble with the latch on the side gate, but eventually I manage to open it. It's years since I've been down this lane and just as many years since I entered the meadow. This time there's no fever to insulate me from the growing cold. It's just me and the darkness: the biting wind stinging my eyes, the swell of the downs rolling like waves in an angry ocean and the knowledge that out there somewhere is my daughter.

This evening, the moon looks almost full. It picks out the tips of the grass in silver as it writhes and undulates in the wind. There's no need for the torch, but the grass is thick and coarse in places, conspiring to trip me, and I have to look down at my feet as I run through it. My phone is ringing in my pocket, but I don't stop to answer it. It will be Mitch asking me what the hell is going on. He'll want to know why I didn't wait for the police… where I am. If I stop to answer, I'll be wasting time.

The frozen meadow feels endless, the downs behind it never seeming to get any closer. My fingers are numb with cold and my coat is too thin, but I have to keep going. I think of Izzy in her uniform. The raincoat she's wearing instead of her winter coat because she got it muddy and it's in the wash. She will be shivering. Her cheeks red with cold. I stifle a cry. My baby's in danger and it's all my fault.

My phone is still ringing. Insistent. Demanding. Stop it! Stop ringing me! As I drag it from my pocket, it slips out of my bloodless fingers and onto the frozen ground. With every ring, the number flashes. It's not Mitch, after all. It's a number I don't recognise. I press 'accept' and wait, my breath coming in gasps. Maybe it's the police. Maybe they're ringing to tell me that they've found Isabella and she's at home with Mitch and Sophie. That I've been mistaken. It's all just been an innocent mix-up.

It isn't, though. The voice on the end of the phone is one that sends a chill down my spine.

'You came.'

I stand stock still, staring into the darkness. 'It's you.'

'Yes.' Freya's voice is as I remember it from all those years ago.

'Tell me what you want.' I struggle to keep my voice level. Hoping against hope that she can't hear the fear in it. 'Tell me what to do. Just give Izzy back to me.'

I can hear a faint crying and I know it's my daughter. She's with her somewhere and I just want to hold her in my arms. Tell her it will be all right. But I can't.

'Please tell me my daughter's safe.' I hear Freya sigh and remember how she would often tire of our conversations if they didn't go her way. I try to keep my voice upbeat. 'Where are you? Let's meet. We can talk. We used to be sisters, Freya. We used to be friends.'

'Did we?' She sounds bored. 'Is that why you told them what I'd done? Is that why you lied about me and had me sent away?'

'I didn't tell them, Freya. I never told your secret.'

'Are you sure about that? Not even your husband?'

I wonder how she knows. 'Please,' I say again. 'Where are you?'

Pressing my mobile against my ear, I strain to hear something that will give me a clue. Traffic. A television. Anything. But all I can hear is Isabella's plaintive voice. *Where's Mummy?*

'You always thought you were better than me, didn't you?'

'That's not true. I didn't…'

She cuts me off. 'With a father and a mother who wanted you. Do you know what it's like to have nobody?'

I struggle to find the right words. Ones that will placate, rather than anger her. 'They didn't love me, Freya. They never did. After what happened, they froze me out. They didn't want me either. Can't you see that it was you they loved?'

For the first time, I think about what it must have been like to be Freya. Arriving in a strange house. Needy. Damaged. Desperate for love. In many ways we weren't that different.

There's a catch in Freya's voice. 'You really don't know anything. You think you do, but you don't.'

The wind is sharpening, tugging at my coat. I fight to stop my teeth from chattering. Crouching down in the long grass, I wrap my arms around my body, wanting the waving grasses to engulf me. But then I hear Isabella's voice again. So small. So afraid. *I want Sophie.*

'She's just a child, Freya. Sophie will be missing her. Let me take her home to her sister.'

There's silence. In the distance, somewhere in the band of trees on the ridge, I hear the mournful hoot of an owl. In the few seconds I wait for her to answer, I pray she'll say she'll let her go, but she doesn't.

'No, Kelly. There are things you need to understand and the only way I can do that is to show you. Without Isabella, Sophie will know what it's like to lose the other half of herself. Her sister. Her twin. And you will understand what real loss feels like too.'

'Where are you, Freya?' I shout into the phone. Desperate. Pleading. 'You have to tell me.'

'I don't,' she says, 'because you already know. Can you still run?'

'I don't know what you mean?'

'I'll count to twenty slowly. Maybe you'll make it in time.'

'Please, Freya. I don't—'

The phone goes dead. I stare at it, a vicious gust of wind catching at the edges of my coat, making it flap. I was right. She wants me to find her.

I also know she'll have started counting.

In the distance is the brick wall of the rifle range. It's not so very far away, but my feet are rooted to the ground and it's like I'm looking through the wrong end of a telescope. However hard I try, I can't move them. My vision blurs. There's ringing in my ears. For the first time the numbers that will calm my panic refuse to come.

And through all this, the never-ending grass ripples and eddies in slow motion. The wind whistles eerily through the naked stems.

My baby is in danger and there's nothing I can do to stop it.

CHAPTER FIFTY-EIGHT

Kelly Now

My hand is at my throat where my locket hangs. I can feel it through my jumper. Unbuttoning my coat, I pull the fine chain from its woollen prison and, with frozen fingers, fumble at the clasp until I manage to open it. My beautiful girls smile at me from their heart-shaped frame and I feel my limbs start to thaw like a princess in a fairy tale.

This time, when I tell my feet to run, they obey. I take the path that cuts directly through the meadow and it's like I've gone back in time. No longer am I Kelly the wife and mother with no confidence in herself. Instead, I am the fourteen-year-old girl from the athletic club whose limbs are strong and sure. Whose feet can cover ground faster than the others. The moonlight guides me, and I keep my steps measured. My breathing even.

I *will* get there before Freya has finished counting. If I don't, I will live with the consequences forever.

I've reached my goal. The wall of the firing range is in front of me and I stop. Despite my run, I'm shivering, though whether it's from cold or fear I can't tell. I place my hand on the cold brickwork, steadying myself. Making myself breathe. This wall is the only thing between me and the iron framework of the targets in the markers' gallery. The only thing stopping me from seeing what's waiting for me there.

Above me, the birches shiver, but where I'm standing the wind is mute – replaced by a bone-chilling stillness. It smells of damp and decay. Of death. Panic tightens like a band across my chest. I'm no longer certain this is the place. What if I've made a mistake? What if it's not the Gemini symbol on the wall of the rifle range she wants me to go to. What if she's waiting for me at the Gemini tree? I glance up at the band of trees on the hill. However fast I ran, I'd never get there in the time she's given me.

'Isabella. Are you here?'

I stand and wait. Rigid. Listening. Wanting, yet not wanting, to hear a reply. When there's nothing, I force my feet to move. Keeping as close to the wall as I can, I inch my way along, the torch lighting the way. I reach the end but am scared to turn the corner. Freya said there was a price to pay for what I did and I've no idea what that will be. Now I wish I'd phoned Mitch when I had the chance. Would do anything to have him here with me now. But there's no use wishing for something you can't have. I've learnt that to my detriment.

With stomach clenched hard as a rock, I step into the gallery. To my right is the long wall, its graffiti fighting for space, to my left the target frames. Lifting my torch, I aim the beam at the farthest end and sweep its light from one side to the other. Picking out the curve of a letter, a rusted strut.

There's nothing here. The place is empty.

Dropping my arm to my side, I bend my head, the crushing pain of losing my child releasing the stopcock of my tears. As I slide down the wall, joining the fag ends and the bottles, I know the keening noise I hear is coming from me.

'Mummy.'

At first, I think I'm imagining Isabella's voice, but then I hear it again. It's coming from the derelict target store to my left.

'Isabella? Izzy?'

Pushing myself up, I run to the entrance and sweep my torch across the concrete space. I see her straightaway. She's crouched in the corner, her arms wrapped around her body, reminding me of Freya when she was first with us.

I'm next to her in seconds, hugging her to me. Kissing her hair over and over. 'Are you all right? Are you hurt?'

I feel, rather than see, the shake of her head. I want to believe her, but I can't. Holding her at arm's length, I study her face and then her body until I'm satisfied nothing has happened to her.

'I'm scared, Mummy. I don't like her.'

I smooth back the hair from her face. It's wet with tears – hers and mine. 'Did she say anything, Isabella? Do you know where she's gone?'

For the second time, she shakes her head.

There's no sound. It's as if the very earth is holding its breath. Is she still here? I'm just wondering what to do, when Isabella holds out her hand. There's something in it. It looks like a page from a newspaper.

'What is it? What do you have?'

'She told me to give it to you.'

I want to leave this place, go home to Mitch, Sophie and Noah, but something tells me this is important. Tucking the torch under my arm, I unfold the page. I expect it to be another horoscope, but it isn't. When I shine the torch on it, I see it's a newspaper article.

The heading is bold. *Gemini Twin Allowed to Die*. As I read, my heart slows, and fresh tears start in my eyes. The article is about a mother who gave birth to identical twins. Twins who were joined at the abdomen and who shared a circulatory system. The stronger of the twins was called Freya and it was her healthy heart that was pumping blood around her ailing sister's body.

I read on, my hand trembling. The doctors had told the parents that, without an operation to separate them, both twins would die within months. But the parents hadn't wanted the operation.

They couldn't bring themselves to sacrifice one child so the other could live.

My hand is at my heart. What if I'd had to make that same choice when the twins were born? I remember the days watching Sophie in the special care baby unit, yellow with jaundice, her little lungs fighting to take in enough oxygen. Would I have sacrificed Sophie so that her stronger sister could live? I realise it's something I can't answer. Something no one could answer unless it happened to them.

The article finishes by saying that, after weeks of wrangling, the appeal court judge decided that the twins should be separated. Two months after the operation, the weaker twin died.

I close my eyes, remembering the day in the swimming pool changing room when I'd seen the pink, shiny scar on Freya's skin. How she'd press her body to mine whenever she crept into my bed at night.

Now it all made sense.

And so did her secret. Freya blamed herself for her twin's death. Yet it wasn't her fault. No one was to blame. If the operation hadn't gone ahead, neither twin would have survived. I try to remember what I know about Freya's parents. Her father left and her mother had a breakdown. Going through what they did, it's hardly surprising.

Freya blamed herself for her sister's death, and I didn't question the truth of it either. I treated her like a killer, when she was a victim.

Perhaps that's why she was always pushing me away. If only I'd been told the truth.

There's a sound at the entrance to the rifle range. A rustle of leaves at the end of the wall as if someone is pushing their way through. Taking Isabella by the hand, I pull her behind me, melting back into the darkness so that whoever it is won't see us. My heart's thumping in my chest as I wait. There's the slap of shoes on concrete, a pool of light from a torch. Is it Freya? Has she changed her mind and come back for Isabella?

The footsteps move closer and I clamp my hand to my mouth to stop from screaming. Behind me, Isabella whimpers.

'Shh,' I whisper, reaching behind me to feel for Isabella's hand. 'Stay as quiet as you can.'

The torch beam disappears as its owner walks the length of the shooting gallery, but I know they'll soon be back. They'll light up the corners of our hiding place and we'll be found. We're sitting ducks. With Isabella close to my side, I creep to the entrance of the target store and look out. A dark shape is standing at the end of the gallery. It's hard to tell, but I think their back is to us. There's a woodpile next to the squat building where we stand and, behind it, the sharp scarp slope of the hill. If we can just get to it, we could use it as cover and disappear between the trees.

'Run as quickly as you can, Izzy,' I say.

But we've only run a few steps when there's a shout and we're trapped in the torch's beam, like actors on a stage about to take their bow.

'Shit, Kelly. Are you all right?'

It's Mitch's voice and I think I might die of relief. He's running now, his footsteps echoing against the empty walls of the gallery. Picking Isabella up, I run to meet him, desperate to feel his arms around me.

He takes Isabella from me and presses her cheek against his.

'Ow, Daddy. That's scratchy.'

I look at Mitch over the top of her head. 'Where's Sophie?'

'She's with Maddie in the car.'

From the way he's said it, I know he's worried about how I'll take this, but I know now how stupid I was to be jealous of her.

'That's good. I'm so glad you came, Mitch. How did you find us?'

'Your mother told me where you'd gone.' Putting Isabella down, he puts his arm around me. 'You're shivering. Let's get back to the house and you can tell me what the hell happened today. Freya didn't…' he rubs at his chin, struggling to say the words, 'do anything? Hurt her?'

'No. She didn't hurt her.'

'Then why take her?'

I try and remember what she said in the phone call. 'I think it was because she was angry that I'd had everything she'd always wanted. She'd thought she had it too and then I spoilt it for her. If only my mother had sat me down and talked to me about Freya before she came to us, things might have been different. But she never did. She was too obsessed with getting the perfect child to worry about how it would impact on me. Freya wanted me to understand what loss feels like… and now I think I do.'

'Why would she go to such extremes? She's insane. A crazy stalker. The lengths she went to…' Mitch stops, disbelief written across his face. 'How did she know about the kids? Where we lived?'

'She saw your letters to my mum, Mitch. There wasn't much you didn't tell her.'

The pain Mitch is feeling is written across his face. 'I put you and the children in danger. I'm so sorry. And I should have believed you when you told me all the things that had been happening. She's dangerous.'

'I don't think she is.' The newspaper article is still clutched in my hand. 'Something happened to Freya when she was very young that made her desperate to be loved. She just didn't know the right way of going about it.'

I hold the article out to him, and he takes it. Training the torch on the writing, he reads. When he's finished, his hand drops to his side. 'Bloody hell.'

'I know. It's awful, isn't it.'

Mitch runs a hand down Isabella's hair. 'And you think this had something to do with why she took Isabella?'

'It could be.' I've nothing else to go on.

'Well, all I care about is that you're both safe.'

I can't stop shivering. Taking off his jacket, Mitch places it over my shoulders, but it doesn't help. Isabella is safe, but I'm still on edge. I don't think Freya means to harm us, but why bring Isabella to this place? Why go to the trouble of leaving the clues for me to find? I want to believe that this is the end, but I'm not sure it is.

Taking the torch from Mitch, I light the way along the gallery, and as the beam picks out each tag and picture in turn, I see it. Two vertical lines of green paint with a horizontal arc along the top and bottom. I stop and stare at the Gemini symbol Freya sprayed on the wall the last time I was here. The paint has faded over the years, blending in with the other graffiti, but now there's something different about it.

Moving closer, I train my torch on it and immediately see what it is. I give a strangled cry and step back. For hanging from the arc at the top, in fresh black paint, is a rope. On the end of which is a hangman's noose, just like the one on the Gemini tree.

'Oh, God,' I whisper. 'Please, Freya, no.'

Now I know what Freya wanted me to find. And it wasn't just Isabella.

CHAPTER FIFTY-NINE
Kelly Now

My torch swings wildly as I force my legs to conquer the grassy slope beyond the rifle range. My chest is tight. My breathing heavy. Above me, is the wood Freya and I played in all those years ago, the trees spectral against the indigo sky. I stop to catch my breath, looking back down the hill, the way I came. There's nothing to see, but I can hear the sigh of the waving grass and Mitch calling my name.

When I left him in the rifle range, I knew that he wouldn't be able to follow me. Not with Isabella. He knows the direction in which my thoughts have run and has heard enough about Freya's instability to know what she's capable of. If we're right, there's no way he'll let his daughter be a witness to that. I'm relieved. This is something I must do alone.

I press on, wondering what Mitch will do now. The most likely thing is that he'll call the police to tell them Izzy's safe before taking her back to the car where Maddie and Sophie are waiting. When he's done that, he'll come after me. There's no time to waste, and I run again, my torch picking out the safest route along the rutted path.

The gate that leads into the trees appears sooner than I expect it to and I push through, jumping as it clangs shut behind me. Everything is still again. The air cold and silent. I know I must go on, but my fear, and the darkness that presses in, holds me back. Makes me hesitant. Even the beam of light from my torch is no comfort. Above my head, huge bunches of mistletoe hang like chandeliers from the birch trees and the bare branches glisten with frost where the light catches them.

My heart is racing uncomfortably. The sweat growing cold on my back.

'You can do this, Kelly.' Without realising, I've spoken the words aloud and I stop, listening for an answering voice. There is none and I don't know if this makes it better or worse.

Ahead of me is a clearing. The trees thinning to reveal the open space Freya and I once played in. It's bathed in moonlight and I switch off the torch. In the clearing's centre, standing mute and ghost-like, is the Gemini tree.

Instinctively, I close my eyes against the stuff of my nightmares. Imagining the Medusa-like roots taking hold beneath the frost-hardened earth. Fighting the panic, I count under my breath, leaving little space in my head for the terror to take hold.

But even as I'm counting, I know I must look. It's the only way to bring an end to all this.

Finding an inner strength I didn't know I had, I open my eyes again and force myself to look. It's now I see what I didn't when I was eight. The Gemini tree is not one tree with two trunks at all, but two trees. They've grown so close together that their silver-grey trunks have joined where they touch – just as Freya's and her sister's had.

It takes all my strength to make my eyes move to the long low branch that spreads away from the trunk. To force them to see. To understand. Freya knows that the clue she left me at the rifle range will have led me here. This time there's no lightning. No sleeping tablets muddling my thoughts. What I see is real, not something I've conjured up.

The long rope hangs – just as it did when we were children.

Just like it did the day I thought Freya had died.

Today, though, the noose at the end hangs empty and I cover my face with my hands in relief.

'Kelly.'

My hands drop to my sides and my blood freezes at the sound of Freya's voice. My eyes strain to see her.

'Where are you?'

'Where do you think?'

I see her now, her blonde head luminous in the moonlight. She's leaning against one of the trunks, her palm pressed against the bark. Caressing it.

'What do you want from me, Freya?'

Freya looks at me. She steps forward, her hands outstretched. 'I don't want anything from you.'

'Then why have you been doing all this? Isabella showed me the newspaper article and I understand why you took her. But why leave the final clue. Why lead me here?'

A sudden gust of wind shivers the leaves of the trees that ring the clearing and the rope swings slightly. My skin puckers with goosebumps and my pulse thrums at the base of my throat. Have I made a mistake? Was it me Freya wanted to hurt all along?

Seeing where my eyes have rested, Freya gives a sad smile. 'You still don't trust me, do you? You're frightened of me.'

My eyes snap to hers. 'Of course I'm frightened of you. You moved Noah's pram, you left your locket inside his covers, you put newspapers through my door that I never ordered and you let yourself into my house. I thought I was going mad.' I'm angry now. 'You took my child, Freya. How do you expect me to feel now that I'm standing alone with you in this awful place?'

Freya shakes her head. 'You've got it wrong. You don't need to be scared. I'm not going to hurt you.'

'Then why bring me here?'

'I wanted to warn you.'

I'm confused. 'Warn me about what?'

'Not what... who. I'm talking about that woman – Karen. She's evil. She duped me into thinking she loved me and she'll do it again. Even now, she'll do anything to have that one perfect child. She'll worm her way back into your life and take yours. Not in the way I did, but she'll have her ways. She'll pick a child and turn them against you. Favouring one, making them feel special and loved, while all she'll offer the other is indifference. When I read your husband's letters, I knew she'd find where you lived. That she'd reach out to you. I wanted to save your daughters from the pain we both went through.'

I'm trying to process all the information. Make sense of it. 'But why go to so much trouble? If you were that concerned, why not just phone me or speak to me in the playground instead of leaving your locket there?'

'Because you wouldn't have believed me. I had to get your attention. I did it all to remind you of the past. To get you thinking about how bad it was. How much your mother manipulated us. How she duped us both.' She frowns and folds her arms. 'The only thing I don't understand is why they kept you.'

In the distance I hear my name being called. It's Mitch. He's on his way to find me. I look in the direction his voice is coming from, then back to Freya, distracted.

'What do you mean, *kept me*? I was their daughter.'

Freya sighs. 'I didn't know whether to tell you or not, but when your husband said in his letters that he wanted your kids to know their grandmother, I knew it was time you learnt the truth.'

'The truth about what?' I supress the urge to run. To find Mitch and get as far away from this place as I can, but an inner voice tells me that what Freya is going to say next is something I need to hear.

'Important documents should always be kept in a locked filing cabinet, don't you think? Especially ones from the fertility clinic. You see, Kelly, Karen and Andrew couldn't have children of their own.'

It's said without malice, but with those words, my world comes crashing down as I realise everything I've known about my childhood has been a lie. I stand, immobile, the shock spreading through me.

'It's not true. You're lying.'

But I know she isn't. It's like a jigsaw piece has fallen into place. It explains so much. The way my mother looked at me. The way she acted. When they'd adopted me, my mother must have thought I was *the one*. I wonder how old I was when it became clear I wasn't.

Freya steps forward and holds out her hand. 'I did it to protect you. Nothing more.'

A memory stirs and I draw it towards me. I'm eight years old and am staring at a waif-like child who stands in the doorway of our living room – a new sister I conjured up with the blow of a birthday candle. She's scared and lonely, her life changed beyond recognition by a tragedy I won't know about, or understand, until many years later. She took my hand that day because she thought she'd found an ally.

But I let her down.

I look at Freya's hand now, reaching out to me in the moonlight. Stepping towards her, I take that hand and hold it tight in mine.

'Karen isn't evil. She's just sad and lonely.' Despite what I've just said, I can't bring myself to call her my mother. Not any more. I look at Freya's face, carved white in the moonlight. 'What will you do?'

She shrugs and smiles. Her bravado back. 'I'll be fine. You don't need to worry about me.'

I do, though. I always have. 'Will I ever see you again?'

She shakes her head. 'I don't think so. It's better this way.'

There's the sound of twigs snapping underfoot. A rustle of branches. My name called again.

Freya turns and walks away, just as Mitch reaches me.

He pulls me to him. 'Are you all right? The police are on their way.'

I force my head around. 'Freya. Wait…'

But it's too late. She's disappeared between the moonlit trees.

CHAPTER SIXTY
Kelly Now

It's a beautiful day, the sky a clear cobalt blue, the sea below the promenade foaming and hissing up the stones. It's the first run I've had in a while and I've missed it.

For the first time, in a long time, I feel as if life is getting better. I'm going to be starting at the girls' school as a classroom assistant, in the new year. Just part-time, but it will give me something to focus on outside of my family. It was Mrs Allen who told me about the job as Miss King is leaving to move up north to be with her boyfriend.

After discussing it with Mitch, I went to see my GP and I've already had two sessions with someone who specialises in OCD. She's told me that a desire to count actions or objects isn't unusual in people suffering with anxiety. It even has a name – arithmomania. Together, we're working out a plan to help curb my desire to count, but since my meeting with Freya, things have become a lot better. Sometimes, I wonder if somewhere deep down in my subconscious, I knew that she was still alive. If it was what was triggering my anxiety in the first place.

Ahead of me is the Palace Pier. Despite the number of people who are milling around the entrance, I see Mitch straightaway, standing with the buggy. A little way away, Sophie and Isabella have their feet on the bottom bar of the blue railings and are inching their way along in a game that's making them giggle.

When he sees me, Mitch waves and calls to the girls who jump down and run to me.

'Look what I've got.' Isabella thrusts a postcard into my hand. It has a picture of the pavilion on it – it's where we're going to take them after lunch. 'Daddy says we can write on it and send it to Gran.'

I take the postcard from her and look at it, thinking of the letters and photographs Mitch sent to Karen. Not realising the consequences. Freya wanted to warn me against involving my adoptive mother in my life again, but she didn't know that I'd already pulled away from her. Had already made that choice.

Mitch and I have talked about it. Decided that when things settle down, we will go and visit Karen – let her know how her behaviour, when I was a child, affected all of us. She should have told me the truth about so many things: my adoption and Freya's past. Who knows? If she had, it might have helped her too.

In a strange way, I feel sorry for Karen. She's never known what it feels like to hold her own baby in her arms and, even though we aren't her flesh and blood, we are the only family she has. But whatever happens in the future, there will have to be boundaries. I'll make sure of that.

'I think the postcard's a lovely idea, Izzy,' I say, handing it back to her.

Mitch pulls me into a hug. It's what he wants – for us all to be a family again. If we work at it, I think we'll be all right. *We're* talking more too. It's something we've both taken away from this – the importance of communication. He's opened up about some of the things that happened when he was at the children's home and I've told him more about my childhood. He listens now. Knowing that it's not always about fixing but about being there.

Reaching up, I take my husband's face in my hands and kiss him, his stubble scratching my skin. Then together, as a family, we make our way along the promenade towards town.

'I forgot to ask,' Mitch says as we walk. 'Did you enjoy your run?'

'I did.'

It's only now that the pavilion has come into sight, its creamy-white domes looking exotic against the winter sky, that I realise why. On my phone is a message Freya sent me this morning. Two small words that have changed everything.

Forgive me.

That simple message will help me find the strength to carry on. What Freya did was terrifying, but she acted out of desperation. She couldn't help what happened when she was born and how it made her view the world.

Of course, I forgive you, Freya.

It's not just forgiveness, though. Freya's actions opened my eyes to what happened in my past and how the fallout caused toxic ripples that spread into my future. I should thank her for that. I just hope she receives help to come to terms with her own past.

I have a feeling I won't see Freya again, but if I do, I have her locket with me in my bag. I thought of asking Karen for a photograph of the two of us when we were children but have decided against it. Instead, I've left the locket empty. I like to think that one day Freya will have someone of her own to love and it will be *their* face she sees when she undoes the clasp.

It's getting dark now, the street lamps flickering on, and as we walk, I realise that for the first time in a long while, I'm not counting the number of steps between them. I look at my family and smile.

No, the only thing I'm counting is my blessings.

A LETTER FROM WENDY

Firstly, I would like to say a huge thank you to everyone who has read *We Were Sisters*. If writing one novel is exciting, then writing a second is even more so. A writer needs readers and I hope you loved reading *We Were Sisters* as much as I loved writing it.

If you did enjoy it and want to keep up to date with all my latest releases, just sign up at the following link. Your email address will never be shared and you can unsubscribe at any time.

www.bookouture.com/wendy-clarke

Setting has always played an important role in my writing. In this novel, the action takes place in Brighton, where I used to live, and also in a fictitious village in West Sussex based on the one I live in now. As a dog owner, I walk a lot. One of my favourite walks takes me through a combe where, in the summer months, the grass either side of the path can be nearly waist high. In the distance are the South Downs, a band of woodland stretching out along the ridge, and if you investigate further, you will find a disused rifle range covered in graffiti. The whole area is wonderfully evocative. No wonder I chose to use it.

For those of you who recognise the location but think things aren't as they should be… you'd be right! In reality, the area is beautiful: the woodland well-managed, the combe full of orchids in summer and the rifle range cleaned up and undergoing conservation to retain its history. I've changed things, moved them around, embellished them to create a sinister place – more in keeping with a thriller. Some would say I've used up my quota of artistic licence!

I hope you loved *We Were Sisters* and if you did, I would be very grateful if you could write a review. I'd love to hear what you think, and it makes such a difference helping new readers to discover one of my books for the first time.

I love hearing from my readers – you can get in touch on my Facebook page, through Twitter, Goodreads, Instagram or my website.

Thanks,
Wendy x

wendyswritingnow.blogspot.com

@WendyClarke99

WendyClarkeAuthor

wendyclarke99

ACKNOWLEDGEMENTS

I am so lucky to have a supportive and talented network of people around me and what luck when my editor, Jennifer Hunt, decided that she loved my writing enough to offer me a contract! Not only that, but her help, guidance and editorial skill has helped to make this second novel the best it can be so thank you, Jennifer – being a published author has made me happy beyond my wildest dreams. Thanks also to Kim Nash and Noelle Holten for their tireless work getting the novel in front of readers and the rest of the Bookouture team for their support. I know when I've landed on my feet!

As always, I need to give special thanks to my fabulous writing buddy, Tracy Fells, who's shared this journey with me – the highs and lows, the times when I've wanted to scream and the times I've wanted to shout with joy. Many mugs of coffee have been drunk, many teacakes eaten… none of them in vain. Thanks also to fellow Bookouture author, Liz Eeles, who must be sick of my constant questions, and my other lovely RNA writing chums. Where would I be without our monthly catch-up and writerly chat?

Not all the people I know are writers of course and I'd like to thank 'The Friday Girls', Carol, Barbara, Jill, Linda and Helen for their friendship. Every week, for more years than I care to remember, we've walked the route my heroine, Kelly, runs when she's a teenager. I bet you never knew our weekly forays would make it into a novel!

Thanks also to local ecologist, Petra Billings, who gave up her time to talk me through the flora and fauna of the downland.

Even though only a small amount of the information was used, I've learnt so much and now no one can say I had cow parsley growing in the wrong place!

My family are the people who make it all worthwhile – my children, my stepchildren and their partners, and my mum. My husband is probably thinking I've forgotten him, but it couldn't be further from the truth. He's the one who acts as a sounding board when I'm thrashing out my plots, who isn't scared to tell me when I've written rubbish and, just as importantly, when I haven't. Thank you, Ian!